How the Body Prays

Other Books by Peter Weltner

The Risk of His Music
Beachside Entries / Specific Ghosts
Identity and Difference
In a Time of Combat for the Angel

How the Body Prays

A NOVEL BY

Peter Weltner

Graywolf Press
Saint Paul, Minnesota

Publication of this volume is made possible in part by a grant provided by the Minnesota State Arts Board through an appropriation by the Minnesota State Legislature, and by a grant from the National Endowment for the Arts. Significant support has also been provided by Dayton's, Mervyn's, and Target stores through the Dayton Hudson Foundation, the Bush Foundation, the McKnight Foundation, the General Mills Foundation, the St. Paul Companies, and other generous contributions from foundations, corporations, and individuals. To these organizations and individuals we offer our heartfelt thanks.

Published by Graywolf Press
2402 University Avenue, Suite 203
Saint Paul, Minnesota 55114

www.graywolfpress.org

Published in the United States of America
Printed in Canada

ISBN 1-55597-288-8

2 4 6 8 9 7 5 3 1
First Graywolf Printing, 1999

Library of Congress Catalog Card Number: 98-88486

Cover design: Scott Sorenson
Cover art: Edwin W. Dickinson, *The Cello Player*, 1924–1926, Fine Arts
    Museums of San Francisco, Museum purchase, Roscoe and Margaret
    Oakes Income Fund, 1988.5
Cover photograph: Barnaby Hall, *Nude Couple*, Photonica

For Atticus Carr

and

To the memory of Wright Morris (1910–1998)

The elders have ceased from the gate, the young men from their music.

—Lamentations 5:14

If we love one another, God dwells in us, and his love is perfected in us.

There is no fear in love, but perfect love casts out fear: because fear has torment. He that fears is not made perfect in love.

—I John 4:12, 18

Contents

Andrew Stafford Odom   3

Louisa Marie Odom   9

Aaron Rose Odom   39

Anna Ruth Odom   53

Andrew Willingham Odom   79

Andrew Lane Odom   133

Michael Anthony Benedetti   167

Joshua Aaron Rose   233

Max Appleman   241

How the Body Prays

Andrew Stafford Odom

Elisabeth always knows what to play. When I hear a Bach prelude, I feel I might want to live forever. In everything she touches, the soul of her mother inhabits her. The dead must live on somewhere. As Elisabeth plays, Christa plays with her. I want to hold her again, but as I stretch my arms out to embrace her, Christa stops playing. I can hear only her daughter Elisabeth playing alone.

I am an ancient, nothing but walking bones. Hope molders in me like a brave man in his grave. Body is hobbled horse, toothless dog, clawless crawfish. Heart is cow with milkless bag. Soul is blind, hungry owl, beak and talons no longer red with shrew or rat. My father would say, "The bitch Sphinx lies waylaid on her rock, but pay her no mind. Whatever her riddle, man was never the answer."

Father would say, "The world is a prison. Its iron bars are fear. Its iron locks, cowardice. Only pride sets you free." He preached, "In the beginning, God sent down an angel with a flaming sword to guard the Tree of Life. At the end, the same fiery blades will protrude from between His teeth. Jesus came not to bring peace but to unsheathe another sword. God is Law. The Law is strife."

The breeze this afternoon is fragrant with blossom. I watch the petals dance and glide to earth. Butterflies whirl in the sunlight.

I was born, my father boasted, on the day Scott marched his

troops into Veracruz. My days total more than 34,000. Throughout them, war has followed war. Yesterday, the Japanese began a new offensive in the Philippines. Bataan. Corregidor.

All things flow. Only river, moon, winds abide. Life is sere leaf. Life is melting snow.

When I was nine, I rode with Father on horseback to Charleston, farther from home than I had ever been before. The ride was long, hard, hot, and dusty. We were often hungry and sore. Whenever early in the journey I cried out in discomfort or fear, Father struck me with his crop. I quickly learned to cry out no more.

In Charleston, Father sold fur and hide or bartered them for seed. While he traded, I watched the other trade in slaves. No Odom owned slaves. No Odom ever would enslave another man or let himself be enslaved. I had been born sworn to woods and game, to track and to hunt squirrel, possum, fox, deer, boar, bear. At home, Father had told me local tales of black men bloodily lashed, of a mother whipped from her child, of a sister ravaged from her brothers, of weeping babes. The Law commands, give me your son, brother, father. Give me your daughter, your wife. "The Law must be disobeyed," Father said. "Pride is freedom from all laws," Father said, "except for the law you yourself have made."

In Charleston, I saw my first caged bird. The abasement of pigeons, Father declared, was as metaphysical as slavery. The pigeon was also a slave to man.

Across from our boarding house was a stable, part of which was used as a residence by the family who owned the horses. The youngest son had built a small coop beneath a wisteria thicket next to a shed. He loved his pigeon with an openhearted sentiment I had witnessed previously only in neighbor girls who played with dolls. He held it, petted it, cooed to it, fed it with his fingers, and let it peck his neck and nestle in his lap.

One morning, he and I were watching an old slave exercise

two colts in a ring. The day was clear and almost windless. Yet an old tree suddenly, unaccountably toppled over onto the shed that dropped several planks onto the small coop. It fell over, freeing the pigeon that did not hesitate, but immediately soared away.

The boy and I hunted for it all the rest of that day, finding it at last only a few blocks from the stable. It lay near a tall iron fence that guarded a house larger than any I had ever seen. Its distinctive green markings were vivid, almost garish in the sun. Its feathers were puffy and bloodied. It held its useless wings outstretched.

A cat arched its back and hissed, a few feathers scattered at its paws. The boy said nothing. He uttered no cry, but began a search. When he found the rock he wanted, the cat seemed unsurprised. He hurled it at its head, but missed. The cat pounced on the pigeon. Its teeth pierced the bird's neck. Sickened by the sight of his tormented pet, the boy fled.

Back on the street, we separated. I chose never to see the boy again. I had already shot dozens and dozens of living creatures. But when I returned to put it out of its misery the pigeon was already dead.

"Your little friend," Father said to me that night after I had told him the story, "has a lot to learn about pity."

"He's not my friend," I said.

I was fourteen when I saw Father killed. One ball, then another, then a third struck him in the back. He'd been leaning against an elm and holding an open map, surveying the terrain. The Yankee attack was swift and thorough, the quickest I had yet witnessed. He wavered for a few seconds between life and death before he fell. I heard him gurgle and sputter. Blood bubbled out of his mouth and foamed. I tore my shirtsleeve and soaked up what I could.

When the skirmish was over, I and two others were all who survived. From Father's tent, I removed his copy of Tacitus, which he loved, and of *Ivanhoe*, which he loathed yet nevertheless also always carried with him to read and reread. After the war, I studied them both and much else Father had owned.

Father's life was too short. Mine has been too long. His father's was long. My son's was short. For over six generations, no Odom has propagated more than one son or fathered a daughter. "That is the Law," Father would say.

My apportioned son Andrew was born in my fiftieth year. I did not love his mother, but she was young. I taught him to hunt and to fight with his fists. I taught him to love work and honor. I taught him to play the violin to my cello and his mother's piano as together we learned the trios of Haydn, Spohr, and Brahms. I taught him Odom arrogance. I taught him Odom pride.

During the last war, my son fought the Germans with Major Whittlesey and the Lost Battalion. His war was as chaotic as mine and perhaps still more ruthless. But life without war is also pitiless. "Our own artillery is dropping a barrage directly on us. For Heaven's sake, stop it!" was the message Whittlesey wrote and entrusted to the pigeon Cher Ami, whose battle-ravaged body is currently encased like a relic in the Smithsonian for everyone to see. Andrew escaped unwounded, returned to the line, and, when there was no more line to defend or penetrate, came home. The Germans had not been his enemy. The French and English were not his friends. He fought as an Odom in spite of folly out of pride.

Three years after the Great War ended, Major Charles Whittlesey, equally honored and disgraced by his battles, drowned himself. He had embarked from New York to Havana on the liner *Toloa*. Late at night, immaculately dressed in evening clothes, he leapt into the sea. What is the attraction of those waters? Did he, like that besotted poet Hart Crane, also wave as he fell? Shall I?

A year later, my son stuffed his pockets with rocks and stones and walked into our river. Elisabeth discovered his body the next morning where it had been caught in the branches of a hickory that had fallen during an ice storm the previous winter.

Before her husband's funeral, she played me Bach's Sarabande from the A minor Partita. Then, hand in hand, we strolled to the oak grove and through the gate to the cemetery. With her other hand, she guided little Drew who was still learning to walk right. She guided him, too, when wide-eyed, he dropped a clod of clay on his father's coffin, where it lay dark in the dark earth.

I regret it is our law that the boy must bare Elisabeth's father's name as the middle part of his. "Willingham," coward and rogue, impotent scoundrel, is unworthy of my grandson. Elisabeth cannot be her father's child. No man could have sired her. She is Christa reborn. Christa in whose womb my seed was secretly sown and always died, burned alive. Christa my pride.

Less than a month after Pearl Harbor, my grandson enlisted, quitting the house one morning so early it might as well have been still night. He caught the train for New York, the same train he had taken initially at my insistence, then entirely on his own, to see and to hear what he could neither see nor adequately hear at home: Wagner, Wagner, yet again Wagner, the greatest artist the world has ever known.

Before the war, on Saturday afternoons, he and I used to tune our fine radio to the Metropolitan and listen to our master. Sometimes, if Drew was away, Elisabeth sat across the room, as attentive as her son. Once, during a performance of *Tannhäuser* (with Flagstad and Melchior, Tibbett and List!), she sang along with the Pilgrims' Chorus, the words as familiar to her as a vaudeville song to a more common sort. Before she'd emigrated, her mother had sung in the chorus in Munich and Bayreuth. But after she arrived here and married the vulgar Willingham, she would sing only to her daughter. "And to me," I yearned to confess.

Although several rooms and a thick floor separate us, I can see

Elisabeth as she plays as if she were sitting in front of me, her head immobile, leonine, and proud. Only her arms and fingers move. Her face betrays no emotion.

In a few minutes, she will be living here alone. She is not the only one who welcomes solitude like a friend. No one knows better than she how to manage this farm.

Life is an untilled land full of dark caves and rushing streams and rivers. But no bird is to blame for the song in my brain, no locust for the whir in my heart.

"God is strife," Father said. Yes, and God is cat. God is pigeon. God is man. God is beetle and worm. God is iron. God is rust. God is music. God is thunder, whirlwind, storm. God is tree. God is the son caught in the tree's arms. "If you look for God," my Father warned, "if you try to find Him, you will be like the dog sniffing in the tunnel from which the fox has already escaped."

The music stops. It is exactly five o'clock. Elisabeth has always been punctual.

I hear her footfalls and the stairs' creak. She pauses on the landing, finishes her climb, crosses the hall, and hesitates by my door. Elisabeth knows how to wait.

I dip my pen in ink for the last time. When she knocks, I turn in my chair without taking my eyes off this page. My body strains, fighting against my will.

She raps gently. "Der Alte?"

Louisa Marie Odom

Since Anna and I weren't yet two years old when she died, I don't remember Mother at all really, except perhaps for her soft hands and her long, braided hair, dark as Aaron's. But I cherish one picture of her in my mind, as clear as it would be if I had displayed it like a photograph on my dresser all these years. She's simply standing by the pond as we four children play. The water's surface is as flat and shiny as a silver dollar, though close to the bottom it was always dark and cold as snow. Since there was no wind, I could see her face reflected in it even as the water mirrored the black pine that forested the two hills bordering it on the other side.

Aaron and Andy loved to swim there, frisking and frolicking, happy as two dogs. But Anna and I were too timid to venture out much beyond the reach of Mother's arms, and I didn't like the feel of mud oozing between my toes. We played close to her, pretending she was a princess and we were her entourage, making necklaces out of wildflowers or transforming twigs and stones into wands and jewels to present to her. I deeply admired the way she bowed when we offered her our gifts.

But, vivid and real as it is, my only picture of Mother is false. She never stood by that pond. She had already died when Mutti first took us four there.

Ten years ago, without warning us of her intentions, Grandmother ordered the dam destroyed, so the pond is also long gone.

All that survives is the creek that fed it and some scattered rocks. Although Andy still swims when it's warm, he can do so now only in the river whose strong currents killed our grandfather.

When we were six or perhaps seven, Anna and I decided that we would marry our brothers. Anna said she preferred Aaron. "Good," I said, "then I'll marry Andy." But then Anna changed her mind. She wanted to marry Andy instead. "Good," I agreed, "I'll gladly marry Aaron." But then, changing her mind once more, she decided she ought to marry Aaron after all. "Do you mind, Louisa?" she asked. "It really doesn't matter to me," I said. "Either way will be fine. But what if they never ask us?" I worried. "Then we shall ask them," Anna said.

Our old Odom house is a hodgepodge. Great-great-great-grandfather Odom chose its site because he wanted to be able to see the river from the front door. But the river, pursuing a different plan, soon shifted its course to flow almost due east nearly half a mile away. Between the house and the river now lie the fields where our cows like to graze.

Great-grandfather started the dairy while he was still almost a boy, shortly after he returned home from the Civil War. The house he'd inherited was small, only five or six rooms. Great-grandfather slowly added to it: first a second floor; then the verandah with its gingerbread trimming; next the two minaretlike cupolas; several years later, after he'd returned from an excursion to New Orleans, two balconies with wrought-iron filigree and many gem-colored stained-glass windows; and finally a wing for a new kitchen and dining room with noble columns to grace the entrance way. Even Mutti contributed a few more rooms, which today number seventeen, not counting the attic with its dark nooks and narrow dormers, perfect for children to hide in. The bricks and the clapboard are painted the same seashell white, and every shutter, no matter its age, shines in the sun like mother-of-pearl.

Three days after Andy was born, Mother, only twenty-four-years old, died of toxemia. She had wanted Andy to be born at home, in this house, in the same bed where Aaron had been born three years before and Anna and I, in that order, only a year after our older brother.

Mutti told us the story as she sat in the chair Anna calls her throne, its dark wood and darker leather looking grim enough for a medieval prioress to have rested in while imposing disciplines upon the devotees of her order. Over her shoulder hung Great-grandfather's portrait, his scowling face as forbiddingly spiritual as a Spanish saint's in one of Mutti's art books.

Perhaps with such a forebear, we children could not help appearing occasionally aloof or severe. And our grandmother, Anna and I were certain, did not want to soften her appearance or to make it more acceptable to the world but strove for severity. It was part of her art. Even when she was most admiring, even loving, she was as remote as Her Majesty the Queen. Once she finally decided to answer our questions about our mother's death, she told us the story almost impersonally, as if it had not happened to us only nine years before but to another family far away and long ago.

"Poor Penelope had always been quite frail, of course," she began. "The Lanes have never been strong or especially healthy. I warned Drew. But after he returned from the war he was so thickheaded I don't believe he ever heard a word I said.

"Perhaps, as he claimed, there really was no other suitable woman in the county. Penelope's brother had been killed late in 1944, on some tumultuous island 6,000 miles away. The Lanes were still grieving. Drew sought them out. A week or two later, he and Penelope foolishly decided to marry.

"Poor Penelope. She and Drew settled here, of course. Where else could they go? Drew had no money of his own. His grandfather had chosen to settle all his estate on me, you see, since my son had never shown the slightest interest in working the farm. My father-in-law meant no slight to his grandson. He was being practical, as in one sense he almost always was. As the Lanes never were. They were newly paupers, victims of the Depression and their own ineptitude."

Grandmother heaved a sigh and pinched our cheeks. "Poor, poor Penelope," she repeated. "Whenever I expressed my mildest uncertainties about this or that I invariably left her helpless in tears. My questions, however careful, invariably seemed to torment her. But I will say that she possessed spirit. Your mother had a backbone. For surely it was she who chose to name her firstborn Aaron Rose Odom contrary to our Odom tradition, though somewhat maliciously, she liked to pretend that the choice had been Drew's. I decided not to explore which relative of hers she had so wished to honor. Why should I? The mistake had been made. The child had been baptized." As she sighed again, her splendid bosom rose and fell.

"A few months later, your poor mother was pregnant again, with you, dear girls." Her right thumb touched a bead of her amber necklace and rubbed it like a charm. "I didn't attempt to conceal my alarm. People said that the war had changed everything. Certainly Drew and his wife seemed determined to behave according to that assumption. But how could I continue to protest when the issue was so wonderfully you, my lovely granddaughters?

"Yet just a little more than six months later Penelope took to her bed again, ill and weary and once more pregnant. I berated my son for days. What could he have been thinking of? Had the war eliminated from him all self-denial and control? But of course it was too late for me to have interceded.

"When his time came to be born, Andy, like some stage-frightened actor clinging to a prop off in the wings, simply refused to appear. He would not budge. Penelope was already so frail, so weak. Her labors had always been hard. Drew could not bear to see her suffer. She clutched my hand as if it were all that might keep her from drowning. I could feel her struggling. But I was not strong enough to save her by myself. Even as Andy finally consented to show himself, she started to slip beneath the waves. Three days later she died. 'Of poisons,' the doctor said. I had my own interpretation of what poisons he meant.

"At first the Lanes objected. But I prevailed. We buried her at the base of the oak where Drew, too, shall someday lie, near his father, my husband next to whom I'll confront eternity in our portion of the Odom graveyard." Grandmother clasped her hands in her lap, her knuckles bone white. "The next afternoon, Andrew Lane Odom was baptized. It was your father who at once began to call him 'Andy.'"

She rose immediately out of her chair and clapped her hands together. "So. Now you know. Anna. Louisa." She patted us both on our heads. "Life expects us Odoms to be brave, the Odom women most of all. Whatever happens to you in life, I ask only that you be brave and proud. It is time for you to play, girls," she said, dismissing us from the room, "go somewhere outside and play quietly. Your grandmother wants to practice a new piece, a little sonata, perhaps too difficult for aging fingers."

I had hoped as I left the parlor that the dismay I felt then would eventually be transformed into some more bearable, more grown-up emotion. But nine years had not yet fulfilled that wish. Some part of me remained dismayed and despairing. Perhaps it always would. But since Aaron's return home after our older brother's expulsion from school, I had felt especially afraid. Grandmother had once more made Andy her ally. Father had joined forces with Aaron. Sides were being more rigidly defined. Increasingly, Anna and I were expected to choose.

"Anna," I wondered aloud to my sister as we were cleaning up after a breakfast during which Father and Grandmother had argued even more bitterly about Aaron, "do you think Grandmother and Father care for each other anymore?"

"Dearest, she might as well be his worst enemy. It's been twenty years at least of cold war between them."

"Do you believe she's Aaron's enemy as well?"

"I don't think she means to be. She simply is. She believes she's right. She shares that conviction with the draft board in town. But Mutti has never been one to be troubled by self-doubt."

"I wish he'd never gotten himself expelled. I wish he'd never been involved in that disturbance."

"Disturbance? They kidnapped three people, one of them a dean of something. They set fire to files."

"I never thought Aaron could be so wild."

"He's always been different from the rest of us, Louisa."

"I hardly recognized him in that newspaper picture, with his fists clenched and his face all distorted with rage."

It was only early May, but the air was as thickly hot as it is in late July. A buzzing fly repeatedly collided with a windowpane. Anna's forehead and arms were sparkling with sweat. I opened the window next to the kitchen hutch where Mutti displayed the family's oldest crockery, each piece tobacco-spit brown or yellow-white like weathered wood. When I peered out the window, I noticed her standing on the verandah, staring into the fields beyond the barns.

"What do you suppose she's looking at?" I wondered.

"Who knows? The trees. The shadows. A sick cow."

"She seems suddenly very old somehow."

"She is almost seventy, Louisa."

"Do you think she truly loves any of us?" I dabbed my forehead with the hem of my apron.

"Great-grandfather."

"I know that, Anna. But he's long since dead. I mean, any of *us*."

"She loves Andy. She has hope for him. But I'm sure it would be better for him if she didn't."

"But she cares for us all, don't you think? That can be love too, can't it?"

Anna twisted the sink's faucet. "I suppose."

Pipes shook, the tap coughed, and a little water spat into the basin. When it began to flow, I filled the kettle. After the water had boiled, I poured it into the pot for tea.

We sipped it sitting at the small oak kitchen table. As Anna brought the steaming cup to her lips, her fingers trembled. Then her whole body shook. But she didn't cry. Even when we were little girls, neither of us ever cried. We had made a pact between us to leave the tears to our brothers. Anna carefully set her cup back in its saucer. With great concentration, she quieted herself. As I stared into her eyes, I might have been watching two thin blue flames flickering and dimming. Outside, several mourning doves fluttered, rose, hovered over the verandah's rails, and finally settled on the bushy boxthorn.

I said, "I wish it would rain. I wish it would cool."

She combed her fingers through hair that was as golden as all Odom hair except for Mother's and Aaron's. But Anna's hair was especially beautiful, sunshine bright strands highlighting it even when there was no sun. "We must take a clear side, Louisa. We must choose."

"For Aaron?"

"Yes. And Father."

"They drove off so early this morning in such a hurry. I wonder where they were going. You know, don't you?"

"Yes." Anna rose from the table and gazed out the open kitchen door. "Andy is riding Suzy too recklessly again. She's not a jumper. He's going to land in a gully soon, with a broken arm or leg or fractured spine. He's even more stubborn than his brother."

"I didn't ask about Andy, Anna."

"They're in town. On business."

"We mustn't hate Elisabeth. We mustn't detest our grandmother."

"But I don't. God's law rules over her just as it rules over us, I imagine. Yet when that law is wrong, when Elisabeth is wrong, we must oppose her. And Andy too, of course."

I glanced out the door. Several years ago, Grandmother had ordered a statue of herself carved for the Odom graveyard. Someday, she boasted, none except our heroic Great-great-grandfather's will stand higher than hers among the oak and cypress. I didn't doubt it. When she turned on the verandah to face me, her eyes were already stone. Had she heard what Anna and I had been saying?

I whispered to Anna, "She knows."

"Don't be silly," Anna replied. "Of course she does. She always knows everything."

After the sink had slowly filled with hot water, Anna and I washed the dishes just as we had washed them after every meal since we were ten. This morning, it was Anna's turn to dry them and put them away. I handed Anna a dripping plate. "Mutti said last night that it was Aaron's education that had tricked him into believing he had choices when he really didn't. Do we have choices, Anna? If we do, I wish you'd let me know what they are."

Anna inspected the dried plate for spots. "Do you remember how Mutti struggled to teach us piano?"

"She was almost patient with us, don't you think?"

"But we just wouldn't learn. We simply refused to learn."

"I think I regret it now. Don't you? Don't you wish you had some real talent for music, Anna, like Aaron or Father or Grandmother? I do."

"I think we should learn to say no more often. That's what I think."

"Then we wouldn't have a friend in the world."

"We haven't any now. Odoms don't have friends."

"Andy's popular. He's good at sports. He dances handsomely I've heard girls say."

"He brags too much, Louisa."

I dunked another dish into the soapy water. "Father plays violin so beautifully, almost as well as Aaron plays the cello. What do we do? Wash dishes. Garden. Clean house. Sew. Do the laundry. And occasionally read."

Anna dried her hands on a towel. "You know, I don't much care for music. What has it done for Father? He sulks. He's morose. And Aaron's been nearly as unhappy much of his life. I blame music." She flung her towel onto the rack. "It makes people miserable. Or like Grandmother, impossible. I won't cry, Louisa. Whatever happens, I won't. And neither will you. I'm going for a walk. Do you want to come or not?"

"And neglect our chores? Of course."

But it was already past noon when Anna and I did finally begin our walk and an hour later when we crossed the ridge that gently sloped down to the river. All during March and much of April, we had been hoping for spring, tired of the brown fields, and of the bleak naked trees that covered our land. Even the jessamine and crocus had been delayed. By the last week of April we noticed on one of our treks how the dogwood were almost ready to bloom. As soon as their buds appeared, the rhododendron also swiftly flowered, and all the trees leaved at once, as if they'd received on the same day the order to color the world green at last. The birds, ducks, geese, and heron returned simultaneously like miraculous creatures God had commanded to descend from heaven in a choir all together. I spotted a fox with its fur again golden red like a rooster's brightest feathers and two black snakes twisted together on a warm flat rock by the river. As Anna and I wandered, we delighted in a patch of lady's slipper or a thicket of wild rose or the sinuous curves of dozens of jacks-in-the-pulpit. The moss on the trees had turned velvet green, the grass was green as mint, and the air smelled pungently green, sharp as resin in late summer. But the pleasures of spring are always too brief.

"It's already unpleasantly hot today, isn't it?" I complained, wiping my cheek with the sleeve of my blouse. The river had flooded up to the bank. We kneeled beside it and splashed our faces with its still chilly water. "It's been such a perverse spring, hasn't it, Anna?"

On the pasture that bordered the river's opposite bank, Andy's horse galloped riderless back toward the stable. We watched it disappear over the ridge. Anna held my hand as, following the river's curves, we approached a bend where pine and dense brush grew to the water's edge. We pushed our way through.

Stripped to his plaid undershorts, Andy was lying on the broad trunk of a fallen oak, sunning himself, asleep. We had already started to walk away when he summoned us back. "Louisa! Anna!" We turned to face him again. He offered us a mock salute. "What a surprise!"

"We haven't been looking for you," Anna said, "if that's what you think."

He smiled pleasantly. "Why should I think that?"

"Isn't the water still much too cold for swimming?" I inquired.

"You get used to it fast."

"You mustn't take too much sun at once," I warned. "You're already a little red."

"Am I?" He pushed a thumb down on his thigh. "I guess you're right, Louisa."

My sister forced some more brush aside and walked around me. "Andy. We need to talk."

"Do we?"

"Yes. I want you to stop quarreling with Aaron."

He sat up, reached for his T-shirt where he had hung it on a hook of a branch, and slipped it on. "I'm just trying to prevent my brother from further disgracing himself. And us."

"Aaron's no coward."

"I never said he was."

"Didn't you? I was there last night, remember? I heard what you said."

"I said a real Odom would never refuse a fight. That's all."

"That's Grandmother talking, not you," Anna said.

"Grandmother speaks for all of us," Andy said. "History is on her side."

"Yet what Aaron's already done protesting this horrible war is braver than anything you've ever accomplished, isn't it?" Anna said angrily. "Answer me truthfully."

Andy scratched behind his ear and grabbed his pants, socks, and boots off the boulder where they lay. We turned away as he finished dressing. Tree limbs snapped and weeds whipped against his jeans as he approached. Gently, he kissed the back of Anna's neck, then mine. "Don't be angry. Father is already furious at me, isn't he? But why? He joined the army during his war, didn't he? I'm only saying Aaron should do the same."

"And live up to the family honor, as Mutti demanded he do? Don't make me laugh. The Last Gentleman, she calls you. What in the world can she mean?"

"I know I'm not worthy of her praise yet," Andy said. "But please don't mock her, Anna. Or me."

The three of us started to walk through the woods toward the house. When we reached the grove, Andy clasped my right hand in his left, Anna's left hand in his right, his grip as insistently tight as I had ever felt it. "I don't have a choice," he said.

We continued walking. "Of course you do," Anna said. "All you have to do is pretend you're not her grandchild at all. I do it all the time." She halted. "Listen, Andy. This war is evil. There's no honor in it. We must support Aaron in whatever he decides to do because Aaron is right. Or, if you can't agree to that, if she's so blinded you that you can't see that, then at least be quiet until he's escaped. Then you and Mutti can lament the shame he's brought upon the Odom name morning, noon, and night if you like because in a few days Aaron will be safe." Anna's face was flushed with rage. "Do you understand what I'm telling you, Andy?"

"Yes." He walked away from her. "I'm afraid I do." He climbed over a stile into the pasture. Several dozen cows were grazing near the dairy. A lone bull stood guard by the gate. At the door to the stable, Mutti was talking to two workmen. She caught sight of us, waved, and quickly returned to her conversation. Andy dashed toward her, fast as Suzy.

"Andy!" Anna shouted, but he did not look back. She faced me. "I've said too much. Oh Louisa, I've revealed too much."

"Tell me then, Anna. Please. What's about to happen."

Andy rounded the silo. Al and Carl Tibbetts held out their hands for him to shake as he approached them. The three of them entered the dairy behind Mutti.

"He's going to tell her. He's going to snitch. I know him. He will."

"Tell her what?"

"Tomorrow, or the day after tomorrow, Aaron will be leaving for Canada. He's going into exile, Louisa. He and Father are right now consulting with people outside of town. People who know how to help boys resist the draft."

"Oh, thank God! I've prayed for this. But Andy can't stop him. Neither can Mutti, can she? Aaron's determined, isn't he? He and Father both?"

"I'm such a blundering fool when I'm angry, aren't I?" was all the answer Anna offered me as we headed directly for the house.

At twilight, the air was still as hot as it had been at noon. As they stepped out of the car parked at the end of the drive, Father and Aaron looked soaked, their shirts dripping. Frowning, they walked down the path to the verandah and paused at the stoop, still talking softly, but earnestly to each other.

I stood near an open kitchen window where the odors of baking pie and roasting meat mingled with honeysuckle and gardenia. I nodded to Aaron and Father as they passed me. Aaron was wearing bib overalls and a T-shirt, his black hair slicked back. Father was dressed in his usual natty dark gray suit, though because of the heat he had loosened his tie and was carrying his jacket draped over one arm.

The screen door shut behind them. Just a few minutes later, I heard two showers running upstairs. Anna called to me from the kitchen. Andy was in the sun porch watching the news. He'd turned the volume high enough that everyone in the house would have to hear the whir of the helicopters, the burst of bombs, the screams and shrieks of the frightened or injured.

When he was a boy, Andy enjoyed lightning more than any-thing, especially if a storm struck just after sunset. The winds that occasionally toppled trees and ripped through flowers, stripping them of their petals, the lightning cracks and thunder rumbles, the pelting rains that beat some bushes to their knees, the clouds blacker than the sky at midnight all terrified me and Anna and Aaron too. They scared our herds sometimes, but at the first sign of a tempest Andy would race outside. Through beads of water that the wind crushed as it blew them across the windows, we'd watch him dance as each new bolt somewhere in the distance struck the ground like a knife falling off a counter onto the floor.

After the rains had stopped, he'd stay outside to trap fireflies in glass jars. One of the old hands had told him that fireflies were born from lightning, like maggots from meat or beetles from dung. Despite Aaron's admonitions, Andy would keep the filled jars next to his bed. Even when he remembered to punch holes in the lids, the next morning when he awoke all the fireflies would be dead.

Once, in our early teens, Anna and I followed him and Aaron across a pasture to a twist in the river where they liked to fish. Near the path, Andy discovered a small brown rabbit pitilessly caught in a briar patch, strung up by the vines and thorns as if something deliberately cruel had trapped it, its eyes white as a blind cat's. The dew on the wild grapes sparkled in the early morning light, golden with bees. Wood mice scurried across a split log into a thicket of fireweed. As the breeze blew from the east, the air smelled like wet stones. When it shifted and blew from the west, it was sweetly sour, like the barn. On the other side of the field, where rocks were numerous, Andy found one big and heavy enough to do the job right. With all his strength, he thrust it upon the rabbit's head, crushing it. Its blood spattered his chest and face.

I was horrified, Anna enraged. "He didn't want it to suffer anymore," Aaron explained. "He's got more guts than I do."

Just a few days later, returning from the county fair, they boasted how they'd spied a woman, naked to her waist, who was paid to let snakes coil around her arms and breasts.

It was Mutti who caught them smoking cigarettes near the dairy and forced them to scrub the whole dairy clean, a job that took them weeks. Andy borrowed a gun from Al Tibbetts and taught Aaron how to shoot it. When Mutti found them taking practice shots at one of her milk cans they'd set on a boulder, she boxed their ears. But, a week later, she gave each of them a new rifle. Aaron never used his, having hidden it somewhere in the attic. Andy hunted with Charlie Sutton and a few of the other town boys, though he insisted they had to eat whatever game they killed.

I heard a woman's voice trying to sell toothpaste on a commercial. Andy turned the TV down. After King had been murdered just a few weeks before, Anna and I vowed never again to attend to the news. That the world was cruel and violent was enough for us to have learned at home and in school. Together, we promised each other never to leave the farm. Why did our promise give us hope? Neither the farm's past nor present could be described as peaceful.

"But perhaps we might make it so someday," Anna proposed, hinting, without actually saying, that she meant "when all the others are gone." Was I more pleased or alarmed by Anna's suggestion? Did my sister really believe that this land and its buildings where we had worked like servants for much of our young lives someday might be all ours? "It's a lovely dream," I said to her.

Mutti sang to herself as she prepared food. I peeked through the kitchen window. Anna was tossing a salad. I walked noiselessly down the verandah to the outside stairs that led to the second floor. Down the hall, Aaron's door was open.

He sat cross-legged on the floor, his eyes closed. Was he meditating? "Aaron?" I quietly shut his door behind me. "Aaron? I know. Anna told me. I agree with your decision. I believe it is a tremendously brave thing to do." I couldn't help sounding a little thrilled. "It's like the antebellum underground railroad, isn't it?"

"Is it?" Was he annoyed with me, or with Anna for having revealed his secret? He opened his eyes, stretched his head back as far as it would go, uncrossed his legs, and jumped up.

I glanced at the top of his desk. On it lay scattered papers, some official looking and ominous. "Has it been arranged? When do you leave? Are you going to tell Grandmother? You won't let Mutti or Andy sway you, will you?"

"What do you think?" he said, but his voice was weak, almost tentative.

I said, "This awful war has brought suffering into everyone's life, hasn't it?"

He glanced out the window at a cardinal, perched on a pine limb. "I don't fault Andy. Not really. He infuriates me sometimes. But he's only talking like Mutti's boy. He's always been her favorite. It's easy to see why."

"And you've always been Father's favorite."

"That leaves you and Anna out, doesn't it, Louisa?"

"Anna would say we prefer it that way."

"Andy's just turned eighteen," Aaron observed. "He'll change. He'll surprise us all someday."

"You've already surprised us."

"Have I?" He smiled sweetly at me. I had never in my life seen a smile sweeter or more fond than Aaron's. "At least you and Anna stay wonderfully the same."

"Do we?" I curtsied. "Why thank you kindly, Brother."

His cello rested against the wall next to his bed on which he had already piled clothes to be packed. He reached for his bow where it lay on his dresser and rubbed its horsehairs with rosin. "Father and I have prepared a brief farewell concert. A sonata for cello and violin by Ravel. But you mustn't let on you know it's a farewell concert. You and Anna, stay mum," he warned. "I'm not sure my nerves right now could weather another family storm."

Back downstairs, I checked the dining room. Anna had already done all my chores for me, and the filled wine carafes sat before Mutti's place at the end of the thick old oak table. (Mutti had always insisted that we drink wine. In so doing, she undoubtedly meant to scandalize the town folk and all its right-thinking Christians, but how could any of them know enough about our private customs to be sufficiently offended by them?) The candles in their holders were set out, waiting for Mutti to light them. The napkins had been correctly folded and precisely placed. The three tall vases filled with fresh-cut flowers stood where they always stood, even during winter when dried ones replaced what her gardens could no longer provide.

At Father's instructions, Mutti, Andy, and Anna had already gathered in the parlor by the time I arrived; "as always," Anna would be thinking, "a few minutes late." I took my customary seat next to the huge green urn filled with an assortment of peacock feathers, bold eyed like ancient Egyptians and twice as gaudy. Anna sat impatiently in the antique rocker. Mutti and Andy, huddled together, occupied one end of the sofa, their backs supported by plump embroidered pillows Mutti had worked on during what she called "Drew's war," though Father repeatedly insisted it had been no war of his, not his war at all.

Both her hands clasped Andy's right one in her lap. He

frowned with irritation as he did when he was ill or exhausted. He'd neglected to brush his hair. Mutti wore hers in a loose knot that she gathered in back with a lacy net she tied to the crown of her head. Anna rocked to the rhythm of the pendulum of the clock that stood next to the bookcase, which was filled with Great-great-grandfather's editions of, among others, Burke, Scott, Mrs. Radcliffe, and Maturin. When I tried to read one once, its cracked leather binding crumbled like dried mud in my hand. Over us all, Great-grandfather's portrait glowered down, although his gaze seemed to be directed as always toward Mutti's grand piano.

Father entered first, carrying his fiddle and bow in one hand. Aaron closely followed, holding his cello by the neck in one hand, his prized bow in the other. He had changed his coveralls for a fresh black shirt and newly pressed black slacks, exactly like Father's. As we applauded, they both bowed and walked to the piano, where they stood facing each other a few feet apart.

Father cleared his throat. "We had intended to play for you the Ravel Duo Sonata," he announced. "However, this is going to be a very brief concert because . . ."

"We'll only be playing the third movement," Aaron continued.

"The rest is still too difficult for us. We were just practicing the first movement again and . . ."

"It was a disaster," Aaron said.

"My fault. All my fault," Father said.

"Please," Mutti said, "no more excuses. Just play what you have to play. Let us be the judge."

"Of course, Grandmother," Aaron agreed.

Father lifted his violin into position. Aaron sat in his customary straight-back chair that could support his lanky body as it vigorously danced in place while he played. Mutti looked at Andy, the skin of her face a white veil of crisscross lines, and patted his knee reassuringly as she used to long ago when he had brought her an unexpected gift she probably didn't like, a delicate blue feather, say, or a tiny smooth pebble formed by erosion into the shape of a heart.

Father nodded. Aaron began to play, a lovely, somber, lean melody rising from the cello's lowest register. Father's violin entered and repeated the same simple, plaintive tune. Slowly, the music gathered momentum, becoming increasingly intense. Then the two voices again sang almost as one, a rocking figure moving from one instrument to the other. I heard no counterpoint or any real difference between the two instruments. Instead, the music sadly conversed, its two voices singing as if they were one, although neither ever quite merged into the other.

Applauding heartily when they were done, Mutti exclaimed, "Bravo!"

"Encore!" I demanded.

Father and Aaron bowed once, soberly and correctly. Still clapping, Grandmother rose from the couch and approached them. "Drew. Aaron. Neither of you has ever played better. Fortunately, the literature for violin and cello is small since otherwise you would never require my participation in your music making ever again. Perhaps very soon you will favor us with it all?"

Aaron blushed. "Thank you, Mutti."

"Now, with your permission," she said, seating herself on the piano bench, "I have a little surprise of my own." Father opened the lid and propped it. She rested her fingers on the keyboard. "But like my son and grandson, I am this evening prepared to play one movement only."

In the beginning, I thought I could detect the music's wavering uneasily from minor key to minor key. But even when it began to sing in the major, its song was more resigned than hopeful. A surprising cadence appeared. Moments were deeply agitated. But the song returned, simple yet sorrowful, sorrowful yet noble. Above all, it was noble. I didn't want it to end, though through it all Anna fidgeted restlessly, impatiently rocking her chair. Suddenly the music stopped, unfinished. Mutti merely quit playing. Without explanation, she pushed back the bench and stood up. She glared at Father, then Aaron. "It is late. It is hot. You must all be hungry."

Father took her arm. "You'll also play the whole sonata for us soon, Mother?"

"One never knows." She folded a hand over his. "Perhaps."

They vanished into the long dark hall, Andy swiftly following them, leaving Aaron, Anna, and me alone. "She knows," Aaron said softly to Anna. Their two shadows mingled on the wall. I switched on the overhead and clicked off the two floor lamps. "That piece she just played. It was the second movement of Beethoven's Farewell Sonata. The movement's titled 'Absence.' She knows," he repeated more desperately.

"If she knows, she knows," Anna responded. "You mustn't waiver."

"Tell her I'm not hungry. Tell her I don't feel well."

"I won't. She wants to frighten you. She means to scare you. Don't let her."

"I'm no coward, Anna."

"Of course you aren't," I interjected. "But if you leave tomorrow then this will be our last meal together for who knows how long. I'm sure it will be nice. Please don't disappoint Anna and me, Aaron."

"I don't know," Aaron said. "I don't trust her."

"She's not a cruel woman," I said.

Anna shot me her most contemptuous look. "Isn't she?"

"I'm certain deep in her heart she loves us all." I seized Aaron's hand. "I insist. I really do insist because later it will mean so much to everyone."

In the dining room, Andy was capturing a moth that had been fluttering around one of the candle flames. As Father opened the screen door, Andy freed the moth back into the night.

Mutti carved the roast and poured the wine. Food bowls were

passed around the table. Andy grouched about an incompetent umpire who had unfairly called him out during a game he'd played the previous Wednesday. He praised a new Beatles song titled "Lady Madonna" that he'd heard at Charlie Sutton's. Aaron remarked that he'd always preferred the rawness of the Stones over the Beatles' polish.

"What about the Doors?" Andy asked.

"Jefferson Airplane's better," Aaron answered.

Mutti appeared mystified. She worried aloud about another calf she'd found dead near Bethel Creek and speculated about the likelihood of toxic runoffs from the Hightower farm. Father reminded her of the dead calf she'd found last season in the ravine where the pond used to be. "Calves just die sometimes," he said. "Mysteriously."

"Maybe Felda Hightower's do," Mutti said. "Mine don't."

"Remember that terrible time thirty years ago, Mother?" Father said.

"What else do you think I've been worried about, Drew?" she replied testily.

"Perhaps you should experiment with organic methods of raising alfalfa and hay and corn," Anna suggested.

Mutti snorted. "I'll give you an acre to experiment on all you like, Anna. If it works out, we'll talk more. The same goes for any of you. I'll never oppose a good idea. But first show me some proof it will work."

Father wondered what operas the Met might be broadcasting the next season. "Why don't you just go to New York City, Father?" Anna said.

"And take us with you," I added. "I would love to see New York once."

"So would I," Aaron said. "More than once."

"Not me," Andy dissented. "The Old South is good enough for me. It always will be."

"Oh, Lord," Anna said.

"But New York!" I enthused.

"It's tempting," Father allowed.

"Drew practically lived in Manhattan before the war," Mutti informed us. "Weeks and weeks on end. I thought he was never to come back home. But he always did. Whatever did you find to occupy you up there, Drew?"

He shrugged. "More than has ever interested me here. Concerts. Museums. Galleries."

"Did you want to live there forever, Father?" I asked.

"'Forever?' That would have been a little too long, Louisa."

"You should have stayed, if you wanted to," Aaron said.

"I don't believe I'd ever want to live anywhere but here," I said, "but visiting elsewhere would be heaven."

Father shifted in his chair and stared past his reflection on the window out into the night. "Sometimes I do wish I had stayed. But things happened. The war came."

"Yes, the war," Mutti said, pondering. "You almost did what you had to do, didn't you, Son?"

"Almost?" I asked.

"Hush, Louisa," Aaron said. "Don't encourage her."

"Encourage me?" Grandmother rapped her knuckles against the tabletop, gripped the edge, slid her chair back, and rose from her place with an actor's skill at silencing her audience and directing attention to herself. As theatrically, she reached for the snifter and took a sip of brandy. "A toast! To Andrew Stafford Odom, my beloved father-in-law, my tutor in life." She set the brandy glass back on the table and began a little speech, as she had often done in the past after a meal she regarded as important. "'Elisabeth,' he instructed me, 'the most ancient wisdom is still the best. Air struggles with earth, earth with water, water with fire, fire with air. The truth of all life is struggle and war. The only God mortals know is strife. Whatever is most beautiful swiftly blows away. Every petal fades in an hour. Only the wind stays.'" She rapped her knuckles still more emphatically on the tabletop. "The day before I married Andrew Martin Odom, Father Odom summoned me into his study, that room we now keep empty upstairs to honor him. 'Elisabeth Reinertz Willingham,' he said, 'you are about to become an Odom. In honor of that happy event, I want to share with you a secret. It is our family motto. *Pone metum.* Lay aside fear,'" Mutti quoted yet again as I watched Anna mouth the too familiar words to herself. "'No Odom must be afraid to live,' he told me, 'no Odom must ever be afraid to die. Courage is the source of all our pride. Men die, my daughter, only when they cannot connect their end to their beginning and therefore die and die and die.'" She leaned over, blew out a candle, and to complete her brief scene, apparitionlike glided out of the room.

Anna snuffed out the remaining candles and pinched their smoldering wicks with her moistened fingers. Father clicked on the chandelier. "My mother has never forgiven me for not having gotten myself decently killed twenty-five years ago," he said bitterly.

"I don't think that speech was directed at you, Father," Aaron said. "Not this time."

"What if Great-grandfather was right?" Andy said. He rubbed his thumb hard against his perfect, rigid jawbone. "What if a man's not a man until he's faced death and either lost or won?"

"You can't believe that," I said, horrified. "You mustn't."

"But I think he does believe it. I think he's swallowed everything Mutti has taught him, haven't you?" Anna said to provoke him. "You do believe her, don't you, Andy?"

"See if I don't."

Aaron stared him in the face. "What does that mean?"

Andy folded his arms across his chest defiantly. "The town kids wanted to hate us, didn't they, Aaron? All the townspeople have always hated us. The high and mighty Odoms, they say. But I made them all admire me, even if I had to fight each boy one by one until he begged me to quit. I fought all our fights for us and won, didn't I? Didn't I, Father? I reckon I can fight another one without too much fuss."

Father touched Andy's shoulder. "Don't talk nonsense."

Andy pulled away from Father's hand. "Don't you worry about me. I'll be fine. You can be sure I won't shame the family name."

"Andy," Father implored. "You're much too young to understand what you're saying."

"Am I?"

Father studied him carefully. "What are you contemplating, Son? In just a few weeks you'll be graduating from high school, your future before you. What are you thinking about? What do you mean to do?"

"Right now, I mean to go to bed," Andy said. "I'm tired. Real tired. So good night." At the door, he turned back to face his brother. "Good luck, Aaron. I mean that. I love you. I'm sorry we've quarreled so much these last weeks. I wish you the best. You do what you have to do. So will I."

"Aaron?" Father said after Andy had left.

"I'm all right."

"Are you sure?" Anna asked.

Aaron smiled wanly. "As sure as I'll ever be, I guess."

"You must be certain," Father said. "Absolutely certain."

"Don't ask for too much. I'll never be as certain of myself as Andy," he said. "I should go to bed, too. So should you, Father. Tomorrow will be a long, difficult day."

But instead of following his older son to bed, Father helped us clean the table and wash the dishes until, having chipped a second plate, he let us gently shoo him away. Our work done, Anna retired to her room, I to mine, though it was barely ten. Had I already fallen asleep when I heard, mingled with the crickets, tree frogs, and owl, the crying of a child? Was it Aaron? Or Andy?

I dreamed again of Mother. Father was leaving for work while we five gathered on the porch of a tiny, plain brick house in town to wave him good-bye. Our frisky spaniel barked. The two cats merrily pounced into the leaf pile Andy and Aaron had raked.

It was a golden fall. Mother relaxed on the stoop, sipping her steaming coffee, her cheeks blushed by a chill breeze. Anna tugged on one pleat of Mother's skirt while I gripped another. Her black braids reached halfway down her back. A passing car tooted a greeting. Mother waved.

Children were playing in our yard, giggling, dancing in circles, turning clockwise and counterclockwise. Wearing a droopy straw hat, a boy sat on an old stump, a grin brightening his freckled face. Playing tag, other children chased one another from yard to yard.

Off in the distance, cowbells were tinkling. Willows shivered, their lacy stems glittering in the sun. Mother rested her mug on the porch rail and alternately braided my and Anna's hair, tying it, when she was done, with bright red ribbons. Aaron and Andy squatted in an old lawn chair and sucked on rock candy. She kissed them. She kissed us. And, as I woke, I felt in her kisses not just her care for us but her care for everyone in the whole world, her love for everything she did or touched.

Someone was rapping frantically on my door. "Louisa?" Anna said hoarsely.

Frightened, I rolled onto my side. "Yes?"

She walked in and opened the shades. The sky was a deep blue, a "serious blue," Father would say. Two finches pecked at the tray of the feeder that hung from my window ledge. Downstairs, I could hear Father, his voice uncharacteristically loud and shrill. But I couldn't make sense of his words.

I sat up straight. "What's happened?"

Anna was dressed for church. "It's Sunday morning," I

thought to calm myself, "and I've overslept again. Father's very angry." But why?

Anna tossed me my clothes. "Andy's left," she said. "Gone."

"Gone? Gone where?"

"He snuck away in the night and rode his horse to Charlie Sutton's. He took the morning train. Would you please try to dress more quickly, Louisa?"

"I can't help it. My fingers are shaking so."

"Charlie carried a note from Andy to Mutti, but Father intercepted it and read it first." She assisted me with the buttons on my right sleeve. "Andy's volunteering to fight in Vietnam."

"No!"

"We must protect Aaron, Louisa. That is our duty now." She grabbed my brush and brushed my hair. "Charlie rode Andy's horse back. Aaron's driving him home now."

"Listen," I said. "Father's no longer shouting."

"She must have just left for church," Anna conjectured. "She'd drive herself if she had to, she said. She was just putting on her gloves and pretty hat as I left the parlor."

"I must see Father," I said.

He was standing almost motionless, framed by the parlor window's stark linen curtains, its pleats in the morning sun stiff as bars. His hands clutching the sill, he leaned his forehead against a pane and stared out. Andy's note lay unfolded on the leather-top table.

Dear Grandmother,

I feel as happy as I felt last spring after I scored the winning run in that game against North Fork for the divisionals. And I'm as grateful to you as I was when you bought me Suzy. See that someone takes perfect care of her, will you, Mutti? And don't be upset at Aaron anymore. There's no need now, is there? Each

*war demands only one Odom, and maybe it's more
than luck that this time I'm the one. I'll hurry home as
soon as I can. Please give my love to everyone.*

Your devoted grandson,
Andrew Lane Odom

"Has Aaron read this?" I asked. Anna nodded. "I wish he
hadn't," I said.

"She's gone to church by herself, hasn't she?" Anna said to Father. "She believes in a hard God."

"Hard as Abraham's," Father said. "She hears him speak only
in thunder and music and sacrifice. I should know. The same man
who taught her how to listen to God's voice tried to teach me,
too." He checked his watch. "It's almost eleven. Aaron and I were
supposed to be at the Evans' house in Catawba by noon. What
can be keeping him?"

He quit the room abruptly. I sat next to Anna on the couch
and took her hand. "Think of the good times, Anna, please. Think
of how she used to hug Aaron after his recitals. Of how she
cheered Andy during his baseball games. Remember how she
helped us sew our first dresses and of the books she loaned us to
read. How she read the Brontës aloud to us and Virginia Woolf
even before we could understand them and made us listen and
love them anyway. How she held our hands during storms that
scared us. How gently she spoke to us about what it meant for
our bodies to bleed. Think of everything she's taught us about
this farm. Us, Anna. Not Andy. Not Aaron. Us. Please, please,
Anna, think of all that and so much more. Hating her would be
too terrible." I released my grip. "I feel a need to take a long walk.
Do you want to join me?"

She shook her head. "Not now, Louisa. I need to be alone for
a while."

I wandered in circles until twilight, occasionally resting in a bed of warm grass along a bank of the river. Half of the after-noon, one of the Tibbetts' old hounds followed me, wanting to play until another dog finally distracted him away. I hid in the barn for a while, until I heard some of our dairymen returning from church. I found a jar of milk in one of the dairy's refrigera-tors and drank it fast, surprised at my thirst. As I leaned against a tree trunk on a knoll near the house, I studied its obvious failures in design and debated with myself if any counterarguments could be made for its aesthetic success. I gave the cows grazing in the pasture names and considered what life must be like for creatures that possessed bovine brains and stomachs. Hilda and Gladys, Kay and Mary Beth.

As I approached the stoop, I saw Father half sitting, half lying in the swing that hung from the ceiling of the verandah. Was he asleep? Or was he still waiting for Aaron? "Father?"

He lifted his head. "Mutti's prepared a little dinner. She left it in the kitchen. Have some when you're hungry."

"I'm not hungry. Is Aaron home yet?"

"No." He shook his head in despair. "Not yet."

"Maybe he's gone to the Evans' on his own. Maybe he didn't want to endanger you."

"Maybe."

"Aaron will be safe," I assured him.

He stilled the swing. "Will he?"

"If he's not home shortly, the next time we'll hear from him will be his first letter from Toronto or Montreal. You have my guarantee."

But when Aaron's letter arrived it was postmarked neither Montreal nor Toronto. He had mailed it from Atlanta. Other-wise there was no return address, and he chose not to write a salutation.

> *I could not let my brother fight for me. I abominate this war. I despise all war. But I could not let my brother*

fight instead of me, alone. Please do not tell him what I have done. All my love,

Aaron

A few hours after Father had read it, Anna and I found him on the floor of his room. He was very still. Mutti called the doctor. It took more than an hour for the ambulance to appear.

"He could recover completely," Dr. Higham informed Anna over the phone. "It's possible."

"How possible?"

"Well, that depends on Drew, doesn't it?" she reported to me he had said. "He's not all that old, not yet fifty. He's reasonably fit. It's his right side I'm worried about, especially his arm."

"His bowing arm. The one he writes with."

"Exactly," Dr. Higham said.

At suppertime, I carried some food on a tray upstairs to Mutti. "Grandmother?" I said through the door. "I've brought you some dinner."

"How thoughtful. But, no thank you, dear."

Nor did she accept any food the next day or the day after that. "She'll starve," I said to Anna who replied, "Let her."

The following morning, I tiptoed down the hall. When I reached her room, I pressed my ear against the door. Was she listening to music? No, she was weeping, though obviously she was attempting to stifle the sound of it, perhaps with handkerchiefs or her hands or a pillow. After I carried the tray downstairs, I reported to Anna what I had heard.

Both her hands clenched into fists. "I can't accept it. I won't. It's offensive, intolerable. She has no right to grieve."

By noon, Grandmother had abandoned her room and returned to her chores, as diligent and thorough as ever. Just before dinner, I heard her playing Bach in the parlor, one of her beloved Forty-eight, I presumed. I snuck into the room to listen. Although Anna would berate me for saying so, her expression was rapt, and her strong, graceful fingers didn't seem to miss a note.

"Grandmother," I remarked after she had finished the prelude. "That was beautiful."

"Beautiful?" She squinted at me disapprovingly. "It was Bach."

"Didn't you praise Aaron's playing of that Bach cello suite last Christmas as beautiful? I'm certain that you did. Why must you be so disagreeable, Mutti? Especially now, when we're all suffering so?"

"Everyone suffers, dear child, every day. There's nothing extraordinary about suffering. What alone matters is how one suffers. Do you understand, Louisa?"

"I don't know. Maybe. But . . ."

"I don't want you to be sentimental. Odom women must never be sentimental. Your poor mother was, I fear. Suffering scared her to death."

Returning her face to the piano, she lightly rested her fingers on the keyboard, a gesture she often used to signal a dismissal. "Suffering, beauty," she proclaimed. "Sentimentalities from which Bach, thank God, is blessedly free."

Without quite meaning to, I bowed and began to back out of the parlor. She started to play the fugue, her fingers moving as they frequently seemed to move during such intricate passages, as if the score she was reading already inhabited them. I yearned to shout at her, "How dare you diminish my Mother. You've never truly loved anyone in your life." But I managed to persuade myself to vacate the room, perhaps for no better reason than I feared hearing her dismiss me as sentimental again.

Later that afternoon, when I asked her, Anna agreed to walk with me through our woods once more.

Aaron Rose Odom

Two hundred seventy-one. If a man always knows when he is about to die, does a woman always know when she's just about to become pregnant? Would Tu know? Would she tell me? Would she know whether it's mine?

Two hundred seventy-four. "How can anyone bear to be proud," Father writes me in his most recent letter, "when all pride is indistinguishable from the terror it tries to hide? Pride is the ruler who, after savage armies have devastated his lands, looks out over them with joy and declares to himself, 'Let all things pass away.' Pride is the great Polish musician who practices his violin even as the bombs fall upon his Warsaw and the fires begin. Pride is the believer who after all his family has been destroyed by plague will not curse God and die but instead praises Him and His mysteries. The truth of things is cruel, Aaron, but now you know that far better than I. Yet don't let that knowledge make you proud. Pride is the blindfold God ties around our eyes just before He orders His soldiers to fire."

Am I proud of anything? I'm proud of my prick.

Two hundred eighty. I've recorded so many deaths from combat in the last few days and filed them away that, Tuesday, my body died. Until on Friday lust again returned to save me. Thank God for desire. Praise the Lord for hard-ons.

Would my body have ever known so clearly what it now longs for if Tu had not aroused such yearnings in me? Maybe. Several times a week she resurrects me from death. She's my Jesus summoning her stinking Lazarus from his grave.

Her room in Cholon is a cheap, bare, sleazy hut that stinks of rotting bamboo and men's sweat. The sun when it seeps through its shades is always lightbulb yellow and harsh. Her bed is an old battered mattress she hauled in from the street, lumpy and hard. She softens it with piles of cloth that we strip off it like clothes as we screw.

Two hundred eighty-four. The hottest, most humid days on the farm are to Saigon's heat as, say, one of Father Owens's sermons is to a Holy Roller's ranting, as Puccini is to Wagner, as war journalists and TV reporters are to soldiers, as masturbation is to fucking.

Two hundred ninety. The world's arithmetic: 12 mos. + 1 mo. = 13 mos. Nam's arithmetic: 12 mos. + 1 mo. = 12 mos. R and R doesn't count. No one counts the days you're supposed to be unafraid.

Two hundred ninety-five. Some of the old pleasures that I need to write down before I forget them: Playing trios with Father and Mutti or sonatas with just Mutti, especially Brahms's Second and Reger's Fourth. Practicing Bach by myself in my room or in winter on the sun porch. Watching Anna and Louisa prepare a meal, shucking corn, shelling peas, slicing tomatoes, stirring a sauce, their long slender fingers and their long slender necks graceful as dancers'. Seeing them stand hand-in-hand on a distant ridge, the sunshine on their hair bright like light reflected off a mirror. Riding the school bus home when we were all little to where Odom Road enters Route 4. Al Tibbetts waiting for us parked next to the fence, the gate open, chewing on a cigar that

Mutti forbade him ever to light on her property. Skinny-dipping with Andy in the pond after Mutti and the girls had left or, after the pond was drained, in the pool we discovered beneath the cascade on Indian Head Ridge, a good ten-mile hike from the farm. Swinging off the barn's roof from the rope Andy had tied to a limb of the tallest oak and onto the roof of the stable. Even mucking the stable with Andy and the Tibbetts and Simon Trask, showering after when it took an hour to scrub clean. Seeing Father lying peacefully on his bed in his room as he listened to a new record with his eyes closed, his attention to the music so intense it transformed his usual scowl almost into a smile. Getting lost in the woods with Andy and feeling safe no matter how far we had wandered even after we'd spotted fresh bear tracks. Breezes floating through the windows of my room bringing with them the scents of new blossoms, fresh-cut grass, and honeysuckle. Anna and Louisa laughing as they chased each other back and forth through Mutti's boxwood maze. Mowing hay, herding the cows back to the barn, relaxing on the grass afterward, chewing on a blade of it, staring up at the peaceful sky.

Three hundred two. Why haven't I written Father about Tu? I won't. I can't.

Maybe Andy would understand. Maybe, now that he's also surely been changed by this war, wherever he is. Father believes his cynicism, his bitterness about life has freed him from vulgar morality just as Mutti believes her pride has liberated her from all common beliefs. They're both wrong, especially Father.

I've never felt free from him and his judgments. I didn't need Andy's barely conscious jealousy or Anna's cutting asides to see how differently he loved me from the way he loved my brother and sisters. Did he love them less? Or did he merely attend to me more? He was always watching me, no matter where I went or what I was doing.

Even when I was alone, I could sense his eyes on me. In his

heart, he was constantly spying on me through a door he kept always ajar, like an anxious wife, watching her husband in another room, wanting to see everything he did but not be seen herself. I could always feel his gaze, his worried frown, his inescapable concern. Until Tu. Until now.

Three hundred seven. Father's letters are increasingly difficult to decipher. Maybe he should dictate them, like Milton to his daughters.

He reports a fact he's just discovered. There was once a Russian mathematician, Krylov by name, who calculated that the distance from Earth to God must be exactly nine light-years. How? "Easy," Father writes. 1905 was the year the Russo-Japanese War ended, mostly in disaster for the Russians. Therefore, Krylov reasoned, it must have taken exactly eighteen light-years for the prayers of the Russian people for vengeance to reach God and then to be fulfilled in the great Japanese earthquake of 1923—nine years for the prayers to fly to God, nine more for His answer to be hurled back down to Japan.

Father remarks that it must have been Krylov's assumption that it takes war and catastrophe to measure God's distance from us. So a mathematician devises a calculus by which we can measure that distance. He graphs a parabola from wrath to revenge.

Father speculates that this war won't end until 1981. He accuses Kennedy of having begun it in 1963. According to Krylov's calculations, he figures it will take eighteen years for the North Vietnamese and Vietcong's prayers to be answered. "What additional catastrophe will befall our nation in that year?" he wonders almost with glee. "I long for 1981."

Have Father's cynicism, his bitterness, his mordancy, been his only pleasures throughout his life? Or only since Mother died?

Three hundred eight. No one knows where Andy is. Father writes, "Thank God you're reasonably safe behind a desk in

Saigon. Behind a desk is the best place to be during a war." He seems to take some comfort in the word *office*. I'll never tell him what I do in mine.

Three hundred nine. If Andy knows I'm in this God-forsaken country along with him, why haven't I heard a word from him? But how could he know, unless he wanted to know?

Yet I'm sure he knows.

Father once researched a people called the Etoro who believe that every man possesses an immaterial spirit double called an *ausulubo*. He wanted to learn if, when the man dies, his double also dies.

I wonder if, when Andy left, he knew for certain that I'd follow. Or was this a fact that only Grandmother understood? Would she feel prouder if we both died?

Three hundred eleven. I met a sergeant the other day from some outfit no one's supposed to know about somewhere in the vicinity of Pleiku. He was lounging in Saigon on a little R and R. He told me he'd met another Odom just a few weeks ago, thought his first name might have been Andrew. But he wasn't sure.

Seven months ago, I spoke to a guy who claimed he'd traveled here with Andy from Oakland and Travis.

I thought I might have traced him once to a position in the Kim Son valley, but heard he'd been transferred to the Delta. Then I learned he was supposed to be at the Cambodian border, not looking at it from, but back to Vietnam.

A sergeant I encountered in a bar swore he'd drunk some beers with an Andy Odom who was a helicopter pilot or maybe a door gunner flying out of maybe Phu Bai. Blond kid with kind of a snotty-nosed attitude. Talked with a slow fancy drawl like he was putting you on. Used a lot of fancy words. Stuck on himself. "Like you," he said to me, "only he didn't look like you at all."

Andy doesn't want to be found. I don't blame him. Not anymore. I don't want to be found either.

Three hundred thirteen. Stories of more fraggings, some right here in Saigon. The most recent one, a too cool lieutenant from Connecticut by a not so gung-ho Georgia grunt who wanted to live long enough to get back home.

Three hundred eighteen. Bored, staring out the window, tapping my pencil on my desk top, humming a tune. Smithson, passing by, halts. "Bach," he identifies, "Brandenburg no. 5." I hum it again. He's right. Good for him. "Not what I'd expect to be hearing here," he says.

That afternoon, he invites me to his *quarters*, a room he rents to get away from the *noise* and the *madness*.

Like Tu's, it's sparely furnished, but with far finer things: a couple of good chairs imported from the States, a new springy mattress on the floor, some plump, colorful pillows, and a nearly perfect stereo set, all components Japanese, its speakers four feet tall with pitch-perfect sound, much better than anything we owned at home.

Smithson puts on the Goldberg Variations with Glenn Gould. Although it reminds me of Mutti, I don't ask him to play something else. I like Gould. The aria soothes. By the time it returns we've smoked two joints.

He asks me what I'd like to hear. I tell him, the fifth cello suite. I don't look at the jacket. As it plays, I try to guess. Starker? Tortelier? Immaculate. Passionate. I vow never to attempt to play the cello again. I vow never to go home. And fall asleep.

I wake to sirens in the street and the stench of burning tires. Cam Smithson is holding my hand.

Three hundred twenty. I am grateful to Tu. I am grateful to Saigon. I am grateful, God damn it, for my safe office job.

No more pigs rooting among charred bodies. No more phosphorous shells (expensive) or Zippo lighters (cheap) setting fires to villages. No more rows of yellow casualty tags tied to a boot or a body bag. No more danger of jungle rot or blackwater fever. No more elephant grass slicing my skin like a slick blade. No more having to watch a guy whose nuts have just been blown off writhe in agony and terror. No more having to look at a clutch belt and flak jacket with nothing to surround except some guts, a shredded arm, pieces of fingers. No more having to hear someone whisper, "Ambush, ambush. Don't bunch up, damn it. Stay spread out. Don't bunch up."

Just paper, pencil, pen, and typewriter. Not the horrors themselves, but only the names of those who suffered them.

Who is Aaron Odom? A petty bureaucrat in an office dedicated to death. A minor functionary in a mausoleum where the bodies we bury are papers, the blood we shed is ink.

The Vietnamese plant trees to honor their dead. They light joss sticks. I write down the names of ours and file them away.

Three hundred twenty-three. I shot one man in the face, another right through his heart. Those are the two I saw. How many months ago? Four? Five? I heard their shrieks even though I knew they hadn't actually cried out. I heard them scream long after they'd died. But I don't hate myself. I don't even blame myself. Not yet. Why not? Why not?

Three hundred twenty-five. Signal flares machete knife dry socks 3-day rations poncho map compass C-4 explosives M-16 clips of bullets couple of grenades 1st aid kit malaria pills halizone tablets canteen versus a basket boat as tightly woven and beautifully crafted as any tapestry the West has ever made. Versus a sunset you risk your neck to climb out of the jungle onto a mountainside to see.

Three hundred twenty-seven. Smithson keeps inviting me back to his quarters. I keep accepting, even when I assure myself I would much rather be with Tu. Which is more the lure, the music or the dope? I tell myself, Tu needs the time by herself to work. But most of what I tell myself isn't true.

On Sunday, Lieutenant Merrill tags along. "Another music lover," Cam says.

Cam allows him to choose a record from the stack. Tim picks Berlioz, the *Symphonie Fantastique*. "Head music." Smithson winces.

("Hector Berlioz was unquestionably a madman," Grandmother warned me when she caught me borrowing Father's records of *La Damnation de Faust*, "and madmen make terrible artists. No self-control, no sense of form, no discipline at all.")

Tim smokes too much. So does Cam. So do I. Just excess, with no interest in wisdom's palace.

The streets outside look seductively European, like something from a black-and-white movie shot in Paris by a New Wave director. A car is burning, the smoke lustrous, thick, and black as tar, yet somehow elegant. The flowers and leaves are not plants but translucent jewels that chime in the wind like glass bells.

Slowly stripping to the music, Cam doffs all his clothes as Tim applauds. Buck naked, he saunters to the balcony and steps out. He fondles his cock, talking to it, then directs it over the railing and pees, his urine forming a beautiful yellow arc and splashing on the sidewalk below. "Barattatat," he yells. "Blam. Pow. Ooph. Takka takka, takka takka. Take that ape man. Thud. Crunch."

As he begins to climb over the rail, I rush out to grab him, catching him just as he begins to pitch over. I hold my arms tighter around his body and drag him back in.

Tim's rolling all over the floor, like someone whose clothes are on fire, laughing crazily. Cam kisses my cheek and asks me to lie next to him on the mattress. His cock reddens and swells. "Touch me, Aaron."

Tim sits up and quits laughing. He unlaces his boots, stands up, and drops his pants. Underneath his shorts, he's also rigid.

"No," I say.

Tim says, "You mean yes."

"When I say no, I mean no," I say. But I'm way too stoned to return to the street on my own.

Three hundred twenty-eight. Cam walks past my desk like we'd never met. So does Tim. Good. Maybe. Or do they both now think of me as a threat? My time is almost up. I'm afraid of trouble.

Three hundred thirty-two. Joe Acheson, Larry McKay, and I visit a bar that's just opened near our office, one that's been decorated for Americans. They've painted the ceiling in bold stripes of red, white, and blue. But over the walls they've crisscrossed and swirled a jungle of rat-a-tat-tat orange, zowie purple, and bam-bam-bam aluminum. They've created a psychedelic bar, all the music by San Francisco bands singing about peace, love, and getting high.

On the street, two South Vietnamese soldiers accost an old woman who's carrying an ominous looking sack on her back, big as a child. The barkeep turns off the music and stands by the door to listen to the soldier's words. Joe asks him a question in his halting Vietnamese. We all hear the response: "VC."

Had she already tried to trigger the device? Before she can make a second attempt, the soldiers shoot her.

I've never been so afraid in my life. Why? Because I wasn't prepared for fear? At least, I tell myself, I'm no longer afraid of being afraid.

Three hundred thirty-three. Smithson's left a note on my desk. "Don't fight it."

During my next visit to the john, I look at my face in the

mirror over the basin. Unlike Andy, I've never been vain about my appearance. I had no reason to be. I check my left profile, then my right. "Maybe it's not as bad as you thought," I say.

Three hundred thirty-four. Tu touches me all over like she knows I'm going to be leaving soon. How do I respond so she might understand I don't mean to abandon her? How should I hold her, kiss her, fuck her?

I met my first girl outside Tan Son Nhut airport. The second in what passed for a whorehouse in Da Nang. The third inside the Meyercourt. The fourth, too expensive, at a table in the Continental Palace Hotel. Tu Loc was the fifth, the only one whose name I learned.

Does Andy know how much I envied him his girlfriends? He never bragged. He didn't have to, not to me. Everyone envies Andy. He's the beauty of the family. Next to his fancy bloom, I'm a stalky weed, olive dark like Mother with permanent shadows under my eyes, not the sort of boy Alexandersville girls would deign to notice even if my name hadn't been Odom and already off their list of eligible mates. But Andy was so good-looking he dazzled them into forgetting he was one of those Odoms for whom the word *proud* might have been invented if anyone, including the Odoms themselves, had been able to figure out exactly what it was they were supposed to be so damned proud about.

All I wanted was a girl's body next to mine, under mine, on top of mine, all over me. I read book after book. I listened to music. I played music, practicing hour after hour. I talked to Father about God and art. I worked next to Andy in the fields. But all I thought about in my heart of hearts was sex. Yet, until I landed in Vietnam, I'd never slept with a girl. I'd never fucked anything except my hand. I'd never been in love.

When I first saw Tu, she was wearing those silk trousers and orange, filmy *ao-dais* I find so sexy, so enticing, so alluring, as they say. She was working, of course. She's a hard-working girl, a real professional. But I was glad she was a pro. I was still shy. It was easier to be asked to pay. In dollars. She insists upon dollars. She needs the dollars for her mother and her sisters, she says. To protect them. "And your brothers?" I asked. When she shook her head no, she meant to tell me she has no brothers. But I've learned since she has at least two, both fighting on the other side. She's afraid of them. She's afraid of the Americans. She's afraid of everyone.

After I met her, I quit trying to learn Vietnamese. I didn't want a lot of words between us. Words, even if only a few carefully chosen ones like pride, have killed too many Odoms already. I just wanted to make love. The English words she understands are mostly the jargon of her trade. Her art, I sometimes like to think.

Because I was inept at sex and even more naive, she shocked me at first. Then she taught me how to please her so that I would be more than just another customer.

Tramp. Slut. Prostitute. Hooker. Harlot. Whore. Hateful words, which I can't stop thinking. They light up like a neon sign all the time in my head, especially as I'm walking away from her room at night.

This morning, her eyes would not leave my body. She twisted the tight black curls of my pubic hair into knots with her fingers. She licked and kissed my cock while it hardened and pulsed. But, as I attempted to enter her, she clutched her belly and wept and wept.

Three hundred thirty-eight. I never read Mutti's letters but immediately tear them up and toss them out. I only skim Anna's or Louisa's since all either of them talks about is the farm. So why can't I ignore Father's?

In today's, he says he's dedicated the rest of his life to the god of irony. He encourages me to do the same. Father will never change.

Three hundred thirty-nine. A letter from Andy. A letter from my brother.

I wait five hours to read it, never letting it out of my sight. But it's not a real letter. Just a note. He's been sent to a sector only seventy miles up the river from Saigon.

How long had he known where to find me?

"Do you want to see me? Would you like to talk?"

I write back, "Yes. Of course."

"Forgive me?"

I want to write back, "For what?" but don't.

I should have fled to Canada when I had my chance. Or maybe I should have waited out these days in the purity of some jail. Why, as I drove Charlie Sutton back home after Andy had run away on the morning train, did I change my mind? Only because, like my brother, I was an Odom, afraid of being afraid?

Father asks me what I've learned. Two truths, Father. One is that when splattered together a pig's brains and a man's brains look pretty much the same. The other is that of a world which makes such things happen even God Himself is not ashamed to be afraid.

Three hundred forty-one. Cam Smithson informs me about a convoy scheduled to head where I've told him I need to go. It leaves the day after tomorrow at 0500.

He asks me if I'd like to rendezvous with him in his room before I leave. Just once more, before I quit this country for good very soon.

I tell him about Tu. I write down her address for him. "In case something happens to me," I say. "You never know."

"Have you told anyone else about her?"

"Nope. Not a soul."

"I'm flattered." He pockets the slip of paper. "I'll look after her. You have my word." He grins like the boy he probably still was not so many months before. "Aaron."

"It's not really me. Honest."

"You put on a good show of it then. Just an hour," he pleads. "I can arrange it so easily whenever you like. You've seen."

"No, Cam. I mean it. No."

He blushes. "You're going to make me say it, aren't you?"

"Say what?"

"I love you."

What else could I do? I tell the truth. "I love Tu."

Three hundred forty-one. I'm gathering my things from Tu's room, preparing to depart tomorrow to see Andy. Suddenly, she collapses on the floor. She claws at my legs. She bawls and shrieks. Does she think I'm abandoning her for good, already on my way back home?

Its toes spread out on a squat table, an unusually ugly gecko peers at us between slits that reveal eyes as demon-haunted as a cat's. "Tu," I say. "It's my brother. I've got to meet my brother up north. I've got to see him. I have to. We parted badly. It's been over a year. I'll be back."

How much does she understand? I display four fingers. "That many days," I say. "Then I'll be back. Here," I say, pointing to her mattress.

I force myself free of her grip and pry open the door to step out. When I glance behind me, she's holding her belly, hugging herself tenderly, pitifully, like a mother caressing her sick child.

Overwhelmed by her grief, I kneel next to her. "Tu. I won't go. I'll stay. Marry," I pronounce slowly. "Marry me?"

Her tears stop. Her eyes glisten with contempt. Or is it fear? "No. No. Fool. Fool," she screams at me. With the force of her frantic fists she drives me away.

Anna Ruth Odom

"Waiting is maddening," I grumbled to Louisa one day when no letter had arrived for Father from Aaron for weeks and weeks and we hadn't yet despaired of ever hearing from Andy again. "You can't stop hoping even though you're scared to death. Or do you have to hope because you're so afraid? Remember, Louisa? 'Your mother isn't dying, little girls. She's just very tired. Soon she'll be fine and on her feet and in your room, generous as always with her hugs and kisses.' Wasn't that when we learned how to hope, Louisa? While Mother lay dying?"

"We weren't yet two when Mother died. How can you remember so well?"

"And Dr. Higham. Does he really think we're so stupid? 'Your father didn't suffer a serious stroke. Just a couple of little ones. He'll be his old self in a month or two. Be patient, girls. He'll be sawing that fiddle of his again in no time, I guarantee.'"

"He was only trying to comfort us. He meant well. Father has shown some improvement."

"And Andy and Aaron are outside scuffling on the lawn, frolicking and yelping like puppies. They didn't go to war, after all. Look, there are their fishing poles leaning against the screen door and, balanced on the rail, see, the jar of worms they've just dug up."

"Anna, that's mean. Why must you be so mean?"

I should have told her, "Hope makes me mean. It makes me

crazy with worry. Don't you know I'm terrified that they'll both be killed?" But I held my tongue.

Why did we continue to attend church every Sunday morning, Mutti, Louisa, and I? Sometimes, though rarely, even Father, with our help, limped along. Louisa would defend our churchgoing by saying, "You can't be mortal and not pray."

I'd reply, "Only crazy people believe in prayer."

And she'd respond, "Then I guess you're as crazy as I am, Anna."

From his pulpit one Sunday morning, Father Owens read, "Out of the depths have I cried unto thee, O Lord. My soul waits for the Lord more than they that watch for the morning."

I thought to myself, "Well, at least he may understand that much about us. Not one of us sleeps past dawn."

After that service, Grandmother uncharacteristically planted herself on the church lawn and let other members of the congregation shake her hand as they walked past. Was she playing the patriotic grandmother who had inspired her two grandsons to fight for God and country?

"You Odoms have always done more than your part. Have always sacrificed so much," one old biddy, Miss Alice Waddell, praised her. "Your boys are always in our thoughts and prayers."

"Continue to be strong, Elisabeth," old Marian Tate, the pharmacist's wife, advised.

The high-school principal said, "Andrew did what only an Odom boy would do on the eve of his graduation. It wouldn't have been what I'd have recommended, Mrs. Odom, but his gesture honors us all. As does Aaron's remarkable conversion. What an example you must be to your grandsons! You, and all those amazing Odoms before you, of course."

Dressed in a too tight suit, Sam Willetts returned his homburg to his globe-like head and inquired, "How are you good people holding up?"

"I always knew those boys were real smart," Ethel Rae Willetts remarked, "but it's been a blessing upon us to see how they've become such fine moral examples to the rest of our young, so many of whom have lately lost the way of righteousness." Her eyes were almost dewy. "And your son, Mrs. Odom? Faring better, I hope?"

"Quite well, I thank you. I thank each and every one of you dear people," Grandmother said to all, her features finely composed, her stance dignified, her voice noble. Was I the only one to see through the pose? "Your good, kind words sustain us."

"Dear people?" I challenged her a few minutes later in the car. "They despise us, Mutti. Every platitude they mouth drips venom."

Mutti ignored the stop sign at the intersection and stepped more forcefully on the gas. Was she smiling? Since I was sitting behind her in the backseat, I could barely see her face in the rearview mirror. "Never let people understand you, Anna. Let them love you or hate you or not care about you in the slightest. It really doesn't matter. But never ever provide anyone with the opportunity to understand you. As I suggest you not try to understand me."

For the thousandth time at least, I thought the word *bitch* to myself and blushed furiously as I imagined how I had almost just let it slip out.

On Sunday afternoons, Mutti invariably worked as hard as she worked all day every other day of the week. She never needed to remind Louisa and me that without her the farm would fail even though we'd added many of our brothers' chores to those we already performed. Ever vigilant, Mutti ordered, commanded, bossed, and cajoled the dozen men and more who worked for her without their ever overtly complaining. Perhaps they held their tongues because she made a point of paying them well, higher wages than any of them could have earned anywhere else in the county.

Was her insomnia an unsuppressable symptom of some soul

sickness or heart weariness she would never otherwise allow to be shown? Or just more evidence of her exceptional vigor and strength? Father praised her as a stoic in the best Roman tradition. "Listen, Anna. Hear how beautifully she plays Bach or Scarlatti. While she's playing such music, her spirit rises like Seneca's above all suffering."

"And when she's not playing, Father?" Her playing had always infuriated me. What right did she have to rise above the suffering she had so plainly caused?

"'Honor thy father and thy mother that thy days may be long upon the land which the Lord thy God giveth thee.' It's the only commandment that comes with promise of a reward, maybe because it's such a difficult commandment to obey. I must love her, Anna, as nearly impossible as that is for me to do most of the time. So must you."

Father had taught himself to write with his left hand. His self-instruction was imperfect, however. Although his writing gave him something to do with his days, what he produced was a nearly illegible scrawl. It might as well have been an intentional cipher.

But he wrote Aaron often, telling none of us what he had said. Aaron's replies were few, erratic, and evasive, especially after he'd been transferred to Saigon. I wasn't the only one who suspected he was nowhere near so safe as he claimed.

Father wrote more than letters, too. He kept this work hidden in boxes he stored on the shelves next to his bed. When I asked him what his topic was, he answered, "A history of my failures." But then he reconsidered. "I have no topic. There is no topic. How could there be? I'm writing about the irresponsibilities of the heart."

Every so often, he would open his Bible at random. Despite all his professed earlier convictions, had the war made him superstitious? But he'd cheat. He'd place his thumbnail exactly where the book would have to fall open to a joyous psalm. Once, after his thumb slipped and his Bible opened on Jeremiah instead, Father read, "No flesh shall have peace." "No more sortilege for me," he said.

"Can anyone live without hope for signs and wonders?" I asked. "I find I can't believe in Heaven anymore, Father. I'm almost certain I never did. Is that a sin?"

"Ask Father Owens."

"I'm asking you. I think you'll be more honest."

"I was once told the only unforgivable sin was the sin against the Holy Ghost. Against love."

"I may not believe in love either, Father. I'm sorry."

"Sometimes you sound like your grandmother, Anna."

"Yes. So Louisa has often remarked."

The summer following the summer after the spring when Aaron and Andy had run away in the night like two frightened boys chased by ghosts was the hottest on record. Our workers repeatedly announced that fact as if it were a statistic to be proud of. But why should anyone be proud of circumstances that owe nothing to anything human? Mere endurance of nature's whims is no reason for pride.

Trees drooped and sagged. Protected by whatever shade they could find, the cows chewed their cud as if they were conscious of their exertion, as if moving their jaws wider than necessary might cause the poor creatures to keel over. The river merely trickled. Rocks lying exposed on its bed appeared to have been burned white like old bones. Corn and sorghum shriveled to stalk and stem. The men plowed it under. The dairy's generators worked night and day. Every afternoon, Mutti scanned the heavens, anxiously awaiting the heavy gray clouds that had always rumbled across our skies in August, bringing whipping winds and torrential rains. But rain clouds did not darken the heavens until late September when one afternoon the sky blackened and lightning flashed quick and bright, like a filament burning out. Thereafter, it poured and poured for weeks.

Mutti, Louisa, and I were either always sopping wet or busy changing our rain-soaked clothes until, as suddenly and arbitrarily as the rains had begun, they quit. Apparently some weather-god had determined that the earth had been watered enough for a while. The air cooled. Fall began. Despite the drought, the leaves slowly mutated from green to red, orange, yellow, or rust and when they fell they descended to earth as beautifully as flowers in their last bloom.

I was working in my little vegetable garden, the plot Mutti had finally granted me for my experiments with organic methods, when I spotted a dull gray-green car driving along Odom Road to our long driveway, which it crept up as cautiously as it might have during a winter ice storm. The soldiers parked to the north of the verandah where Mutti was already waiting for them as if she'd been warned they were coming. The young driver stepped out of one side, another mere boy, equally sad faced and wearing a nearly identical uniform, out of the other.

Mutti accepted the envelope they handed her with a bow. While the taller of the two talked, she listened intently. The other spoke at greater length, holding his hands open, palms out, like someone offering an apology. But even after he had delivered his message she remained silent and tight lipped. When two big crows cawed in a nearby pine, she glanced up to spot them, but the sun shone in her face. She covered her eyes with her hands like a visor and stood very still for several minutes. Slowly, her arms returned to her sides. She again bowed to the boys as they backed deferentially off the verandah.

Mutti watched them drive away and returned into the house. The expression on her face told me not to approach or question her yet. She would have to tell Father first.

I didn't hesitate. I dashed to the stable. Billy Akers was currying Suzy as Louisa treated her with an apple. I caught my breath, clutching a crossbar on the stable door. "Louisa! Come! Come!"

We met Grandmother on the front staircase landing. She had

just left Father's room. At her silent bidding, we followed her into the parlor where she sat in the chair beneath Great-grandfather's portrait and formally folded her hands together. "It was Aaron." She didn't need to add, "He's been killed. He's dead. Your older brother's dead." Her infuriating poise sufficed to inform us of that.

Both Louisa and I resembled her more than either of us had ever dared to admit out loud, of course. Neither of us cried. Neither of us wept. Neither of us screamed out of grief and rage and loss. Rather we quietly sat down side-by-side on the couch. Louisa took my hand in hers.

Was Mutti nibbling on her lower lip? Had I ever seen her do so before? She rose from the chair. "Drew has never been a strong man. I may have failed to prepare him carefully enough for the news. I may have told him too quickly, girls. I've called Higham, as a precaution. But I ask you not to go up there. Not yet." She walked into the hall. "He's responded in a way I could not have predicted."

I called her back. "Grandmother?"

She paused under the lintel, her back toward us. "He was riding in a convoy, northwest of Saigon. It was early morning. A tree had fallen, or more likely been felled, across the road. All the trucks had to halt until it was removed. Some peasants were walking along the shoulder. Guerrillas. Their grenades destroyed three of the trucks, including the one Aaron was riding in."

She stopped, but still did not look at us until Louisa said, "Oh, Mutti."

She turned, her face clear white like the best old porcelain. "Those two sweet boys were pathetically ill-prepared for their job. They could hardly bear to tell me that Aaron's been dead for weeks and weeks. Papers were misplaced." Did I detect a slight tremor in her hands? "His body, what remains of it, was lost for almost a month. Such things happen during the disarray of wartime, of course, but . . ."

"Grandmother," Louisa said, rising to comfort her.

To my surprise, Mutti accepted her embrace. "Soulless. Soulless and base and small. That is what the world is like in this new age." She shook off Louisa's arms and glided down the hall.

I said, "We must see Father."

"But Grandmother . . ."

"We must."

His room was lined with hundreds of books and thousands of records he had rarely revisited since Aaron and Andy had gone. Unused, his violin lay in its case in a dark corner on the floor. The leather upholstery of his chair was flaking like paint. His right arm dangled uselessly. A trace of saliva oozed between his lips.

He began to curse, vile imprecations full of the foulest language Louisa and I had ever heard. If we had perhaps read such words somewhere or somehow become aware of their existence, they nevertheless had never before been spoken in our presence, not even by our workmen at a stubborn mule or cow or intractable machine, nor by the cruder boys or men in town. No one would have been so rude or deliberately vulgar in front of us.

But Father hurled them at us. He meant to offend. He meant to hurt, to wound. They spewed from him. Louisa clapped her hands over her ears and shrieked.

I reached out my hand to touch him, to perhaps appease him, but with brute force his left arm struck my hand. He raged obscenely against God. Louisa pulled me back, away from his reach as his oaths turned into a childlike high-pitched wordless scream.

How long had Mutti been standing behind us? "Anna. Louisa. It is not right for you to be here. You must go. Drew, stop it. Stop it. Now!"

Slowly, he quieted. His eyes turned gray and bulged like the back of a spoon. Mutti glanced anxiously at the clock on Father's dresser. Grabbing my hand, Louisa dragged me out.

The ambulance didn't arrive until another hour had passed.

Once more, it carried our father to the hospital in town. Mutti rode beside him, holding his hand. That night, at my sister's request, I slept next to Louisa in her too soft bed with the frilly canopy I'd long ago removed from mine. We stared into the night it seemed to hold.

"Do you think Andy knows?" she wondered.

"No. I don't know. Maybe."

"If you were to die somewhere away from me, I'd know immediately. The instant you died, I'd know. My soul would feel it."

"Do you think so, Louisa?"

"Yes . . ." She touched my wrist. "I dread every day now. Every day is a day I dread."

I pecked her dewy cheek. "Try to sleep."

"Will we ever part, Anna, you and I? Surely someday you'll want to marry."

"Don't be silly, Louisa. What man would ever want to marry me?"

"I believe God must be like nighttime mist or fog," she said. "Something that the sun burns away almost every day. Or maybe He's like a dream we can't quite remember in the morning."

"Perhaps it would be better for our family, Louisa, if God did not exist. He does not seem to care for our family."

"Do you think Mutti is ever afraid?"

"Of what? Of God?"

"Of anything?"

I rolled away from her, annoyed by the question. "I don't know. I really don't want to think about her right now."

"*Pone metum*," she muttered to herself.

"Arrogant nonsense, Louisa."

"I'm scared to death."

"Are you?"

I could hear her breathing. "Forgive me. Just one more question. Then I'll let you go to sleep. Do you really think some day we'll own this farm, just you and me? I was just wishing it might be so. It's a silly question, I know. You needn't answer."

The same ambulance that had carried Father to town brought him back home to the farm three weeks later. Four days afterward, a hearse rolled down the same road to turn not up our driveway but into the wide horse trail that led to the family cemetery. At his request, the Tibbetts brothers and Billy Akers moved Father's bed and much of his furniture from his old room to the previously empty one that had long ago served as Great-grandfather's study and that looked out over the lawn through the gardens to the graves.

Although Mutti had insisted the graveside ceremony be private, she also made certain that the army would send an appropriate honor guard. From a safe distance, closer to Mother's mossy headstone than to Aaron's sparkling new one, Louisa and I watched them strut and swagger. "They've been over-rehearsed," I whispered to Louisa as they removed the flag from the coffin on which it had been draped, folded it, and stiffly handed it to Mutti. Although I had never heard her express any particular devotion to her country, she embraced the flag with fervor. Perhaps she believed that Aaron's death had made it worthy of her.

Al Tibbetts, the two Trasks, and Billy Akers lowered the coffin into the grave with ropes. As they began to shovel dirt over it, Mutti, Louisa, and I tossed in a few clods. Was Louisa also thinking about Mother? Father Owens read from the Book of Common Prayer, but I refused to listen. We'd left the plot before he was quite done.

As my sister and I reached the house, I pointed up to a window of Father's new room where his nurse, Sue Evans, was holding him, her strong arms stretched around his thin chest. He wasn't yet fifty, but he looked as worn as a man of eighty. He'd once lamented that, since his father had died so young and his grandfather had lived so long, it was his fate to have to live until he was very old. But fate was unreliable. It liked to play tricks on our family.

Mutti stepped decisively across the verandah. Was she hearing drumsticks on a muffled drum and a bugle in the distance playing taps? Father pressed his face against the glass, flattening his nose and lips. His nurse tugged him back.

"He won't outlive the winter," I predicted to Louisa.

What use are anyone's prognostications? It was early spring when Mutti suggested that Father's record player and some records be moved to his new room. Father didn't object. He rarely talked, and the few words he spoke were often abrupt, disjunct, or random, as if he were jumping in his mind from place to place or time to time without regard for his listener, as events occur in a dream with no concern for the dreamer. He could still write with his left hand, though more laboriously than ever. If Louisa or I questioned him about his work, he refused to answer. It wasn't intended for us, he said.

One rainy afternoon, Louisa selected the Mahler First to play for him. She read aloud the conductor's name, Dimitri Mitropoulos, and lowered the tone arm, but kept the volume soft.

Father nodded in recognition. "Heard him. Carnegie Hall. Went to the Met too. Heard all the great ones. Melchior. Flagstad. Thorborg. Kipnis. Tibbett. Björling. Milanov. Grandfather insisted, 'Only German operas.' But," his eyes glinted, "snuck many Italians in. Pinza. Martinelli. Gorgeous stuff. Loved Tchai . . . Tchaikov . . . Tchaikovsky," he managed to say. "Beautiful. Beautiful melodies. One of my. Favorites. Don't ever tell. Mother." His eyes explored the dark ceiling, tracing its exposed beams. "Aaron." He started to weep.

"Father," Louisa said, holding his left hand.

"Wanted to compose. Talented. Songs. Sonatas. Working on long piece. Lamentations. But the war . . ."

"I didn't know," she said.

"Gentle. Kind. Didn't love enough. Couldn't. Afraid, maybe."

He shut his eyes. As his body shook, the sheets and pillowcases rustled. It might have been the sound of the rain on the leaves outside.

Sue Evans stepped into the room, rolling in the tray, and, having lifted him to a sitting position, she slid the tray over his lap and laid out a row of pills, some small, some tiny. With his left hand, Father effortfully picked one up and placed it on his tongue, reached for the glass on the tray, drank from it, and swallowed. Twice he repeated the exercise. But on the fourth attempt a minuscule white pill slipped out of his fingers and dropped onto the white sheet. I retrieved it with my forefinger and thumb. "Open wide," I said to Father and placed the pill on his tongue. As he retracted it into his mouth, his tongue accidentally licked my hand. The feel of it was hot and slimy. Recoiling, I backed into Sue Evans who started to speak, her breath on my back as intolerably warm and intimate. When Louisa grasped my wrist, her palm was sweaty. "I must see about dinner," I said to excuse myself, and fled.

But I didn't see about dinner. I didn't need to. Mutti had offered to prepare it that night. Instead, I wandered out to the verandah to watch the rain. When it started to pour again, I kicked off my shoes, ran east of the house to the nearest wide clearing, held out my arms, stretched my neck back, and opened my mouth. The drops were cool and pure. I performed a little madcap dance, my toes relishing the ooze of mud and the tickle of tender grass, and whirled around and around, like a child trying to make herself dizzy.

Once the rains had subsided, I headed for the cemetery to lie down beneath an old oak and rest my head on one of its roots. Although they had been pounded by the storm, petals torn off and scattered, fresh flowers lay on Aaron's grave. Who had left them there? And when? Mutti never honored her dead with impermanent things like flowers. Only marble and gilded monuments sufficed for her. And Louisa surely would have told me if she had brought them there. An anonymous mourner, then, I decided. But I didn't really care who it had been.

Yet the gesture incited me to action. "The libation bearers," Mutti took to calling me and Louisa a few weeks later. We raked and cleaned, cleared and pruned. With an old scythe from the barn, we mowed the grass more scrupulously than Jim Trask had ever managed to do with his cumbersome power mower. We scrubbed the marble, erasing the moss, until all the headstones gleamed, their chiseled, haughtily Latin inscriptions much easier to read and ponder. *Media vita in morte sumus,* one said. *Et ego sicut foenum arui,* warned another. Had ours ever been a hopeful clan? Vengeful and proud in life, our great-great-grandfather remained threatening in death: *Et perdes omnes qui tribulant animam meam.* Only the women were silent and did not speak from their graves. All their stones recalled of them were their birth, death, and faithfulness as wives. Yet Louisa and I toiled throughout the cemetery as if all our ancestors spoke for us until every stone shone like silver and every plot was scrupulously neat.

When Al Tibbetts reported to us that Cambodia had been invaded and students killed on campuses, we barely heard what he said. We knew, of course we knew about other riots and horrors, massive bombings, prisoners captured, slaughters and maimings, atrocities, the massacres at My Lai. But such news was to us no more terrible and unreal than our spending all our spare time attending our family's cemetery.

"Maybe it was a girl," Louisa speculated as side-by-side we sat on a bench Billy Akers had built for us and secured between two pines near the cemetery's gate. "Maybe it was a girl who placed those flowers on Aaron's grave all those months ago. He might have had a girlfriend, a town girl, and never told us."

"He might have. But I don't think so. Not Aaron."

The early winter afternoon was chilly, the sky icy blue. It had been weeks since a northern wind had stripped the last leaves from their branches. Her fingers undaunted by the cold, Louisa was knitting a sweater. "For Andy," she'd said. "For when he finally comes home."

"Great-grandfather's statue looks particularly Roman today," I observed. "Clear-eyed and fearless. He should especially thank us for the fine job we did on his noble nose."

"Would you like to spend some time in Rome one of these days?" Louisa inquired. "I think I might. Some place truly ancient would suit me, I believe."

"We've been overeducated, Sister," I said. "Sometimes I feel I've been around the world too many times already."

Louisa set her knitting on her lap and cupped her hands over her eyes against the wintry glare. "What's that? There," she pointed, "beneath Aaron's headstone."

We walked over. I bent down and picked up a candle holder containing the burned nub of a candle, and a little wooden box. I opened it. "It's hair. Very pale blond hair."

"It could be ours. No. Not ours. It's too white. Andy's. Anna, do you think . . . ?"

"Someone else probably left it. Maybe whoever left the flowers." I slipped the box into my coat pocket. "It doesn't mean that . . ."

"Oh, I know. But wouldn't it be wonderful, Anna, if Andy had come home?"

"Not a word to Father. Or Mutti," I warned.

"Of course not," Louisa agreed.

Had it been Andy? Had he really been here? Would he return? If I'd waited for him inside the house after Louisa had gone to bed, Mutti would have wondered why I was not also asleep. It was impossible to hide from her. Only the deep woods and distant hills were safe from her surveillance. Because the nights were already frigid, I wore a heavy sweater under my overcoat and a scarf on my head as I waited on the cemetery's bench. There might have been only an hour or so of dark left before dawn when I heard the faraway clopping of horse hooves. An owl hooted. A wild dog barked. Then the night fell silent again. I raced down to the road where it curved sharply toward the barns.

I might not have recognized him right away when he walked round the bend. But he had already spotted me and called out, "Anna?"

He strode closer. He was wearing civilian clothes that fit him badly. Charlie Sutton's? Even as he kept his distance, the moonlight was bright enough for me to see the scars on his face. Around his neck, he wore a peace medal that bounced on his chest as he walked closer. When he bent to kiss my forehead, I flinched from his touch.

He stepped back. "I see."

"No, you don't see, Andy." Even though it was still night, I could tell how he had darkened, all but this hair. "Do you know Father's sick?"

"Charlie told me."

"How long have you been here?"

"Two days. I fly back to Nam day after tomorrow. I'm not a coming-home soldier. I want to go back."

"You've been wounded."

"Yeah."

"Why do you want to go back, Andy?"

"I don't know." He kicked a stone. "I was in California for a while last year. I liked it there. I'll probably settle down there when the war's over. Get me a nice little place in the back of some canyon where it's quiet."

A bat and a few nocturnal birds swooped over head. Otherwise the night was as still as after a winter storm when the branches are too burdened with snow to sway or creak and the air is too cold to stir anything.

"Father will want to see you," I said.

"I doubt it."

"And Mutti."

"No."

"Were you here before, Andy? Was it you who left those flowers on Aaron's grave?"

"It was Charlie. I asked him to." He stuffed his hands into his jean pockets. "Everywhere I was, I always made it my business to learn where Aaron was. I always knew where he was. Always.

"He was killed on his way to see me. My year was almost up. His year was almost up. I knew it was risky. But I had to see him. So I sent him word where I was because for a few weeks I was going to be close to Saigon and my assignment was fairly safe. I didn't want to ask him to forgive me. How could I? I just wanted to tell him I was scared."

"Don't expect me not to blame you, Andy."

"I don't expect anything from you, Anna. Or anyone else here. It wasn't you all I came home to see."

"Not even Mutti?"

"Let me tell you about our grandmother, Anna. She cheats. Even when she's holding all the trump cards, when she knows she's going to win anyway, she cheats."

Andy's left ear had been sliced. Had the same blade also ripped his neck? Had a different slash reached his nose, then cut down to his jawbone? What further scars did his clothes conceal? Would they also boast and strut like the ones I could see, a show-off's deliberate wounds like the ones that decorated the faces of Mutti's dueling German ancestors? Yet they had aged him and streaked his face like drips of wax. "Why must you go back, Andy?" I asked again.

"It's safer there than here."

"Was that Charlie's horse you were riding?"

"Yes. How's Suzy, Anna? How's the old mare?"

"Billy Akers has been taking good care of her. Riding her every day. She's fine."

"That's good." He turned away from me, walked to the gully, jumped it, then faced me from the dark of the woods. "I came to

talk to Aaron. I have some things to tell him I didn't have the
nerve to say to him last night. Go on to bed, Anna. It's almost
dawn."

"I insist you see Father, Andy. Before you go, you must."

"No."

"For Aaron's sake. You know he'd want you to."

"You cheat too, Anna."

"Do I? Only when I have to, Andy."

"Say hello to Louisa," he said walking off.

His feet kicked at the leaves as he moved. Although I thought
I'd dressed warmly enough, I shook from the cold. As I reached
the path to the house, I noticed Mutti standing in an upstairs hall
window she had cracked open. The moon colored her face and
hands chalky white, but her dressing gown might have been cut
from cloth made out of the night. As I reached the stoop and
glanced up again, she shut the window and seemed to have
faded from sight, though I could still see her breath on the pane.

Louisa was waiting for me in my room. I didn't switch on a
lamp but stood by the window, waiting to hear the horse's
hooves clomping on the bridge's wooden planks.

"You've become as secretive as Grandmother, Sister," she
complained.

"Have I? Louisa, I'm tired. I don't want to quarrel. I've just
seen Andy, if that's what you want to know." I opened the curtains wider.

"That was selfish of you."

"You're right. It was." I let the curtains drop. "You may sleep
here for what's left of the night," I offered.

"No, thank you. It would no longer comfort me, Anna," she
declared as she quit the room.

All the next day, Louisa and I didn't speak. But silence had
become so customary in our little community that we might
have all taken a vow. Father lay in his bed each day weaker, as I
was convinced was his intent, using what little strength he had

left to deprive himself of that much more. If one of us tried to engage him in conversation, he would turn his head away from us toward the window. I could imagine his wanting to fly out and perch on an oak branch over Aaron's grave, where he would refuse to migrate, waiting for snow.

Louisa and I were preparing Father's dinner tray in the kitchen when we heard a strange car on the driveway, steps, and a brash knock on the back door. Louisa dropped a bowl of applesauce on the floor.

It was Charlie Sutton, gat-toothed and handsome as a politician running on his looks alone. The missing three fingers on his right hand reminded me that he'd also fought in the war, one of over three dozen boys from Alexandersville who'd gone to Vietnam. But only Aaron and Chester Madden, the great-great-grandson of slaves, had been killed, and none of the white folks had ever grieved much about Chester, who had been labeled a troublemaker when he returned from Washington in 1963. Alexandersville was a vicious town. I could never understand why Andy spent so much time there, especially with Charlie Sutton.

"Andy's waiting out in the car," Charlie said. He was chewing tobacco. Every time I'd ever seen Charlie, he'd always been chewing something, usually gum, and grinning, showing off the gap between his two front teeth. But now the grin, like the gum, was gone. "He thinks this is a big mistake, Anna. But I persuaded him it was worth a try. It's his dad, for Christ's sake. Blood's blood, isn't it?"

"Thanks, Charlie," I said.

He leaned over to kiss Louisa's forehead. "It's been a long time, girls. How many years?"

"Only three, I think. Or maybe four," Louisa said.

"Well, too long," Charlie said and left to fetch Andy.

Andy paused to speak to him as Charlie returned to the car where he'd said he preferred to wait. Slowly our brother wandered up to the house, each step an effort, as if the war had left him lame. When he approached the kitchen door, Louisa opened it. He shook her hand. "Don't I get a kiss, Andy? Charlie kissed me."

"Did he?" Andy pecked her cheek and nodded a halfhearted greeting to me. "I can't stay very long. Where is he? His room?"

"He sleeps now in what used to be Great-grandfather's study," Louisa informed him. "Father asked to be moved so he could see . . ." She caught herself. "He wasn't happy in his old room."

"Best let me go in first," I suggested, passing in front of Andy. "Father's very moody these days and a little unpredictable and easily upset. Be careful, Andy."

He followed me up the stairs, down the hall, and through the open door to Father's bedside where he halted a few feet behind me. Louisa lingered close to the door, not wanting to crowd us. "Father?" Did he stir? "Father?" I lay my hand on his right shoulder and slowly, inch-by-inch helped him roll onto his back. "I have a wonderful surprise for you, Father. Someone we've all been praying to see." His eyes gradually opened. I stepped aside.

Andy bent forward and gently kissed his forehead. Tears dribbled down both sides of Father's face, staining his pillow. "Father," Andy said. "Father. I'm so sorry."

Father opened his mouth and tried to speak. He tried and tried again but succeeded in emitting only a slight gagging sound. His body tensed. He blinked fiercely. With great effort, he drew his left arm out from under his blanket and sheets and held it up high as if he meant to offer his son a blessing. But instead he beckoned him closer.

Andy gently slipped his arms around him and lifted him to his chest so that Father was almost sitting up for the first time in weeks. His head was nestled between his son's scarred neck and shoulder. Was he smiling?

My heart pounded. What was I afraid of? Father turned his

head to kiss his son's cheek. "Son," he whispered. I moved closer to hear better. "Son. You're home. Safe."

"Yes, Father." Andy was also quietly crying. "Yes."

"I'm so glad. I'm so happy. Aaron. Aaron. You're home. Safe."

I glanced behind me. Louisa, with a gasp, had fled the room even as Mutti entered. Her eyes were red. Had she really been weeping? When I turned back to the bed, Father was lying down on his back and Andy had retreated several yards. "I'm Andy, Father. Andy. Aaron's dead," he said. His arms flailing, he stumbled out of the room. As Mutti reached out to touch him, he shoved her away from him. She fell against the armoire. Father twitched and quivered. "Sue!" I cried out.

I darted into the hall. Louisa was running toward me, Sue Evans only a few feet behind. The three of us raced back into Father's room.

Father died in the middle of the night. None of us was certain about the exact time. After briefly examining him, Dr. Higham said there was no point in our trying to move him to the hospital. Grandmother, Louisa, and I kept vigil in his room with the nurse, since Higham had driven home shortly after midnight, saying he'd return before dawn. In fact, he came back several hours after the sun had risen, but Mutti had already phoned him with the news that Sue Evans had confirmed. Father's death had been so quiet none of us knew he had died until it was almost light and we could see his colorless eyes. It was Mutti who closed them.

The day before Father's funeral, I asked a new young hand whom I knew only by name, Cal Stanfield, to drive me to town. All the way there I promised myself I'd learn to drive soon. "How do you like working for three women, Cal?" I asked him.

"I can get used to anything if I have to."

"Do you have to, Cal?"

"Yes, ma'am. I sure do."

"'Ma'am'?" I thought to myself. Had sorrow so aged me? Louisa and I were not yet twenty-three.

Charlie Sutton wasn't at home, but his mother suggested I'd find him for sure at the ball field near the high school where there was a picnic of some kind going on, though she didn't see how anyone could enjoy a picnic in the freezing cold.

There was no picnic, of course. Just Charlie and some of his high-school buddies, several of them veterans like him, sitting around, smoking cigarettes and drinking beer. "Andy's long gone, sweet thing," Charlie informed me. "He'll be back in country in a day or two. Might be there already, for all I know. Real eager to go. It's hard to figure. I never expected Andy to be so gung-ho. I can tell you this for sure. I don't ever want to see that goddamn hellhole of a country again."

"You know where to reach him?"

"Nope. Not anymore. Not until he writes me again."

"He knows Father died?"

"Yep."

"Do you think he'll ever come home again?"

He squinted at me and two-fingered a cigarette out of the pack in his coat pocket. "What do you think?" He dipped his other hand into the cooler. "Like a beer?"

"No, thanks."

With the thumb and forefinger of his otherwise fingerless hand, he struck a match and lit his cigarette. "You're a nice-looking woman, Anna. You and Louisa both. Ought to get out more. See the world."

"Should I take that as an offer?"

"Would you like it to be one?"

"No. Of course not."

"Then it wasn't." Several of Charlie's pals were playing football in the muddy field, hooting and swearing. "You know something, Anna? The Suttons aren't much in this world, we weren't the first folks to lay claim to the land in this county or anything like that, but I thank my lucky stars I was born a Sutton and not a goddamn stuck-up Odom. You all suffer from a bad case of what a pal of mine in Nam called officer mentality."

I curtsied. "Why, thank you so very kindly, Mr. Sutton," I said, batting my eyelashes.

"Except Andy, of course." He drank fast and tossed his empty can and burning cigarette into the trash. "He used to be really OK," he said and strutted out onto the field to play.

All the way back to the farm I glowered at Cal Stanfield as if it had been he and not Charlie who had insulted me. "Don't take it personally," I advised myself.

Mutti, Louisa, and I stood as still as the Three Fates at the foot of Father's open grave as Father Owens tried his best to console and comfort us. So did the few townspeople Mutti had allowed to attend.

Directly after the ceremony, Mutti retired to the parlor. Now that Father had also died, two-thirds of her trio gone, she played the piano more than ever, hour after hour, day after day. For the first time in her life, she neglected her work.

"Perhaps what I mistook for ice in her soul," I remarked to Louisa, "is really crystal."

More and more, Louisa and I assumed Mutti's role as master-mistress of our house and lands. We gradually assimilated her duties as one after another she ceded them to us without saying a word. When she was not playing the piano, she read her favorite Greek, Roman, or German writers or poured over scores in search of music her fingers could still learn. Occasionally she would roam over the property as Louisa and I used to do when we had more time for idle wandering. She visited with us only at meals, which she ate with more diligence than appetite.

Although our workers accepted the new regime, they only slowly granted us the deference they had long ago conceded to Mutti. Both Louisa and I had repeatedly to remind ourselves that we were, after all, still very young. But slowly our profits increased. We raised our workers' wages. We hired more men. Finally, even my sister and I ceased being astonished at our success.

Saigon had just been renamed Ho Chi Minh City when we decided at last to give away most of Father's things, donating them to the church for use by refugees. Grandmother insisted on retaining all his books and records. Almost every day, she would take another book or record off its former shelf and carry it to her room to keep.

We were belatedly clearing out another crowded closet when Louisa discovered the two boxes resting on a high, dark shelf in the back where Sue Evans must have placed them at Father's request. It must have been Sue Evans, too, who had carefully secured them with tape after Father had scrawled "For Aaron Rose" over the top of each. I shook them and mentally calculated their weight. "His life's work," I guessed. "Do you suppose this is all of it?"

"I don't want to read it," Louisa said.

"Obviously he meant it for Aaron, not for us," I said.

"Perhaps Andy would like to have it," Louisa said, "whatever it is."

"I doubt it."

"We can't throw it away, Anna. Father didn't, even after Aaron died."

"I wish he had," I said.

"Andy can throw it away if he wants to. He doesn't have to read it simply because we send it to him, does he?"

"We don't even know where he is."

"Charlie might. It's worth a try."

"Perhaps you're right." I shook both boxes again. "I wonder what they say? Aren't you at least a little curious, Louisa? It's not like you not to be curious."

"I'm too busy to be curious anymore. We both are," Louisa said. And of course I agreed.

Since Louisa had learned to drive before I did, she claimed

Mutti's car as hers and always drove whenever we traveled to town. Charlie Sutton had opened a used-sporting-goods store in a small shopping center on the far side of Alexandersville just after he'd married Lurleen Williams nine months too late.

The store was empty of customers when we walked in, perhaps because it was still early. Charlie was standing by the cash register. I handed him the two boxes.

"What's this?" he asked.

Louisa said, "Don't worry. We're not going to ask you where he is. If he ever wants to see us again, he knows where we are. We aren't going any place. But we think perhaps he should have these."

He read Aaron's name out loud. "I don't know."

"They were brothers," Louisa said, as if that fact explained everything.

"He hasn't written me for months."

"But you know where he is?"

He scratched the back of his head. "Yeah, sometimes. He only writes me because he's worried about that old mare of his."

"It's Billy Ackers's horse now, Charlie. We had to fire Billy. He was shirking. Riding some of our other horses when he should have been in the fields plowing. We warned him and warned him. He left us no choice. But we let him have Andy's old horse. After we'd been feeding her for seven years we figured she was ours to give. Billy really loves that horse. You can tell Andy so."

"I already did."

"It was best for Suzy," I said. "Andy's in California, isn't he?"

"Louisa said you two weren't going to ask me that, Anna." He set the two boxes on a shelf beneath the counter. "All right. I'll send them to him. After I do, I'll probably never hear from him again, but I'll do it."

"Thanks," I said.

"It really is for the best," Louisa said.

We turned to leave the store. Uniforms cluttered one corner.

Golf clubs, bats, rackets, and rifles hung from a wall. Pennants dangled from the ceiling. "One more thing, you two," he said calling us back as we reached the door, which had opened on its own as we stepped off the carpet onto the rubber mat. "He asked me a while back to give you a message. He said, if you ever see my sisters again, please ask them to tell our grandmother that someday I intend to scare her to death with the wickedness of my ways, even if I have to rise out of my grave to haunt her."

"Wicked ways?" Louisa scoffed. "What could he mean?"

Charlie grinned in a way only men ever grin. "I could guess."

"Please don't," Louisa said.

"Do me one more favor, will you, Charlie?" I said. "When you mail those boxes, you tell him if he has anything to say to Mutti he'll have to come home and tell her himself. Louisa and I can't be bothered with his nonsense. We've got much too much work to do."

Andrew Willingham Odom

Drew hadn't known what a funeral was until his mother told him one night. His father's funeral, she said, would take place the following morning. All he had really understood was that his father wasn't here any longer and wouldn't be there. His father was gone, his mother had said, he'd left them. But no one should be sad because he had done what he wanted to do. Yet Drew was sad. His father had held his hand while he was learning to walk and to climb stairs and had jostled him on his knee in the swing. Tickling his sides, he'd kissed him when he put him to bed.

His mother dressed Drew in the clothes he wore to church and brushed his hair. She covered his play table with toys and tenderly touched his cheek. She wouldn't be gone long, she said. A little while later the music began. Sometimes when he'd heard the music before, he'd been allowed to watch them play if he promised to be very quiet. He didn't mind because he liked to be quiet.

But that morning Drew wanted to see them playing the music very much. He crept out of his room and down the hall to his grandfather's study, which he'd been forbidden to enter unless he'd been invited. The door was closed. He pressed his ear against it and listened. But it was an uncomfortable posture and he didn't like the music so he crawled away, down the stairs and through the hall to the front lawn.

His mother found him sitting in the middle of a mud puddle next to the verandah. He was filthy. She had to bathe him and dress him all over again. After he was clean, she hugged him until he stopped crying.

At the cemetery, his grandfather, his mother, and Drew stood next to the hole the big box was already lying in. His mother handed him some dirt from the pile beside them. "Throw it in the grave, Drew. Say good-bye to your father. Dust to dust." His grandfather frowned.

He let it drizzle like water through his fingers onto the box. As it fell, it sounded like rain. Reaching for more, he tossed it down hard. His mother squeezed his other hand. "That's enough now." His grandfather patted his head.

Little Drew was angry. He hated dirt. He hated mud.

Growing up, Drew made no friends, not one. He was called too "stuck up," too "conceited." He thought of himself as shy. He attended school erratically or not at all.

Most of his education took place in his grandfather's library, at his grandfather's knee, or by his grandfather's side. His grandfather believed all any man required to live a proud and noble life were freedom, land, the classics, music, and a knowledge of mathematics. Although he called himself a Jeffersonian, he acknowledged to his grandson that his metaphysics were, as he said, considerably more eristic than the clockwork theology of the sage of Monticello.

The old man tutored Drew in everything he knew from Hesiod to Augustine. He taught him to play violin. He taught him algebra and geometry and how to milk cows. Boasting of the prizes he'd won for dressage when he was still young, he tried to teach Drew how to ride like a knight in a tournament. Although he'd proclaimed history to be a record of nothing so profound as tragedy but only of man's pathos and folly, he encouraged Drew to read as much of it as he could "stomach." He offered him art books to look through or study.

But his grandfather disparaged all journalism, all reportage, all attempts to chart the passage of the ephemeral and everyday. He subscribed to no magazines and vilified the few newspapers he deigned to read.

So, disobediently, Drew would hitch a lift to town with Mitch Akers whenever Mitch went to Alexandersville on an errand for the farm in his Model A. In the public library, Drew would study copies of, among other magazines, the *Saturday Evening Post*, *Life*, and *National Geographic*. He especially admired the photographs and illustrations.

To him, pictures in magazines were like a dream or nightmare his waking mind could never have imagined on its own. An old man wearing striped coveralls, like those chained prisoners were forced to wear while working on the roads, was holding onto the brim of his cap as his whole body leaned against a wind that was blowing dust across ragged stubs of corn stalks poking out of cracks in the earth that appeared as hard as concrete. Far away, close to the horizon, stood a building the caption identified as a grain elevator. It looked to Drew as much like a temple as a soaring shrine he'd seen in a picture taken in a land he'd never before heard of that the caption called "Ladakh." Australian aborigines, their bodies heavily painted and scarified, stood in a ceremonial ring and watched as a boy, a member of their tribe, screamed and writhed as he was being circumcised. The Spanish artist Dalí had been photographed with a flower adorning each tip of his waxed handlebar mustache. He was dressed and arched his back in the manner of what Drew's grandfather would have derided as a dandy or poseur. Yet when Drew laid the two pictures side-by-side it was clear how Dalí's eyes were as wide and shockingly white as those of the tribe's elder, watching a pubescent boy's foreskin shorn with a flint knife. Thousands and thousands of people were jammed into a soccer stadium in Santiago or a football stadium in New Haven, lined the streets four- or five-deep during a Nazi rally in Munich, packed the sidewalks along Parisian boulevards on Bastille Day and waved to parading veterans of the Great War, jostled one another on Fifth Avenue sidewalks in the snow just before Christmas in New York, filled every inch of a square in Rome to cheer il Duce. If he looked closely enough, if he studied each picture with the little magnifying glass he'd borrowed from the librarian Mrs. Talbot, Drew was certain that he could see many of the same faces inhabiting every picture. Was the world really so full of repetitions and uncanny resemblances? Or did such similarities appear only in dreams and magazines?

After he'd seen photographs of Italian troops occupying Addis Ababa, of the Germans remilitarizing the Rhineland, of trials in Moscow, of the Japanese in Manchuria, he said to his grandfather, "There's going to be another war soon. But I've decided I'll refuse to fight. I'm a pacifist, Grandfather."

The old man regarded him crossly. "War is inevitable. For you. For everyone."

"I refuse to believe that."

"Believe what you like," his grandfather said. "War doesn't care what you believe."

Among historians, his grandfather particularly admired Tacitus. He praised his style for its objectivity, terseness, and difficulty. He lauded his themes, particularly as they were manifest in the *Annals*: cruelty, the ruin of innocent men, friends' treacheries, betrayals, and denunciations, the wheel of man's destruction turned over and over by the same dull hands.

"Tacitus clarifies, as does no other writer, that a man's nobility of temper and magnificence of soul are reason enough for others to accuse him of every imaginable crime. Do you know what true virtue's reward always is, Drew?" Drew shook his head. "Death," his grandfather said. "Annihilation. Oblivion."

His grandfather enjoyed telling the story of the Flavians' fight against the Vitellians in imperial Rome. As they watched the cruel show, the Roman people clapped and shrieked and cheered one side or the other as if the war were merely a mock battle. Although all the soldiers were determined to inflict as many wounds and shed as much blood as possible, most of the loot they stole in the midst of the struggles ended up in the hands of the mob. Yet, even as men were being slaughtered, whores continued to ply their trade. Diners continued to eat in restaurants next to which bodies lay stacked like logs ready to be burned. Dancers danced, actors acted, musicians played their instruments and sang. While the city was being sacked, its citizens went on holiday.

The most steadfast Flavians held the praetorian barracks where the heaviest fighting was taking place. They shouted to one another that the Senate had been returned to the people and the temples to the gods. But the barracks, they rejoiced, were theirs alone, for the barracks and the field of battle were the soldiers' true home and only country.

Their enemy, the Vitellians, were by then as doomed as they were outnumbered. Because they were doomed, they cried havoc. Their aim was no longer victory, but bloodletting and desecration. Most of them died hanging from towers or walls. But a few Vitellians survived to attack one last time the oncoming victors. As each Vitellian fell, his wound was always in front. "To face the enemy at the moment of death, even if the enemy is Death Himself, is the meaning of honor," his grandfather said.

After he'd heard his grandfather repeat the story for the sixth or seventh time, Drew asked him why he'd told it to him so often. Angrily, his grandfather replied, "Some day, perhaps, you'll understand. God likes to repeat everything. He's an ironist. So was Tacitus. So am I."

By his eighteenth year, Drew had become an adept, an exalted master of self-abuse. While an unskilled novice in his younger years and thus still susceptible to puberty's alarms, he feared mishaps and terrible side effects. Because he'd been warned by stories circulated surreptitiously among his contemporaries, he feared disease and madness, some terrible malformations of his palm, skin, or brain.

But when, despite his daily frenzies, month followed month and year followed year with no ill effects at all, he lost faith in such threats.

What was he longing for? As he fondled himself and thrust and pounded, what was he yearning for? What images did he see? What did he want from his hands? Nothing. No one. Just pleasure. Just release. Just ecstasy.

Only after his grandfather had clicked off the radio did Drew hear the steamlike hiss of the fire burning in the hearth of the old man's den. Already it was dark. Reflected on the windows' panes, the flames appeared to be licking the snow-covered limbs of the trees outside.

His grandfather rested his head against a cushion of the maroon overstuffed chair where he always sat when he listened to the opera on Saturday afternoons. The fire colored his white hair bright yellow, like the blond hair in his portrait that hung in the parlor downstairs or like Drew's own hair.

Books filled every shelf, shelves lined every wall. Covering many of the rugs as well as the hardwood floor, oversized books lay stacked throughout the room. Others cluttered his pine desk. All their bindings were an umber so dark and roughly textured that they might have been bound in bark.

They had listened to the music without speaking for over

three hours. When the opera was over, Drew's grandfather pinched the bridge of his nose between his eyes. Had so much concentration again caused a headache? The old man often complained of headaches after he'd been practicing his cello too long as well, whether alone or with Drew's mother or with Elisabeth and Drew too, in their trio.

He slowly opened his eyes and seemed disappointed in what he saw. "Das Wunderreich der Nacht," he quoted from the opera. After he'd paused for a moment, he said, "How sentient, how plangent, how true Melchior is in all he sings. How perfect was the lyricism in Hofmann's Marke. And Bodanzky's conducting stirred even Flagstad into a profound anguish and an almost ethereally agitated ecstasy at the end, wouldn't you agree?"

"Yes, sir," Drew said.

"Wagner's love song to the night. Only two days into the Year of Our Lord nineteen hundred and thirty-seven and I may hope no more from this or any other night."

For his eighteenth birthday, his grandfather gave Drew a round-trip ticket to New York City and sufficient money for cheap lodgings and the most inexpensive opera tickets. He heard *Lohengrin* with Flagstad, Branzell, Maison, and Hofmann, *Das Rheingold* with Branzell, Maison, and Schorr, and, to his grandfather's irritation, *La Traviata* with Sayão, Kullman, and Brownlee. It had been wonderful, of course, but he'd admitted to his grandfather that he'd been disappointed. No singer was as beautiful as her or his voice. Nothing he saw on the stage was as fine as what he had imagined listening with his eyes closed at home.

Two nights, he attended the ballet on his own nickel. His favorite was a dance called *Classic Ballet* by Dollar and Balanchine. The dancers' bodies were all very beautiful and moved with a purity which, unseen, he could never have imagined. Nothing he could have fantasized would have been more lovely. But as he sat in his seat he felt it would have been intolerable, unendurable, if anyone onstage had sung or spoken. Such physical perfection would have been utterly undone by the sound of words.

Drew's mother asked him what he liked best about his first trip to New York. Did he answer honestly and say the noise, the smoke, the grime and soot? The thousands and thousands of roaming people? The bustling bridges, the massive ships docked at the piers? The whale gray stone buildings, the ravenous streets, the avenues wide as parade grounds, the pinnacled skyscrapers? The museum galleries like palaces ripe for looting by the eye? The golden theaters and movie houses? The music?

No. He preferred to irk her. "There wasn't any grass to cut," he said. "There weren't any cows."

In the early fall of the year, some of the Odom herd fell prey to a mysterious illness, first visible in their bloated udders and distended teats. The veterinarian declared it something strange, different from hoof-and-mouth disease. Before those scary days, Drew had not known that animals could scream in such prolonged agony, a misery far more horrible to hear than the brief shrill squeak of a stuck pig.

As a cow became ill, his mother or grandfather shot it. But they refused to destroy the whole herd. Just as they had never let Roosevelt tell them what to do with their milk, they would arm their workers if need be to prevent the government from invading their farm. They sent the cows they hoped were not infected to distant pastures where they stayed until the sickness had run its course.

Watching his mother shoot the last sick animals, he heard his grandfather mutter, "A cruel God is truer to nature than no God at all."

As blood poured out of the cow's mouth and nostrils, Drew

jumped off the fence where he had been sitting and bent over the ditch to vomit.

Drew loved watching his mother bake bread. She'd dribble cool water onto the flour, ground in a neighbor's mill, and mix flour and water slowly into a dough that she'd fold over and over. She'd add yeast and slap the dough hard onto a flat board hundreds and hundreds of times before she sprinkled the salt in and slapped the dough again. After it had risen, she'd deflate it, let it rise, deflate it again, then shape it on a floury linen cloth where, covered, it rose once more until its surface shone like a glazed clay bowl. She'd toss water into the oven and lay the bread on terra-cotta tiles to bake. After she'd taken the bread out of the oven and let it cool, Drew loved to watch her slice it and slather it with their own rich butter and take a taste. If it was good, she'd offer him piece after piece. Whether she was making bread or playing the piano, Drew loved to watch his mother's lovely hands.

Mitch Akers told Drew the story. Two days earlier, a white girl, Josie Banter, had claimed to her best friend that she'd been stalked that morning by a big colored man who followed her across the street from the movie theater and down two long blocks, smacking his lips as if he meant to grab her and kiss her. She wanted to scream but no other white people out on the street seemed to notice his intentions toward her at all.

Although she'd been sworn to secrecy, Josie's girlfriend immediately reported the incident to Josie's daddy. Confronting his daughter, Cecil Banter demanded to know who the nigger was. At first Josie denied everything, Mitch reported to Drew, but when her daddy threatened her with his belt in front of everyone in his store, she said it had been Johnny Sutcliffe, the big colored man who worked in the back room at Merchant's Hardware.

As the first crowds began to gather, the sheriff arrested Johnny and locked him up "for his own good." In the middle of the night, a mob set fire to Johnny Sutcliffe's house. The house burned to the ground. Johnny's wife Mary and their three kids were lucky to have escaped.

Mary Sutcliffe was the cleaning woman at the church Drew's family had been attending for generations, though why they went so faithfully every Sunday morning Drew had never understood. "You better let Grandfather know about this right away," Drew advised Mitch.

His grandfather phoned the sheriff. Two hours later, Mitch Akers drove him and his grandson to a street in the colored part of town. The dogwood was just beginning to bud. Tulips were peeking out of the ground. They parked in front of a bungalow. Mitch Akers hopped out to open the old man's door. As his grandfather aimed straight for the porch, Drew almost had to run to keep up with him.

The screen door's springs creaked as it slowly opened. A tall, thin black woman stepped onto the little porch. Unsmiling, she nodded. "Good day to you."

He tipped his hat. "Lydia." He reached into his coat and pulled out a thick envelope. "For Johnny. It's enough."

Crossing her arms defiantly, the woman shook her head. "He never followed that lying white girl."

"I'm aware of that, Lydia."

"So why are you running him off, making him leave town for good?"

"To avoid a ruckus. There are too many cowards with guns in this county, Lydia. I despise anarchy where I live."

"The world is full of cowards, Mr. Andrew."

"Your nephew can't be numbered among them. That's why I want him to go. He's worth more than the whole lot of them. I've arranged an escort. And Cecil Banter, I can report to you, has changed his mind about the whole incident."

The woman sighed. "Johnny won't take your money."

"Then he'd be a fool after all." He held the envelope out to her.

She accepted it, sighing again. "I'll see what I can do."

"You do that, Lydia," his grandfather said as he stomped off the porch.

Following a few feet behind, Drew was still looking back over his shoulder at the black woman. Her body was still shaking with rage as, not watching where he was going, he crashed into a mulberry tree.

After they'd returned to the house, Drew pursued his grandfather into his den. "The Germans have marched into Austria, Grandfather."

His grandfather sat slumped in the chair he used to listen to music and wiped his face with a handkerchief. "I don't doubt they have." He waved an arm wearily toward his desk. "See that book, boy, the one I left open near the lamp? Pick it up and read me the passage I've circled. I'd like to hear it read out loud by a young voice just now."

Drew lifted the book up and read, "'I cross a broad river on a single reed and trek long roads to a distant mountain in a morning. Though the gourd has bitter leaves and the vine-bean's branches are tangled, I persevere. Why do I wish to return to my own land and kin? Have I not lived among a people who have received many blessings from heaven, where the white clouds were translucent as jade, the pear trees tall, and orioles perched in the mulberries? There, I dined on roast turtle and minced carp. There, I drank clear wine. Yet, half drunk, I departed forever since one must be a Tzu from Sung if one is to marry among them. Friend, if along the highway I catch your sleeve, do not deny me. I wish only to rest soon where before the moon descends the sun has already arisen.'"

His grandfather signaled him to stop. "Sit down, Drew." Drew did as he was told. "You're nineteen now, boy. Old enough to be deciding what you aim to do with the rest of your life."

Drew shrugged. "I guess. But I don't know what I want to do. Maybe nothing."

"Nothing?" The old man arched his bushy eyebrows and laughed out loud. "Nothing?" he scoffed. "You better think more carefully, Grandson. You're nowhere near brave or strong enough to do nothing with your life."

If Drew didn't know what he wanted to do with the rest of his life, he did know he wanted to return to New York as soon as possible. But he had no money, and neither his mother nor his grandfather would give him any. Why should they indulge him in his whims? If Drew sometimes hoped that the vulgar rumors of Odom wealth might be true, he knew the reality was that the farm's expenses consumed most of what it earned. Except for scores and books, his mother and grandfather spent almost no money on themselves. During winters, they sealed off most of the house to reduce the cost of heat. They never traveled. They dressed simply. They rarely used their car. And they never entertained.

To ask his grandfather for a paying job, Drew believed, would be like cheating. Yet people in town were reluctant to hire him. Only after she'd found no one else to take the job did the town's librarian agree to offer him the position she'd been advertising for months. After all, she'd admitted, no one's face had become more familiar to her than Drew's, even if he usually hid it behind a newspaper or magazine.

The library was housed in a small brick building, one of the oldest in town. Some of its rooms smelled like a dusty attic, some like stale water. Drew's jobs were to stack and shelve books, to sweep and dust, to wash the windows, to cut the grass of the library's neat little lawns, to raise and lower the flags, and to assist Mrs. Talbot at the desk as the need arose.

Drew's grandfather had declared his grandson's education a complete failure. His studies at home were over. Yet he continued to sleep in his old room and to eat breakfast and dinner with his mother and grandfather every day. He played his fiddle whenever he could. Every Sunday, immediately after church, the Odom Trio continued to practice or expand their repertoire. The Spohr A minor became his particular favorite.

The evening of the day they'd heard the news that the Germans had invaded Poland, his mother, score in hand, summoned him and his grandfather from their rooms. In the parlor, with no more illumination than the bright light of a fire, they performed an Archduke he couldn't believe was really theirs, so beautiful and pure it sounded to his ears, like music played so perfectly it could have been played by no one at all.

The next morning, having added up what little he had managed to save from his tiny salary, he marked on his calendar a day twelve weeks hence in late November. Faithful to his purpose, on that very day, suitcase in hand, dressed in his only suit, he boarded an evening train headed north. In the city, he rented a cheap room in a run-down hotel.

Ten days later, he hopped off a southbound train onto the platform back home. In his lapel, he displayed a pin inscribed with the words, "I have seen the future."

What had he seen? The Trylon and the Perisphere of course. And Democracity. Lucite, nylon, television. A model dairy, all white paint and aluminum trim. A pavilion shaped like an igloo and the road of tomorrow. A parachute tower, a robot, and Futurama. "Mickey's Surprise Party." What had he seen? Something the fair called progress.

Yet on the American Common where a model of the Moscow subway system and a seventy-foot-tall statue of a Soviet worker had stood before they had been angrily demolished, he'd witnessed a noisy rally encouraging America's entrance into the war and experienced a terrible fear in his heart.

At the dinner table the night he returned home, Drew's grandfather peered at the pin he was still sporting and grumbled.

"You wasted all your money for nothing, boy. You take that fool thing off," he ordered, thumping the pin.

"No, sir."

"What's that?"

"I said, No, sir, sir. I like it."

"Drew," his mother said.

"You ought to know by now your insolence is wasted on me. You at least hear some good music while you were up there?"

Drew squirmed in his seat. He had heard *Meistersinger* with Schorr and *Tannhäuser* with Flagstad. He had watched beautiful dancers in beautiful dances. He had looked at Bronzinos, Vermeers, and Rembrandts. In contemporary galleries, he had studied paintings by Ernst, Picasso, Miro, and Mondrian and felt, the more he saw, increasing joy and excitement. He'd wandered Times Square and visited some bars. He'd explored the Village and listened to jazz while drinking his first beers. Late at night, near the park, he'd seen several women standing on street corners dressed so bizarrely, so provocatively he was certain they were whores. But he wanted to keep it all a secret.

"Well, Drew?" his mother said. "You must have done or heard something worth telling us about. Surely if all you did was just to attend that silly fair you must have been awfully bored."

"No, ma'am," Drew said. But he said nothing more. He stayed mum.

The second Sunday morning in November 1940, Drew sat between his mother and grandfather in the Odom pew. The Germans had occupied most of Europe. They had ceased their daylight raids over London and the other English cities and had begun to bomb and terrorize them in the night.

"Our country is still at peace," the Right Reverend Thornton Welles said toward the end of his long sermon, "and may it ever remain at peace. Americans have no desire to become entangled again in Europe's endless civil war. Yet in such a time as ours the soldier stands for all of us. We hear of terrible battles, of awful conquests, of conflicts that when retold a thousand years from now will still strike terror in all mankind. You have all heard the saying that there are no atheists in foxholes. Perhaps that's true. Perhaps death's imminence would terrify even the profoundest skeptic or most scoffing denier into faith. But woe to those who believe," he preached as his voice grew louder and more stately, "only because they are afraid. Such faith belongs to the devil, not to God, and is dreadful to contemplate. The true believer believes not because he is afraid but because he knows in his soul God's Love is present. Let all who seek Our Lord cast aside all fear. For there can be no fear anywhere there is love. Amen."

Back home, Drew studied his face in the bathroom mirror. What did he see there? "I'm a pacifist," he told himself as if he were speaking to a stranger. "I don't believe in killing anyone. I don't believe in war. I'm not a coward. I'm not afraid to die. I'm not afraid. I'm a pacifist," he repeated, staring himself in the eye. But the stranger to whom he'd been speaking looked unconvinced.

Shortly before his ninety-third birthday, Drew's grandfather had started to slow down. He went to bed earlier, he got up later, he took long naps every afternoon. Leaving most of the farm's daily business to his daughter-in-law, he spent hours alone in his study, picking up one book after another as if he were following some trail of facts that might actually lead him to his long-desired goal. What was he searching for? Drew didn't dare ask. Whenever he peeked into the den, his grandfather would be asleep in his big chair, his swollen legs resting on a hassock. Books were strewn everywhere. Several lay open on his lap.

Early one Monday morning, before he caught a ride to work on a delivery truck, he joined his mother in the kitchen for coffee. "Grandfather was making a lot of mistakes last night." He poured himself a cup from the pot and stirred in some sugar. "The 'Notturno' is an easy piece."

She was standing at the window, staring eastward, her body framed by light. "Yes. I suppose it is."

"His fingers won't do what he orders them to do anymore."

"No. They won't." She sounded distracted.

"I'm taking the train back to New York on Tuesday, Mother," Drew said, seizing the opportunity. "It's taken over a year for me to save enough again, but I've finally done it. Mrs. Talbot is giving me a week off."

"Is she? That's kind of her so close to Christmas."

He set his cup down on the counter. "Mother . . ."

"Not now, Drew. Look," she said, pointing out the window.

He stood directly behind her, easily a half foot taller. Overnight there had been an ice storm. Everything Drew could see from the tops of the trees down to the moss and grass was covered by a paper-thin sheet of glass that seemed to magnify slightly each object it encased. The whole world shimmered and glittered like rippling water beneath a dazzling sun still lying low in a platinum sky.

His mother reached behind her for his hand and clasped it firmly. "Isn't it glorious?" she said.

It was raining hard when Drew walked out of Pennsylvania Station onto Seventh Avenue. Although he'd packed lightly, his suitcase felt increasingly heavy the closer he got to the hotel where he had stayed during his last trip. By the time he reached Thirty-eighth Street and Ninth Avenue, he was sopping. His room stank of wet plaster and rust. But he pretended he didn't mind. After all, if he skimped on unimportant things like lodging and meals, he might be able to stay a few days longer.

But the rain wouldn't quit and each day the air grew colder. The newspapers promised icy sleet or snow by noon the next day. On his way to his third concert, he had to buy an umbrella so he wouldn't have to sit through Toscanini's performance of the Verdi *Requiem* drenched to the bone and steaming in the warmth of Carnegie Hall.

After the concert, it was storming harder. Although all the limousines and taxis had departed and everyone else had at least begun their trip back home, Drew and one other man continued to linger outside the entrance just a few steps off Fifty-seventh Street. Although they stood only a few feet apart, the other man's face was almost entirely hidden by the wide, turned-up collar of his black overcoat, his black scarf, and his broad-brimmed black hat. He might have been playing a gunsel in a movie starring Cagney or Robinson or Raft. His gloved fingers gripped the lapel of his overcoat as he studied the firmament. "It's never going to stop."

Had he been speaking to Drew? "How far do you have to go?" Drew asked.

"Only a few blocks." When he turned toward Drew, the streetlight illuminated his face. His features were sharply thin, but he was much younger than Drew would have guessed. "I hate to get wet," the boy said.

Drew held up his umbrella. "It's brand new, but it leaks." The rain splashed like hail in the flooding gutters "Want to risk it anyway?"

"Why not?" The boy wiped his forehead with the back of his hand. "My uncle's waiting for me."

Drew slid his umbrella open and held it over their heads. "Which way?"

"Right. Then right again on Sixth Avenue."

Several minutes later they reached a bakery with two large windows facing the street on either side of the entrance. The boy tugged on Drew's coat. "This is my stop," he said and laughed.

The neon sign, the windows' lights, all the lights inside were dark, but behind one of the counters an open door glowed. The boy knocked on the door using a signal of taps and pauses that he repeated several times before a big, not quite heavyset man stepped through the light and into the front room to unlock the door. A gold watch chain fit tautly across the vest under his heavy tweed suit. His face was beaming. "How was the great man's concert? Perfection?"

"Not quite," the boy said. "Moscona entered too early a couple of times. Björling made some mistakes too. Milanov seemed scared to death of the high B-flat in the 'Libera Me.' She started gasping for breath bars before she finally hit it, more or less. But, Uncle Joe, it really was beautiful. Toscanini's a genius."

"That he is, Aaron my boy," he said, slapping him on his back. "And he believes in liberty, too." He held out a hand to Drew. "And you are?"

"Odom. Drew Odom."

"I'm sorry," the boy said. "You were good enough to walk with me all the way under the protection of your umbrella and I didn't even ask you your name. Or tell you mine. I'm Aaron Rose. And this is my . . ."

"His uncle Joe Rose. Come in, come in, both of you. Let's indulge in some poppy-seed cake and a cup of hot tea on a cold night, what do you say? Then Aaron and I should be on our way back to Jersey City. Oh, how I love that new tunnel. It makes our trips so fast now, doesn't it, Aaron?"

"I shouldn't stay," Drew said. "My hotel is still a long way away. It's late."

"You're a visitor to our town?" the uncle said. "May I guess? From the South, yes? I did detect a sweet magnolia scent in your voice, sir, did I not?"

The boy rolled his eyes. "The farthest south Uncle Joe has ever been is the boardwalk in Atlantic City."

"This is my third trip to Manhattan," Drew boasted.

"Then you're practically a native. Where are you staying?" Uncle Joe inquired. When Drew told him, he shook his head disapprovingly. "Not so good, son, not so good. Not very wise. A bad neighborhood. You mustn't walk. I'll drive you there. But, first, you must taste the best poppy-seed cake in the whole of greater New York. Rose's was voted the best, the very best. It says so right here," he said tapping a cutting from a newspaper that had been pinned to a cork board that hung on a wall in the huge back room where a half dozen bakers were stirring batter or opening and closing oven doors or decorating cakes. Had the kitchen back home while his mother was baking pies or cookies ever smelled half as sweet? "A family business," Uncle Joe informed Drew as he escorted him and Aaron into the office. "Mine, my brother Theodore's, my sister Ethel's, my sister Eva's. Aaron works here, too, when we can drag him out of his little basement room where he's all the time composing music that he never lets us hear. So does his sister Miriam and their cousins Judith and Samuel. My parents, God love them, started it right here on this very spot over forty-two years ago in 1898. David and Nettie Rosenbaum. Wonderful people. So kind. From Berlin originally. Came over on the same boat when neither of them had yet turned twenty. Out of nothing, they built this thriving business." He slapped his hands against his thighs in pride and admiration. "What don't we all owe to them and their generosity and hard work. They both died too young." His face lost all its glow for a moment, but then he winked at Drew. "Wait until you taste one of our sublime cheese Danishes. Sit down, both of you. I'll bring you some with the cake. We'll eat like gods, drink a little tea, and then I'll drive us all where we want to go, agreed?"

The sky was winter white, the air stingingly cold, but at least it had stopped raining for a few days. Yet by the time Drew reached the bakery from his hotel, it had begun to snow lightly. Three women and two girls were working behind the counters and display cases. Like a customer, Drew waited his turn in one of the lines. When he reached the front, a solidly stout woman whose cheeks had been too brightly rouged, smiled at him. "Yes? What would you like?"

"My name is Drew Odom. I'm here to meet Joseph Rose."

"Joe!" she shouted into the back room. "I'm Ethel Kraus, Joe's sister." She handed a customer the cookie-filled boxes he'd been waiting for. "We'll be leaving as soon as the last custard pie is out of the oven. They're for a banquet in Little Italy tonight. Dozens of them. Can you imagine? But ours really are the best in the world."

On the ride to Jersey City, heading for the dinner to which Drew had been invited two nights before, Joseph Rose, his sister Ethel, and his niece Judith asked him question after question. What were his parents' names? Were his grandparents still alive? What sort of work did his father do? How many brothers and sisters did he have? As one sad fact emerged after another they commiserated, grieved for him, sympathized. He had mentioned he lived on a dairy farm. What was it like? What was life like in a small Southern town? What did he think about the way colored people were treated down there? So many inquiries into his life and beliefs startled Drew.

He was grateful when the car finally stopped in front of a thin, weathered brick house that was almost squished between two much thicker but even more weathered stone apartment buildings. Joe gave Drew a little shove toward the stoop. The front door swung open. As he approached her, the woman standing in the doorway threw her arms around him, squeezed him as a child hugs her favorite doll, and grabbed a thick tuft of his hair. "What a blondie!" She bussed his cheek. "I'm Eva Green," she announced, "and this fellow standing behind me is my husband, Stephen."

"Come meet the rest of our family," Stephen said, inviting him in.

A hefty, balding man stepped across the room to slap Drew

on the back. "I'm Theodore Rose, Aaron's father." He turned around. "And this is . . ."

"I'm Mikla, Aaron's mother." She was sitting a little lost in a huge chair that was pink like the curtains. A sofa was maroon like the valances. The wallpaper almost matched the two wing-backs' crushed blue velvet. The mahogany of the coffee table and the two bookcases was only a little less dark than the room's other exposed wood, much of it meticulously carved lattice work. From nearly every cloth covering a table and from every lamp shade dangled fringe or tassels dyed bright gold. Aaron's mother twisted several loose strands of the linen antimacassar on her chair's arm. Wrinkles had creased her face into a frown even her warm smile could not relieve.

"Dinner's ready," a boy's voice called from the dining room.

They were twelve: the bachelor Joseph Rose; the widow Ethel Rose Kraus and her two children Samuel and Judith; Eva Rose and Stephen Green and their daughter Susanna; Theodore, Mikla, Aaron, and Miriam Rose; and Drew, who had never before in his life dined with more than two others at the table. They ate and they gabbed and they laughed and occasionally everyone would grow quiet as Joe or Ethel or Eva sang snippets of American show tunes or German operetta arias to much delight and applause. Only Aaron said little, and Mikla said nothing at all.

After they'd all finished their lemon-cream cake and cup after cup of coffee, everyone except the girls withdrew to the living room. The three men lit cigars and stood smoking and talking politics in a corner. Eva approached the upright piano. "Stephen?" she called. Aaron grabbed Drew by his shirt. "Come with me. I want to show you my study."

They passed through the dining room and the kitchen where the three girls were cleaning up from the meal and turned right into a pantry that led to steps descending into a dark, unfinished basement. Aaron clicked on a bulb that dangled from the ceiling. "Not bad, huh?" Two desks shoved side-by-side were flanked by two tall bookcases filled with books and magazines. He turned on a lamp that apparently had found its way there after many years' service in a Victorian parlor. "It's the only place in this house I can work. My bedroom's too cramped. But it's all right here, don't you think?"

"How do you read?"

Aaron flicked on another battered antique lamp. "That's better."

Several magazines lay scattered across the top of one desk. "*Modern Music*," Drew read out loud. He thumbed through a copy. "I don't think I've heard much modern music. Does your whole family live here?"

"The Greens rent a flat in the building next door. Uncle Stephen is a haberdasher in Hoboken."

"Your mother's very quiet."

"Mother's from Misocz. When she was still almost a baby, her father and a brother were killed in a pogrom. Father says that late at night she can sometimes hear horses' hooves and the sound of boots stomping across plank floors and feel her mother's hands around her mouth so she won't cry out. None of the Rose clan quite understands her. They all wonder why my father married her. They're happy. They're comfortable in the world and don't think much about religion or God. But Mikla knows better. She blames God for everything."

Drew opened a score with notes sketched on only a few bars. "You've composed a lot?"

"Not a lot. A couple of piano sonatas. A string quartet. About two dozen songs, most of them to poems by Walt Whitman. A piano trio. Some a capella choral settings of psalms. A *De Profundis* for men's voices and organ. The only piano I have to use is that out-of-tune upright you saw in the living room upstairs. Loud, isn't it? That's Uncle Joe playing now and Aunt Eva singing. They love operetta. Their favorite singers are Lotte Schöne, Richard Tauber, and Joseph Schmidt. They all went to hear Schmidt at Carnegie Hall three years ago, the only recital they've attended together in years. They prefer music they can devour like sweets. Who are your favorite composers, Drew?"

"I wish I knew. My grandfather worships Wagner, my mother Bach."

"It's too dank down here," Aaron said. "It would be nicer if there were a window." He fingered a copy of *Modern Music.* "I try to keep myself informed about what's new, but it's hard to do when so little gets performed. My favorite composers are Verdi for the tragic relentlessness of his rhythms, Tchaikovsky for his passionate, heartfelt melody, Mahler for the spiritual profundity of his orchestration, and Bloch for his honest soulfulness. How's that for a list?" he said grinning. "Do you like Bloch also, Drew?"

"I've never heard of him. And Mahler is just a name to me." Drew looked down at Aaron who was sitting in the chair at his desk. Where had he seen a face like his recently? In one of the museums, perhaps, in some somber Renaissance portrait, all browns and umbers and blacks, that had darkened further over the years. And yet it shone. "I should be heading back to the city soon," Drew said.

"My father'll be driving back to the bakery shortly. It's his night to supervise. You can catch a ride with him."

"Aaron?" his sister Miriam called down into the basement. "The concert's over. It's safe for you two to come back upstairs now."

But it wasn't safe. "Ich bin ein Zigeunerkind," Joe was singing in his sweet, surprisingly light tenor. He held both his hands over his heart expressively as Eva throbbed on the piano with glee and surprising abandon.

Judith pulled back one of the heavy pink draperies. "Aaron, look. Look how much it's snowed in just the last hour. Do you have snow where you come from, Drew?"

"You mustn't attempt to go back to the bakery when it's

snowing this hard, Theo," Mikla said to her husband. "Call Harold Bauer. Let him supervise."

Theodore Rose anxiously ran his fingers up and down his suitcoat's lapel. "Perhaps I could."

"The streets are sure to be slick as ice tonight," Ethel said. She glanced out the door and shut it again after a few flakes had flown in.

Joe quit singing. "Fortunately, we can always depend on Harold."

Theodore Rose shook his head doubtfully. "Remember the disaster with the Goldschmidt wedding?"

"Oh, Theo," Eva said from her piano bench, "I've told you a thousand times that fiasco was more my fault than Harold's."

"Excuse me," Drew said, "but I should really be heading back to the city before the storm gets any worse. What would be the best way? The tubes?"

"You can't be serious," Ethel said.

"We wouldn't hear of it," Uncle Joseph said.

Aunt Ethel hugged him from behind. "Darling boy. Don't be silly. You'll spend the night right here, safe with all of us."

"You'll be a lot better off here than in that disgusting flop-house, let me tell you," Joe said.

"You can bunk in Aaron's room with him," Theodore Rose suggested. "It'll be snug, but it should do."

"Aaron?" Drew asked.

"It's OK with me. But it is tiny," Aaron emphasized. "More like a cell."

"Don't listen to him, Drew," Aaron's father said. "He's always complaining."

"We're all a little cramped," Joe said.

"It's cozy," Ethel assured him.

A few hours later Aaron and Drew were undressing for bed in the half-light in the squat attic room. "You're uncircumcised," Aaron observed as Drew stepped out of his underclothes.

Drew looked down at himself. "Does that make me unclean or anything? Do you need to purify me?"

Aaron laughed. "You've never known any Jews before, have you?"

"Nope. You all are my very first."

Aaron clicked off the light. They lay down in the bed. "Do you think America's going to be fighting in the war soon?" Drew asked.

"I hope so. I want to fight Nazis. I want to see them destroyed. For me, it's kill or be killed."

"I don't want to kill anybody."

"I don't want to kill anybody either, Drew. But Nazis aren't anybody. They're evil."

"You know what you want to do with your life, don't you, Aaron?"

"Yes, I think so. What do you want to do with yours?"

"I don't know. Nothing, maybe."

"Nothing?"

"It's the only answer I can ever think of," Drew said.

At the breakfast table, Uncle Joe cut a thick slice of bread from the loaf of rye. "Did you sleep well?"

"Fine, sir," Drew said.

"There's been over a foot of snow," Aunt Ethel reported. "The schools are closed everywhere."

"Why don't you just stay with us for the rest of your vacation," Uncle Joe suggested. "As soon as we can drive back into the city, we'll grab your suitcase from that dive and settle you in here. What do you say?"

Aunt Ethel pinched Drew's cheek. "Such a darling young man. You must, you know."

"Just precious," Miriam said in a mock-Southern accent.

"Don't mind her, Drew," Judith said. "She's wanted to find herself a Southern beau and live the pampered life of a belle ever since she saw *Gone with the Wind*, haven't you, Miriam?"

"I bet I will too," Miriam said.

"See? You better watch out, Drew," Judith said.

Uncle Joseph peered at them over the frame of his glasses. "Girls."

"It's not like that there," Drew said. "It's nothing like that at all."

Shortly after Drew moved in with the Roses, he wrote two letters. In the first he apologized to Mrs. Talbot for his failure to return to his duties when he'd promised and he requested that she be so kind as to hold his job for him anyway if she could. In the second he briefly informed his mother that he intended to be home by Christmas. He included no return address with either.

Two days later the weather warmed considerably and melted all the snow. Every day, Drew accompanied Aaron on his errands for the bakery. On a few occasions, they delivered cakes as far away as Long Island, and they frequently found themselves all over Brooklyn or Queens. In the afternoons, they'd carry sweets for evening parties up and down Manhattan. Yet they were rarely too tired at night to attend a concert, standing whenever they could, and Friday nights and Saturday afternoons they saved for the Met.

Only once did they take a day off and stay at home in Jersey City. Aaron wanted to play for Drew his records of Mahler, the Ninth Symphony and *Das Lied*, both recorded a couple of years before by Bruno Walter, Aaron's favorite conductor. Almost no one else was in the house that afternoon. They lay side-by-side on the thick rug in the living room and did not speak even as the player let another record drop or when Aaron turned a stack over. After more than two hours, the music was finished.

"Unbelievable," Aaron said, breaking the silence.

"I've never heard anything like it," Drew said. "Never."

They were both still lying quietly on the floor when Aaron's mother wandered down the stairs into the living room. Distraught, she was wringing her hands and crying. "Again, Aaron? Why such sad music again? So much sorrow, so much grief. It's nearly unbearable. What were the words you read to me the last time you played it?"

"'The world is falling asleep,'" he quoted from memory. "'A cool breeze is blowing in the pines' shadow. I am waiting for my friend so that we might say a loving farewell. How I would like to enjoy the beauty of another evening by his side. Where has he gone? Why has he left me so long? I wander on grassy paths and strum on my lute alone.'"

She kneeled on the carpet next to him and clasped his hands in hers. "Yes. I remember now. All this afternoon, as you were playing this music again, I kept hearing an old tune my own mother used to sing. I haven't heard that song in years, but now I can't seem to get it out my of my head. Isn't that strange?" She sang the tune, hummed it rather, and wept and wept.

That night, Aaron and Drew went to a movie in downtown Jersey City. The theater showed a newsreel of the ships the British had destroyed in Algiers. In another newsreel, more recent, RAF pilots were shooting down German planes. The audience clapped and cheered as each one exploded into flames and crashed into the channel. Aaron's face was lit by the light reflected off the screen. Tears glistened his cheeks.

Late at night, their backs propped up by pillows, a lamp on over their heads, they read scores from the small collection that Aaron had carried upstairs to his attic room from his basement study. Frequently they sang the music aloud, exchanging different parts back and forth as they attempted to vocalize the Tchaikovsky trio, a Rachmaninoff concerto, or a Bloch quartet. Often they couldn't finish a movement because they had begun to laugh so hard at themselves and their mistakes, beating their hands against the sheets or rolling around on the bed in mock hysterics.

Only after Drew had prodded him time after time did Aaron show him one of his own compositions, a piano sonata. As a baritone, Drew attempted the left hand, Aaron the high tenor the right. Although obviously the music they'd sung wasn't the piece Aaron had written, he admitted that he'd liked what he'd heard.

"It's rhapsodic," Drew commented. "Tuneful."

"You mean formless, don't you?" Aaron tossed the score onto the floor. "I always mangle form."

Drew shivered. "It's really cold up here tonight."

Aaron folded his half of the blankets over Drew. "That should help some."

But it didn't help. Although he was lying under three blankets and a sheet, Drew started to jerk and twitch. "I'm OK," he said to reassure Aaron. "Don't worry. Really. It's all right. I do this sometimes. It's not the cold. It's me. It'll stop soon." Aaron's lips started to move. "What are you doing?" Drew demanded even as he continued to shake.

"I don't want you to get sick."

"You're praying? Don't bother. I don't believe in God, Aaron."

"I do."

"You do? How can you?"

"Don't ask stupid questions, Drew."

Whenever they passed a bum on a New York sidewalk, Drew would try to avoid having to look at his rheumy red eyes, his grimy outstretched hand, or his nails as discolored as a wild dog's. But Aaron invariably put a nickel or a quarter in his cup, handed him a bun or pastry from one of the full boxes they were transporting, and said with all his heart, "God bless."

Aaron and Drew liked to take their breaks at Nedick's. "Please don't tell my family I enjoy Nedick's doughnuts more than theirs," Aaron implored. "They'd believe I was betraying them or losing my mind." He took another chomp. "Uncle Joe says they're poison."

"Could be," Drew said, biting down on his. "They seem to affect the brain. Once I eat one I don't seem able to leave."

Aaron turned on his stool to face Drew. "When do you have to go back home?"

"Soon. They were expecting me weeks ago."

"When are you coming to New York again?"

"I don't know. Soon."

"We'll be in the war soon. Whether England prevails or not, we'll be fighting the Germans soon."

"I promised my mother I'd be home for Christmas, Aaron."

"Maybe I could visit you there in a few months. What do you think?"

Drew studied himself in the big mirror on the wall behind the counter. How much of what he saw in a mirror did he recognize as Andrew Willingham Odom? When he pictured himself, he never saw the almost white blond hair, the bright blue eyes, or high cheekbones and ruddy face every mirror had always shown him. He saw instead someone who looked more like Aaron, dark and fiercely gaunt and knife thin, a squint to his eyes like that which he'd noticed in old men pictured in magazines who had roamed through deserts all their lives.

A waitress leaning against the cash register retied the netting around her graying hair. A baby-faced busboy was flirting with her as he lined up just-washed coffee cups across a counter. She popped her gum and winked at Drew. When Drew looked at himself again, he saw how nakedly he was blushing. "You wouldn't care for my family," he said, facing Aaron.

"You mean they wouldn't approve of me."

"Don't take it personally. They don't like anyone." He placed a quarter next to his saucer and stood up to leave. "We've got three more deliveries to make."

"I could write you," Aaron proposed as he slammed the door of the truck shut.

"You could."

"But?"

"Not at home. At the library. Without a return address."

"I don't understand. Why do I have to be a secret?"

"Everybody needs a really good secret, Aaron," Drew said as he started the truck. "I've never had one. Now I've got you."

"We met after Verdi and now we're going to part after Verdi," Aaron said morosely as they lingered outside the Met on Broadway just after the Saturday matinee had ended. "And after both Björling and Milanov, too. But have you ever heard more beautiful singing?"

"It was great, Aaron. But for some reason my legs are tired," Drew complained. "I got a cramp standing way up there."

"You didn't like *Un Ballo*?"

"I don't know. Too much Italian band music. Too oompah-pah. Too brassy."

"That's what you've said your grandfather would say."

"Yeah, I know."

Aaron pointed to the poster on the wall. "Next Saturday is *Don Pasquale*. I promise to be here, watching it for both of us, if you'll promise to listen to it on the radio."

"My grandfather has said a man should prefer to see himself lowered into his grave than to have to listen to anything by Donizetti. You've no idea how red he'll turn. It sounds like fun. I'll do it," Drew said.

One limousine drove up behind another. A chauffeur was holding open a door for three elderly ladies, all of them dressed in long black gowns and either sable or Persian lamb capes. "I wonder if they heard the same opera I heard," Aaron said.

Most of the rest of the crowd was drifting slowly up or down the street, walking or waiting for a cab. Across Broadway, Drew slipped on a thin patch of ice left on the sidewalk from the previous night's freeze. Aaron grabbed his hand and didn't let it go until he'd completely recovered his balance. On Fifth Avenue, people strolled the streets, enjoying all the decorations and admiring the festive store windows. At a deli on Fifty-first, Aaron and Drew stopped for a hot turkey sandwich and a chocolate ice cream soda.

They arrived at the bakery two hours later than they had predicted to Uncle Joe, but he said he'd been too busy to notice the time. It was always like that during the holidays, he said. All of the family except Aaron's sister had already returned to Jersey. As Drew retrieved his suitcase from the office where he'd left it earlier, Miriam handed him a bag of fresh Danishes, still warm. "For the long ride home," she said and pecked him on the cheek.

At Penn Station, Joe remained behind the wheel of the car and kept it idling so he wouldn't have to hunt for a place to park. Grabbing his suitcase and the bag of pastries off the backseat, Drew slid out of the car. Aaron rolled down his window, rolled it back up again, paused, opened the door, and stepped out of the chugging car. He approached Drew so slowly he might have been wading through high water onto shore. "Drew," he said.

Drew squeezed his shoulder. "I'll see you."

"When?" Aaron pressed him.

"Is tomorrow soon enough?"

"Don't tease me, Drew. What if I have to go to war tomorrow?"

"I'll go with you," Drew promised.

On the afternoon following the morning Drew returned home, he wrote a thank-you letter to all the Roses and posted it the next day. But he didn't write to just Aaron alone and his failure to have done so at once puzzled and troubled him, especially while he was listening to *Don Pasquale* on his grandfather's radio. He'd half expected his grandfather to deny him its use or at least to walk out of the room during the performance, but the old man settled into his chair almost as expectantly as if he were waiting to hear Flagstad and Melchior in *Tristan* again.

"You seem shocked," he said to Drew as Milton Cross's voice poured into the room. "Why should you be? *Don Pasquale* is one of the oldest stories in the world, older than Plautus or Menander even. An old man in love with a beautiful young girl. What could be more absurd? At the heart of Mediterranean sanity is its wonderful sense of irony and the absurd. Even my master Wagner had the good sense to die beneath Venetian light, Grandson."

Neither his grandfather nor his mother asked him anything about his time away or his reasons for extending it, although Mrs. Talbot at the library, gratefully welcoming him back to a job it was clear no one else in town was willing to take, observed with a twinkle, "You've gained a little weight."

Weeks passed and still he would not write Aaron. Every time he tried, instead of writing down his thoughts, the pen he was holding appeared to erase them from his brain or heart. Drew had read about people who had taken pictures of ghosts. But, even though they had sworn that the person they had seen was as clear to them as life, the image always turned out on film to look like mist or clouds. Was Aaron's unaccountable blurring in his mind a consequence of a similar phenomenon?

When he was fourteen or fifteen, Drew asked his mother if she had loved his father. Since she never spoke of him, never referred to him even in passing, he had often wondered. Her answer had been, "I don't know. I've never known, Drew. We were both so young."

Yet Drew persisted. "What was he like? What did he enjoy? What had he hoped for from life? Had he ever been happy?"

His mother sighed. "Oh, Drew, I could lie to you, I guess. But the truth is I barely knew your father."

Four weeks after Drew had returned from New York, a worker's shack near a creek that flowed into the river burned to the ground. The man had been drinking and smoking and had set fire to his bed. Drew and his mother visited him in the hospital. Most of his body had been badly burned. After he'd died, she notified the hospital that she wished to assume responsibility for his bills. She ordered the charred ruins plowed under and saplings planted on the site.

Perhaps, Drew thought, he could write to Aaron about what had happened to that poor man. To describe what had occurred should prove safe and easy. How could he not? But his hand refused to form words. What did Aaron want from him? Why wouldn't Drew's body, dumb as a beast, respond?

Despite Drew's silence, along with his letters, Aaron sent him:

1. The Rose Bakery's secret recipe for custard pie.
2. A program from Toscanini's performance of the *Missa Solemnis* with Milanov, Castagna, Björling, and Kipnis, December 28th, 1940, Carnegie Hall. Madame Milanov herself had autographed it. ("I'll tell you the whole amazing story when I see you.")
3. A magazine picture of Ernest Hemingway, his right profile jutting forward like a plow, and Martha Gellhorn, both all smiles while clinking cocktail glasses together at the Stork Club. (Aaron had scrawled near the bottom, "Two distinguished American writers seriously at work.")
4. A Nedick's menu.
5. A clipping from the *Herald Tribune*, February 9, 1941, of a Virgil Thomson review of a Hindemith concert. German form, Thomson opined, required harmonic progress, which meant a composer always had to go somewhere and make a point. But the French understood that melody was self-sufficient. ("Which it is, despite the French," Aaron had added.)

6. A picture of Tchaikovsky, cut from a book.

7. A picture of Mahler, cut from another book. ("I'm mutilating my favorite books for you, Drew.")

8. Picture postcards bound together with a rubber band of (1) Brooklyn Bridge and the Manhattan skyline, (2) Battery Park and the Aquarium, (3) George Washington's statue on the steps of the Treasury Building, (4) the South Street Fish Market, (5) the lobby of the Empire State Building, (6) the main hall of Grand Central Station with the light falling down onto the floor from the high half-moon windows like light from a dome in a temple or cathedral, and (7) the spires and minarets of crescent-moon-mad Luna Park at Coney Island. ("Look enticing?")

9. A program from the Met for *L'Amore dei Tre Re* with Grace Moore and Ezio Pinza conducted by the composer, Italo Montemezzi. ("A modern masterpiece? Almost.")

10. A pressing of a jonquil. ("It's already spring, Drew.")

11. A note card with a passage Aaron had identified as coming from Spinoza's *Ethics*: "Wisdom is not the meditation of death but of life." ("False," Aaron wrote on the back, "though the reverse is also untrue.")

12. A photograph cut from the *Times* of women from the Mothers' Crusade kneeling in the shadow of the Capitol and praying for the defeat of Lend-Lease. They waved flags and held up signs reading, KILL BILL 1776 NOT OUR BOYS. ("They should all be pouring tea at a temperance meeting," Aaron observed. "When you say you are a pacifist, surely you don't mean this.")

13. Two verses from the third chapter of *Lamentations* printed on a sheet of music paper: "He was unto me as a bear lying in wait, and as a lion in secret places. He

hath turned aside my ways, and pulled me into pieces: he hath made me desolate." On the other sheets were sketches of music for piano trio written in the key of F minor.

14. Two lines of Whitman typed onto another blank card:

> O who is that ghost, that form in the dark, with tears?
> What shapeless lump is that, bent, crouch'd there on
>   the sand?

15. A smudged thumbprint, a trickle of dried blood on a tissue.

16. Olin Downes's review in the *Times* of a Sibelius symphony: Strong, masculine, bardic. ("Everything he denies to the Jew Mahler.")

17. A song sheet for "America First!" words and music by Sara Quinn Hill. ("Your people.")

18. A picture clipped from the *Times* of inductees on Long Island with wooden rifles and broomsticks.

19. A score of Bloch's "Poème Mystique" for violin and piano.

20. A brand new photograph of the Roses, Krauses, and Greens all proudly standing in front of the bakery, all of them smiling and waving beneath the awning. Only Mikla is absent. (On the back, Aaron had written, "Mother's heard more rumors of German savageries and atrocity near where many of her relatives still live. She refuses to leave our house.")

21. An announcement of the forthcoming Met season with December 6, 1941 underlined three times: *Die Walküre* with Melchior. ("Did you know he toured Argentina in 1933 under the sponsorship of Goebbels to promote German art?")

22. Three photographs Aaron had taken of himself while

sitting in a booth in a penny arcade. He'd pulled the collar of his coat up and the brim of his hat down and wrapped his scarf around his neck up to his chin. With both hands, he held a sheet of paper on which he'd printed in tall, bold letters: AARON MISSES DREW.

23. A poem.

> Drew, will man do a homing?
> Hand will wring me a doom,
> Hoarding me woman will'd.
> How mad, armed on ill wing,
> Hill naming wed war mood.
> Wow, Mahler damning Lido!
> Hid red llama now mowing!
> Will made. Now do harming,
> Hold wing. Mail word, name,
> Andrew Willingham Odom!

24. A pigeon's feather cut so it resembled an antique writing quill.

Some nights, lying awake in his bed, Drew thought he could hear the river that usually flowed through the fields as quiet as a creek more than an hour's walk away roaring like a waterfall just outside his door. Although it might be barely past midnight, he could already hear mourning doves beneath his bedroom window. Field hands called to each other across the road. A barn door creaked open. A truck, backfiring, drove off. Listening carefully, he believed his mother might be practicing something by Bach as she did many afternoons in the parlor downstairs, but of course never amidst the city noises he also heard. Packed as tight as horses in a corral, cars hummed at an intersection. A policeman blew his whistle. A street vendor hawked his chestnuts. Somewhere, closer to the piers, a siren sounded and faded away. Although he was lying only under quilts his great-grandmother had sewn, he heard sheets rustling as Aaron twisted in his bedclothes, groaning quietly as he did sometimes in the darkest hours of the night, deep asleep.

Sometimes Drew slept. Frequently he dreamed that he was standing on the bank of a lake, its waters crystalline and icy blue, its many islands black as the pine forests. An amber sun hovered near the horizon in a purple sky. It did not rise, it would not set. A hide canoe waited for him on the pebble shore. Having stepped into it, he pushed off with a pole and paddled toward the farther side. His oar plashed in the lake. Water lapped against his boat. Far off, a solitary bird cried in an empty sky. The water and the air were as dead as the sun.

Shortly after the siege of Leningrad had begun, Drew quit his job at the library. He didn't want to have to look at the war in magazines, he didn't want to have to read war stories in newspapers anymore. As he left work on his last Saturday, Mrs. Talbot presented him with a glass jar full of her famous mints, which were so special, she said, because she rolled them only on fine polished marble. She also gave him a copy of *For Whom the Bell Tolls* that she'd inscribed, "Some valuable lessons in courage for all of us who face the parlous times to come. Yours sincerely, Mrs. R.F. (Sally) Talbot."

Once more at home all day, Drew retreated to his rooms. His grandfather had recommended he follow his example and re-read *The Iliad*, preferably in one of the older prose translations he owned and would be glad to loan his grandson. Since Homer, his grandfather argued, anyone who wrote about battle had wasted his breath. But Drew rejected the offer. All wars, past or present, each day horrified him more.

His grandfather kept to his rooms because he no longer saw much value in pretending he wasn't seriously old. More than ever, his mother occupied herself with the farm, having assumed all of her father-in-law's duties and taken on some new ones of her own devising. Neither chose to attend in any way to Drew's reclusion.

If the weather was clear, Drew went on long and aimless walks. When it rained, he practiced his fiddle. He had learned by heart the first Bach partita, the violin parts of two Mozart sonatas, and a solo piece by Ysaÿe before, after months of hesitation, he finally tackled the Bloch. First he practiced the fingerings, and when he bowed he played quietly so no one else could hear the music. Some passages were surprisingly difficult, in particular those marked *animato.* "Credo in unum Deum!" Bloch had written after "*Moderato assai*" and "Gloria in excelsis Deo" after "*Più lento.*" Could a good tune, lucid and hymnlike, be more effective than prayer? After weeks of practice, one night in early December, suitcase in one hand, violin case in the other, he snuck out of the house, walked to the country road, and hitched a ride to town.

When he arrived at the bakery the following afternoon, a customer munching on a bun swung the door open for him. Drew set his two cases down on the floor and waved. "Hey, Uncle Joe."

Uncle Joe slapped his forehead in delight. "Drew! Why didn't you let us know you were coming?"

"I wanted to surprise you. Is Aaron here?"

Wiping her hands on her apron, Aunt Ethel walked through the back door. "Hello, Blondie. Aaron doesn't work here anymore. He quit months ago."

Uncle Joe shrugged. "He's that age."

Aaron's sister carried a tray of apple tarts to place in the display rack. "Aaron will be surprised to see you," she said as she set the tarts down. "You never wrote him, he said. Why not?"

"I meant to," Drew apologized. "I really did."

"You know," Uncle Joe said, "I may have written three letters in my whole life."

"You don't know anybody to write except family," Aunt Ethel

said, "and none of us ever goes anywhere except home after a long day's work."

"My brother's living down on East Tenth Street near Avenue A," Miriam said. She took a business card from the stack on the counter and wrote his address on the back. "Here."

"He's training to be a piano tuner," Uncle Joe said. "For Schneiderman and Company on West Fifty-first. A fine, growing firm, he tells me."

"Who pay him next to nothing," Aunt Ethel said and rolled her eyes.

"The boy just wants a little independence," Joe said to his sister. "That's all." He winked at Drew. "He'll be overjoyed to see you."

Miriam glared at him. "Don't be so sure."

Drew turned toward the door. "I'll risk it."

"You can always bunk with us in Jersey," Uncle Joe offered.

"Anytime," Aunt Ethel agreed.

"Thanks," Drew said. He bowed to all of them and hurried out onto the street.

Drew rode the subway to Astor Place, walked the few remaining blocks to Aaron's building, and waited on the cold cement stoop for him to come home. Shivering, he watched the sun disappear behind the tall gray buildings to the west, slivers of orange and red shining between them. He had removed a sweater from his suitcase and had just pulled it over his head when he heard, "Drew?" Wrapped in black, Aaron was standing on the sidewalk.

"Surprised?" Drew asked.

"Not really. Miriam phoned work."

"You're not happy to see me?"

"You look very cold, Drew." Aaron mounted the stoop and unlocked the door. "I'm on the top floor." He picked up the violin case. "You've brought your instrument."

"I've learned the Bloch sonata."

"That's good, I guess."

Drew followed him up four flights of stairs and into Aaron's three small, sparsely furnished rooms. "It's nice."

"It's more space than I ever had at home. Pop bought most of the furniture."

Drew pointed to a picture hanging on the wall. "There's Gustav."

"I found him in an antique store on Eighth Street. I had to buy the frame to get the Mahler. I didn't eat much for weeks."

"Not even sweets?"

"Every time I visit the bakery they all try to encourage me to move back home. Except for Miriam. She understands." On the street below, a big black truck, parked in front of a laundry, was spewing smoke from its muffler. "Why didn't you ever write me back, Drew?"

"I don't know. I really don't. I thought of you every day."

Aaron tossed his hat onto a table and unwound his scarf from around his neck. Drew draped his jacket over the back of a chair and lit a lamp. Fingering the cover of a score that lay on Aaron's desk, he asked, "A new piece?"

"From *Lamentations*. I sent you some early sketches."

"I remember." He folded back the cover and read the inscription written on the first page. "You've dedicated it to me?"

"I guess I have."

"It's finished?"

"Some transitions are clumsy. I haven't finished all the vocal parts. Some of the instrumentation needs development." He wouldn't look at him. "I thought you were going to be my friend, Drew."

"I am your friend."

"We must understand the word differently then."

"Does that have to matter?"

"It doesn't have to. It just does."

"We could go to that *Walküre* on Saturday. My treat."

"No. There's too much German arrogance and savagery in every bar Wagner ever wrote. I've never liked him much, but now I couldn't bear to listen to him at all. But . . ." He checked his watch.

"What, Aaron?"

"Panizza's conducting *Traviata* with Novotná and Peerce and Tibbett tonight. If we hurry and if we're lucky, we might still be able to get in. Maybe even find our old spot free."

"What did you think?" Aaron prodded Drew as they headed down Broadway on their way toward the Village for a snack after the performance.

"'Parigi, o cara,'" Drew sang. "We'll leave this city, Alfredo says. The future will smile on us, he says. Then she dies. What could be sadder than hope when there is no future to hope for?" Drew grabbed Aaron's coat and tugged him closer. "It was wonderful."

"Wasn't it?"

They stopped at I Fratelli in the Village for spaghetti and garlic bread and spumoni and wandered through the Square in no rush to get back to Aaron's place even though when they arrived at the building it was nearly two in the morning.

"What time do you have to be at work tomorrow?" Drew asked as Aaron clicked on a light in his apartment.

"Eight. They keep me busy. What nobody else is willing to do is only part of my job."

"You'll need to sleep fast."

"I don't feel like sleeping at all." He opened the door to the bedroom. "You still prefer the left side?"

"I thought I'd just stretch out on that couch in the living room, Aaron. Do you mind? You'll sleep better if I'm not crowding you."

"I see." He reached into his closet, pulled a heavy blanket and a pillow off a shelf, and tossed them to Drew. "I'll try not to wake you when I leave in the morning."

"You'd still like to hear *Walküre* this afternoon, wouldn't you, Drew?" They were finishing their oatmeal and tea early on a wintry Saturday morning. The buildings outside looked dark as iron beneath a sky gray with clouds.

"Maybe."

"So you do mind?"

"Nope." Drew gently punched Aaron's arm. "It's you I really wanted to see."

Blushing, Aaron gazed out the window. Drew shoved his chair back from the table, knelt down next to the couch where he'd been sleeping, fumbled in his suitcase, from a tangle of clothes extracted a stack of seven postcards bound by a rubber band, and tossed them to Aaron who caught them on the wing. "Ever since you sent me those I've wanted to go to each one of those places in exactly that order, starting with Brooklyn Bridge and ending in Coney Island."

Aaron flipped through them. "We'd waste a lot of time doubling back on ourselves."

"Pretend we're on a treasure hunt and that's a map."

"If you say so."

Late that afternoon, they stepped off the boardwalk at Coney Island and onto the beach, still damp from an earlier rain. Alone except for the gulls and a few skittering birds, they slowly crossed the wide strand toward the ocean. "So, Drew," Aaron asked, "how did you like our crazy excursion?"

"I loved it, all of it," Drew said, "but especially the Empire State, maybe because it reminded me of the World's Fair. All of New York's wonderful skyscrapers look like great futuristic ships about to launch into space toward some distant planet thousands of years more advanced than our own and free of all unhappiness, especially the grief of war. Don't you think so, Aaron?"

"I should have remembered the Aquarium had been closed," Aaron said. He pulled down the brim of his hat, rewrapped his scarf more tightly around his neck, and tugged on Drew's jacket as they followed the shoreline's curve. Near the horizon two ships were barely visible. Like children on the crest of a hill they appeared to be waiting to slide down the other side. Aaron nodded toward the water's edge. "Those waves could be rows of men leaping out of trenches and collapsing forward as they're shot."

"Don't, Aaron. Hush," Drew said. He pressed the heel of his shoe into the sand where a wave's last gasp was still trickling and bubbling. Another rushed toward their feet but fell back before it could reach them.

"My mother's cousin Anna Yousselevska lives near here, on Mermaid Avenue," Aaron said. "Mother and I visited her recently. She's heard more stories, Drew, many more stories. Despite everything, a few people escape and talk, though almost no one listens. If ever there was a righteous war, this is it." He wiped his runny nose with his handkerchief.

"It's freezing here, Aaron."

"Yes. We'll get something warm to eat at Nathan's, then head home."

"It's been a great day, buddy," Drew said on the train. "But I'm exhausted."

"I'm sorry to hear that. I was hoping we might attempt the Bloch sonata tonight."

"Brother, I thought you'd never ask," Drew said.

Back in Manhattan, they returned to Aaron's apartment to fetch Drew's violin and copies of the score, hurried to the subway, and rode to Fiftieth Street. At Schneiderman's, Aaron directed them down an alley to a steel door hidden behind garbage bins and wooden boxes. They climbed two long flights in the dark to another massive door that led into a corridor so black that Aaron twice stumbled into a wall before he found his way. He grabbed Drew's hand to lead him into the room.

The lock clicked, the door swung open, Aaron flicked on the light. "That's one beautiful grand," Drew said.

"It's perfectly tuned. My masterpiece so far." Aaron opened up a music stand for Drew to use.

They rehearsed for hours, stopping often to question each other about uncertainties in rhythm, tempo, volume, or pitch, never taking a break, playing the more difficult passages over and over until they got each bar and every note right. Aaron glanced up at the clock. It was well past three in the morning. "Ready?"

"Not really," Drew said.

They played it through without interrupting themselves once. When they had finished, they waited ten minutes and played it all over again.

"That was something," Aaron said after minutes of silence had passed between them. "Almost perfect. Almost as good as Heifetz and Rubinstein could do, I'd bet."

"Yes," Drew said. "How did we do it?" Exhilarated, he mopped his brow and returned his violin and bow to their case.

"I don't think we did," Aaron said. He lowered the piano's lid, set the scores on a shelf, switched off the light, and sat back down on the stool where Drew was already sitting. They both faced away from the keyboard toward the window and the fire escape. Across the alley, a long thin neon sign was blinking on and off, coloring the room in turn watery blue, bright red, shrill purple.

Aaron laid his hand gently on Drew's shoulder. Drew wiped his eyes with his shirtsleeve. They looked away from the window at each other. They held hands. They kissed. Was it a real kiss? Saying nothing, they quit the building. Except for them, their car on the subway ride back was empty and only a few other people were roaming the streets that late at night. They had to drag themselves up to Aaron's apartment.

In their separate rooms, they slept past noon. Even after they had gotten up, they barely moved. Neither had bothered to shower, shave, or change out of yesterday's underwear. Like cats, they napped wherever the sun shone into the living room. Midafternoon, Aaron mentioned a Toscanini broadcast they might listen to, but Drew shook his head. "No music."

"God must have been holding his hand when Bloch composed that piece," Aaron said, "because no one writes music like that alone."

"You know what I'd really enjoy now?" Drew said, clapping his hands together enthusiastically. "An enormous slice of Rose's custard pie."

Aaron checked his clock. "I don't know. They're probably just about closed."

"But someone will be there?"

"Sure. Someone's always there. You want it that bad?"

"I think I do, Aaron."

They washed and dressed quickly and, as soon as Aaron had locked his door behind them, raced down the stairs. As they were stomping across the hallway on the first floor, an old man sucking on a cold stogie, wearing his pants' suspenders over a slightly stained undershirt, poked his head out of his door. "Hey, Rose. Heard the good news?"

As Aaron stopped short, Drew almost bumped into him. "What news?" they both said.

"Those crazy Jap bastards have bombed Pearl. We're at war, boys."

When Uncle Joe answered Aaron's knock at the bakery, his face was bloodless, like brightly colored paper that had faded to gray. "You've heard?"

"You should see all the people gathering together everywhere, Uncle Joe," Aaron said. "Nobody knows where to go or what to do."

Joe waved his hands wildly in the air. "Why should I want to see them? I don't want to see anyone, not anyone. Why do you think I told everyone to go home? We're closing for a few days out of respect for those poor boys who lost their lives. But your mother will want you with her, Aaron. Go home with me tonight, both of you."

"Tomorrow, Uncle Joe," Aaron promised.

Joe squeezed his nephew's face with his fingers. "What are you going to do, Aaron? Enlist? Or wait for the draft?"

"Enlist."

"Good. That's good. If I were twenty years younger, I'd leave tonight. No one is angrier than I am. How dare those people attack this brave and wonderful country like that? The little sneaks, the two-bit cowards."

"Don't tell anyone yet, Uncle Joe, especially not Mother. After I've signed up, I'll tell them myself."

"Sure, kid. I understand." He grasped my arm. "You going to sign up with him, Drew? Or wait until you get home?"

"My granddaddy would have a stroke if I enlisted with a bunch of Yankees."

Uncle Joe laughed. "I guess that's right."

"I thought we were going in together, Drew," Aaron said, "like you promised."

"I've got to go home first, Aaron. I really do."

"Say, you boys want to take a box of pastries home with you?" Uncle Joe asked as he wrapped some up. "There's no sense in letting them go to waste."

"You want to go to a movie, Aaron?" Drew suggested on the sidewalk outside the bakery. "We could see what's playing at the Strand. *The Maltese Falcon* might still be there."

"What are we going to do with all these goodies Uncle Joe forced on us?" Aaron lifted up the three boxes tied together with twine.

"Distribute them to every bum we pass."

"Even the pie?"

"Especially the pie."

Everything was gone before they reached Fourth Avenue. "When I'm ducking bullets in some trench in France," Aaron said, "I'll probably be longing for a cheese Danish even more than sex, but just the thought of eating one right now makes me sick."

They stopped in Bickford's for coffee. The place was packed with people talking, arguing, laughing, weeping, shouting. Neither Drew nor Aaron attempted to speak over the noise. They sat quietly at their table sipping their coffee and staring out the window, which was dripping with steam. "You look really tired, Aaron," Drew remarked as they walked onto the street.

They went to bed early, Aaron in his room, Drew on the couch. How long had he been asleep before he heard Aaron whispering in his ear, "Drew. Drew." He thought he might be dreaming and that it was Aaron in his dream who with both his hands was touching and caressing him over and under his shorts, fondling him until, despite himself, he was excited. When he opened his eyes, Aaron kissed his cheek, his chin, his lips. "Drew."

How long had Aaron been kneeling over him? Drew shoved his hands off him. "Don't. Quit it, Aaron."

Aaron stood up, naked, aroused. He lay down on top of Drew and thrust his rigid flesh against Drew's thigh as he tried to slide his shorts down from his waist. "I love you," he whispered. "Please."

"No!" Drew rolled onto his right side and with all the strength in his arms pushed Aaron off him. He fell onto the floor with a crack and a thud.

He started to cry. "Oh, God."

"Damn it, Aaron. I love you too," Drew hollered at him. "But not that way. Do you hear me? Not like that."

Aaron was sobbing. "Oh, God. I feel so ashamed."

"I'm so sorry, Aaron. I don't want to hurt you. But, Jesus, I had no idea," he lied.

"Shut up, Drew. Please don't say anymore." Slowly, he got up off the floor and stumbling like a drunkard disappeared from the living room into his bedroom.

Drew didn't fall asleep until just before dawn. When he awoke, Aaron was already gone. Although Drew found his note on the kitchen table propped on the sugar bowl as soon as he got up, he didn't read it until, dressed and packed, he was ready to leave. It said, "Please be certain that my door and the door to the street are both firmly locked when you go. I'm sorry if I frightened you last night. I love you. I'll always love you. But I guess I've just learned that humiliation is much stronger than love. I couldn't bear to ever see you again." Drew debated with himself whether he should burn the note or tear it into little pieces, but instead he pocketed it.

He caught the afternoon's first train south, though he had to transfer several times before he reached his hometown. When Drew visited the old man in his room the following evening, all his grandfather said was, "When are you leaving, soldier?"

"Soon," Drew assured him.

But he waited almost a month before he asked his mother to drive him to the station. "If this is how you want to do it," she said to him as he stepped out of the car in the parking lot, "so much the better."

"No crowds, no screaming children, no parades, no marching bands," Drew said.

"Yes, yes, I do understand," his mother said, grasping his hand.

"When I brought him breakfast early this morning, Grandfather advised me before battle always to think of our family motto. 'It's better than any prayer,' he said to me."

"He's right, son," his mother said.

Drew pulled his hand away. "It's all so much nonsense," he said. "Everything you two have ever taught me, it's all completely absurd and useless, Mother." Thrilled at the rush of anger that reddened her face, he hastened up the steps to the waiting train.

When he reached New York, he called Uncle Joe at the bakery. Joe reported what Drew should have known anyway. Aaron had left for training several weeks earlier. "Why didn't you go with him while you had the chance?" Uncle Joe challenged him. "He was so miserable the day he left. You should have, Drew."

"I know that now. Wish me luck anyway, will you, Uncle Joe?"

After Drew had hung up the phone, he decided he wouldn't search for a place to enlist. Rather, he'd let it, like the war, like death, find him. So long as he kept moving from street to street, sooner or later the inevitable would happen. He'd spot the sign in the window or the poster in front of the door. He'd walk in.

Cuius regio, cuius religio. During basic, Drew watched training films, suffered through dozens of inspections including repeated short arm ("Be sure you wash there carefully, soldier"), marched hour after hour, day after day in close-order drill, queued for food. He shot his rifle badly and bayoneted straw-filled potato bags set up on frames. He learned that heavy artillery is like the finger of God, that by firing through trees he could kill men hiding behind them, that on patrol he could keep from sneezing by pressing a finger against his upper lip and keep from coughing by pushing against his Adam's apple. He was warned that almost anything could be a booby trap: books, magazines, teacups, purses, wallets, drawers, tin cans, doorknobs, lamp switches, a lady's hat, panties, a bottle of booze. He was taught when at war to be always attentive as a fox or a wolf and to forget the horrors he'd see because such knowledge is worthless in a fight. Nothingness, a spiritual vacuum, a void in the soul were everyone's best protection against every fear.

Close it up, pick it up, close in. He clambered thirty feet up a rope ladder under the weight of his full field pack and rifle to the top of a wooden wall and then struggled back down again. He swam across a river whose startling currents almost drowned him. He did outpost duty and KP and latrine duty, scrubbing floors with a toothbrush. When it was over, when his training was done, without his protesting, still uncoverted, he was transferred out of the infantry to a clerk's desk faraway west in the Presidio where he would remain, he hoped, throughout the war.

Sometimes, when he had a free hour or two, he'd wander to the hills above the bunkers that stood guard over the Pacific and watch warships sail in and out of the Golden Gate. As he lay in the tall grass and stared up at drifting clouds, he thought he could whiff the wild onion or sweetgum or vetch back home and feel in his back the prick of blackberry brambles. Where was Aaron? Perhaps somewhere awful eating Spam and dried sausage, crackers, cold stew, and candy bars. But, while soldiers around him were chewing gum, playing ball, drinking Cokes, or reading comic books, what was Aaron doing?

Days passed. Months. A year. Another year. Drew filed and typed, typed and filed. His life was almost pleasant, mindless and safe. He spoke to his fellow soldiers only when he was required to speak to them, carefully made no friends, listened to no music, and read little. Occasionally he visited Letterman to do what those who did not understand his reasons might have called some good. He wrote home for those wounded who could no longer write themselves, listened to whoever wanted to talk, held a few desperate, sweaty hands. What sort of men were the Sons of Heaven? he'd ask. "The Japs are all crazy," he was told repeatedly. "They're not like you and me. They don't scare, see?" A kid who had lost most of both his legs to a grenade described a placard they'd hung around the necks of two of his buddies they'd captured during an attack. He had found his friends days later when his platoon recaptured the ground: "It took them a long time to die," the placard read. "No, they ain't human. They can't be," the boy insisted. "Animals, maybe. Lice or jackals or monkeys maybe. But not human." Another soldier, less harmed, showed Drew his bag of Jap teeth, ears, and fingers he'd smuggled in. "Don't listen to that shit," he said. "They scare easy enough. At the point of a bayonet, they scream or shriek just like you and me."

Where was Aaron? Drew wrote Uncle Joe, but received no answer from him or from Miriam when he wrote her later. Perhaps he was already in North Africa. Drew imagined him shot at by a sniper who had caught the sun's glint on the lenses of his sunglasses. But surely one of the Roses would have written him if Aaron had been wounded or killed. Where was Aaron? He might be anywhere, but Drew pictured him most often in Italy. He saw him in the heavy winds and waves of an assault on Sicily and later in Italy's torrential rains, freezing, forging savage rivers, attacking carefully defended mountain passes with only narrow approaches along cliff edges. "A frozen body turns a claret color, just like this," his CO had said to him one evening as, already drunk, he downed another glass of wine in his office while Drew reorganized his files.

Vowing to make killers of them all, basic had taught him to anticipate the confusion of battle, to prepare for war's chaos, and to embrace simplicity. Spared battle, killing, chaos, and death, neither a marauder, an invader, nor a crusader, he did choose to embrace simplicity as the army had instructed him, hoping it might spare him from everything else he feared. Yet, night after night, whether asleep or awake, he would see Aaron slogging through muddy fields or marching along mined roads and trails or creeping through narrow, twisting streets waist-high in rubble. He would envision his wounded body lying near blasted trees or among church ruins. Salerno, the Gustav Line, Anzio, Monte Cassino, the Germans' fighting retreat, the Apennines. Every place Drew heard about or read of, in every battle, Aaron was always there fighting or lying wounded or dead among the other dead in Italy.

Ten days after the war in Europe had ended, Drew read in the *San Francisco Chronicle* how on May 13th Gigli had sung Riccardo in *Un Ballo* in Salerno. The article reported that the public response had been that Gigli was too fat and did not sing well. But Drew preferred to imagine him singing angelically with Aaron in the audience listening.

In that month's *Cosmopolitan*, left open on his desk by another private, Drew read a poem General Patton had written.

> I spare no class or cult or creed.
> My course is endless through the year.
> I bow all heads and break all hearts,
> All owe me homage—I am fear.

Seven months after the Japanese had surrendered, Drew, relieved of his duty, was sent back home. Still a virgin, still a Grand Master masturbator whom army life had made only more inventive and adept, he decided he would marry. All he would need to do was find a woman who would not despise him for his obvious weaknesses and utter lack of ambition and who would not oppose his wish to do nothing with his life.

If his grandfather had died not knowing with what complete, albeit accidental, effrontery Drew had betrayed his name, his mother understood well enough. He had neither fired a gun nor been fired upon in a field of contest. Instead, he had pounded a typewriter and opened and closed filing cabinets day after day, surrounded by what must be among the most beautiful few acres on God's earth. Why had he wished to survive without having been tried? Why had her son chosen to humiliate himself? How could he return home unbowed and unhumbled? Her every look implored him, "How?"

He believed it useless to write Uncle Joe or Miriam again. If they or Aaron had wanted him to know his fate, he would have already heard. He contemplated sending a letter requesting information about Joshua Aaron Rose from the War Department. But, if he had survived, Aaron knew where to find him. Yet whenever Drew said his friend's name he winced with shame.

So Drew married Penelope Lane. She was loving, sweet, gentle, tender, frail, and, since her brother's death, in her heart always grieving. They had a son, twin daughters, and another son. A few days after her last child's birth Penelope died.

Drew knew he ought not to have
Drew knew
His two sons my sons They
I
Not just you
I failed everyone afraid of how he
I never loved anyone enough
Aaron my son you anyone
Aaron

Andrew Lane Odom

"Cool scars," the kid says.

So I say, "Want to kiss them?"

And he says, "Sure." And he does kiss them right there in front of all the other guys cruising each other or just hanging around expectantly midday on the beach hidden by the curve in the cliffs.

"I bet there're more," he says tugging on my T-shirt, trying to pull it free from under my jeans' belt.

I think maybe he's going to rip the shirt. "Hey. Slow down. That's enough now."

The tip of his tongue licks and dots the back of my neck. He nibbles on my ear lobes. He whispers words that I pretend not to hear. I prefer listening to the waves, a sound so old it's like no sound at all. I almost never go to bars anymore. If I can help it, I never go anywhere there's music playing or lots of loud talk. I can't stand noise. I'll ride blocks out of my way to avoid a construction site. Except on the hottest days, when I'm driving the van on the freeways I keep all the windows rolled up. I rented my shack in the back of Dorado Canyon not only because it's cheap. It should be cheap. The place is a dump. But because it sits high and quiet on a ridge all alone surrounded by eucalyptus and a few gnarly oaks, cartoon trees that, though they look like they could talk, fortunately never do.

The kid doffs his shirt and tosses it onto the sand. I think, Not bad. I like a lithe, clean chest, smooth as stone. Both his hands grasp my belt buckle. "What's your name?"

"Jake," I say.

"Mine's Rog."

"Sure it is, Rog."

"No, really. Jake what?"

"Oh, I don't know. How about Barnes? Jake Barnes. That's me."

"Be serious."

"I'm always serious, Rog. You'll see."

He releases his grip on my belt. "You don't want to do this, do you?"

"It depends on what you mean by *this*. Not here. Not in the middle of the day. Not with all these other citizens out window-shopping."

"Why did you climb down here then?"

"To eat my tacos. It's my lunch hour. I had a delivery to make not far away on Catalina Street in Laguna. I deliver flowers for a living. Impressive, huh?"

"You want to come to my place? I live just down the highway, not too far from Dana Point."

I shake my head. "I got a truck loaded with pretty long-stem red roses, Rog. It might as well be Valentine's Day."

He folds his arms around my shoulder and licks the shrapnel slash across my left cheek. "Where'd you get them? Nam?"

"We don't talk about that, Rog."

"Were you a Marine? Really? Jesus, you're so hot."

"Cool down, Rog. I wasn't a Marine."

"Regular army?"

"Something like that."

"Where were you stationed? What was your rank? Where did you fight?"

"Sorry, Rog. I don't play this game."

"I play it well, Jake. Just try me. Just name your scene. There's a cave on the other side of that cliff. Try me."

"Yeah. I've heard about that cave."

"I'm ready, man. Look," he says, tightening his cute little butt and pressing his crotch forward. "Go ahead. Feel. I know you want to. Don't you? Don't you, Sarge?"

"Nope. Don't think I do, Rog. Sorry," I say walking off to the zigzag stairs carved out of the cliff face.

I'd parked the van on the coast highway, across from an Orange Julius stand where I order mine with raw eggs. I drink it slowly, sitting in the van's passenger seat. The coast here is curved like a scimitar and shines like a blade in the sun. I check my delivery sheet. Seven more to go before the day is done. I ask myself, Is tomorrow Thursday? Or Friday?

Back in the war I came from, I made a point of always knowing what day it was. I'd forget the date. I'd forget the month, the year. But I always remembered the day of the week. I arrived there on a Friday. I first went in country on a Friday. I might have killed my first commie bastard on a Friday. Some commie scum wrecked their first revenge on me on a Friday too.

But, stoned as Gracie Slick on one of her wilder trips, I first jerked Dallas Monroe off in a dark corner behind a latrine on a Monday. He reciprocated the following Wednesday. We spent our first night together in what passed for privacy on a Saturday in Saigon.

But he got dusted six months later on a Friday. Or at least that was what I was told when I asked. When I flew out of there and abandoned the war to all the poor bastards on both sides still killing each other on the ground, it was a Tuesday five weeks after the Christmas bombings had ended. But it had been a Friday too when, three and a half years before, my brother had been blown to bits on his way to see me. Fridays are the scariest days. All days are bad. It was an ordinary Sunday when the mine exploded that caused most of my scars, the ones people think were left by a knife or a bayonet. But Fridays are always the worst.

I spot a news rack on the sidewalk two cars up from where I'm parked. I chuck the Orange Julius cup into a wastebasket and read the headlines. That lying bastard Nixon is finally about to get the old heave-ho. The paper says it's Thursday. Tomorrow is the day I should lie low.

But what can I do? At Wild Thing Florists, Friday is always the busiest day. And I like to work. It passes the time. Often the odometer adds up more than two or three hundred miles between nine and five. Most of the time I'm just tooling the freeway this way and that, checking the map only when I have to. I've become a well-programmed rat in the intricate maze they call L.A. Usually I can find the way to where I'm going without a single wrong turn.

At first, Adelaide Wilkins didn't want to hire me. On the morning I answered her ad in person at her shop in Fullerton, I could detect from her worried frown how she was thinking that the left side of my face might be a bit too much of a downer for those usually happy occasions people associate with flowers. And it's only happy times when people see me. I'm long gone before the wake or funeral starts. But Adelaide is a good liberal, distrusting her own impulses, believing all base instincts, especially of revulsion, morally wrong. So, against her own inclinations, she hired me. Now she's glad she did. I've been over a year on the job and never missed a day or a delivery. I quickly learned to walk to every door as I approach some guy I'd like to ball, boldly favoring my great right side.

It's mindless work. But I prefer mindless work. I don't have to talk much or listen to people's crap except for a few seconds here and there considerately spread out over the day, and I rarely have to meet anyone a second time, except for Adelaide and her two daughters, of course. But those three all learned straight away to leave me alone. I was a vet. To them, that meant I was supposed to be moody and brooding and depressed because of the terrible things I'd done and been forced to do and see. It was better that I be uncommunicative and remote than set out on a seven-state shooting spree that started in their shop.

I like flowers. I always have liked them. I like the way their smells, woody, earthy, and sweet, mingle in the van and never quite repeat two days in a row. I like their garish crayon colors as shameless as the colors of tropical birds or of saltwater tropical fish. I like the fact that they don't last, that every gift I bring someone will offer its moment of brief, intense pleasure and then unprotesting, fade and disappear forever.

So work occupies my days, six days a week. Adelaide owns three vans and employs three drivers, but on Saturdays I'm the only one who works. It's how I like it. Jim and Chuy both prefer to spend the whole weekend with their families. I'd work most Sundays if I could.

Nights are sometimes too long. I've gotten used to my dreams. I used to believe that, like newspapers or TV, dreams got almost everything all wrong. Now, if they're deranged, it doesn't surprise me at all. I let them say what they have to say, show what they have to show. They're going to anyway.

I'm usually asleep when I dream. It's when I'm not asleep and dreaming that I get more scared because Aaron is often there watching me, standing at the foot of the bed, sitting next to me on the couch, or waiting by the window, looking straight at me with those dark eyes of his, like Mother's, Father said. He's sad, of course, and angry and disappointed. Maybe he's even ashamed of being dead the way the dead usually are. He never says anything. Neither do I. But, after a while, he leans toward me and kisses me like a brother on the forehead or cheek or neck. Even after I've wiped his kiss off, I can feel the wet spot on my skin. Some kisses are terrible, almost as terrible as Father's the last time he held me. Or held Aaron, I should say.

Every once in a while I contemplate writing Charlie Sutton

to tell him about my life in greater detail. Perhaps I mean to punish him for the crush I had on him all those years. But I never do write him in any detail because Charlie would only misinterpret whatever I say. Most people do. They assume I mean to confess for what I've done or what I do. But without a confessor who can confess? Why should anyone want to?

I like the parks late at night. It's over an hour's speedy drive from where I live to Griffith, but the cruising spots there are L.A.'s best. When the moon is bright, I keep my left side in the shadows and use my enticing right as bait. My scars are not so bad. I've seen lots much worse. I shouldn't complain. Under my clothes they're white and shine like slivers of cracked ice. But those on the left side of my face tug and pull at the skin like too-tight laces on a shoe. Half of my face always feels like it's wearing a rubber mask.

Every Friday day I worry about Friday night. This Friday, it's almost six when I pull the van into its spot in Wild Thing Florists' lot and hurry into the shop to hand Caroline Wilkins the keys and work sheets. Since Adelaide doesn't want her drivers' cars taking up valuable customer space on her lot, I always leave my wreck of a Chevy parked on the street five blocks away in a cute little neighborhood full of cute little bungalows. When I turn the last corner to head down Travis Court I spot the kid from yesterday sitting on my car's trunk. As I approach him, Rog hops off.

"Your employer is indiscreet," Rog says, grinning.

"So I see."

"She described your car perfectly. To a T. All I had to say was that I was your cousin from Alabama," he says, mangling a Southern accent.

"Wrong state, Rog."

"Said I wanted to surprise you. She bought it. She sure is naive."

"I reckon Miz Wilkins needs a little talking to," I say.

"I agree."

"You followed me yesterday?"

"Sure. You wanted me to."

"I did? Maybe I did. So what?"

"I can follow you again. Or you can follow me." He points across the street to a sporty black Triumph. "That's my car."

"Where did you say you live?"

"Near Dana Point. I've got my own apartment now."

"Then I guess you're all grown up. My place is quiet," I say.

"Tell me your real name. I know it's not Jake."

"I'm surprised Miz Wilkins didn't mention it. It's Nick," I say.

"Nick what?"

"Just Nick, OK?" I check him out up and down. He looks too good, like a teen idol on a movie poster. "You queer on wounds, Rog?"

"I'm sorry?"

"Just checking," I say. "You acted like it yesterday."

He's an expert on the freeway, keeping far enough back, but never losing sight of where I am and adjusting with ease to every change I make in lane or speed. As I pull onto the off ramp, he toots his horn and thereafter never misses a turn all the way to the canyon road where, coming back into view after some long curves when we can't see each other, he clicks his lights on and off to salute me, I guess, and let me know he's still there. He parks in the packed dirt drive right behind me.

"Cool place," he says.

"Yeah. It's OK."

"A lot of fuel," he notices looking around the yard. "It'd go up like that," he says snapping his fingers. "If this canyon ever burned it'd take everything you owned."

"Let it."

"I'll help you clean it out in the morning, if you like."

"You planning on spending the night, Rog?"

"Sure."

"You don't talk a lot," he mentions in the morning. Is it a

complaint? We're lying naked side-by-side on the uncovered bed, his left arm draped over my right thigh. A breeze rattles the open window. The eastern sky is rose pink. "You believe in love at first sight, Nick? Or love after the first night?"

"Nope."

"Why not?"

I roll away from his hand and onto my stomach. He grabs my butt and squeezes. "I've got to get to work, Rog. It's a long drive."

"Why not?" he persists.

I jump out of bed. "I have to shower and get dressed."

"I could shower with you."

"You could. But I don't want you to."

Even as I head for the bathroom, he makes no effort to recover his clothes, which are scattered in the other room across the floor. He yawns, scratches his cute behind and boyish chest, and grins like a too eager kid in his high-school-yearbook photo. His body is so slight, so adolescently unharmed and tight, that it occurs to me too late he's probably only in his midteens.

"I'll be here when you get back," he states.

"No, you won't." With both arms, I sweep his clothes off the floor and toss them to him. "You're leaving when I do."

"I thought we had work to do. Cleaning all that eucalyptus bark out," he says as he steps into his dinky briefs.

"Maybe some other day."

He brightens. "Really?"

"No. Not really."

Once showered and dressed, I lock my shack's only door behind us, as he stands moping on the narrow stoop. "Can you ever see all the way to the ocean from up here?"

"Some days. It depends."

He holds my hand too tenderly. "Nick?" He kisses my left cheek. "Can I ask you something? Were you really in Vietnam?"

"No."

He looks downcast, as if he'd just been forced out of a warm house into a cold, hard rain. "Oh. My brother was killed in An Loc in '72. He was older than me by almost nine years. He was a great guy. I was hoping you might have met him."

"How old are you, Rog?"

"Twenty-one."

"Like shit you are. Sixteen is more like it."

"OK. Eighteen. His name was Carl. Carl Matthiessen."

I'm recalling another place that wasn't but might have been An Loc in '72. "Didn't know him."

"No. How could you? You weren't even there, you said. Nick?"

"Hush. You're a smart kid, Rog." I open the door to his car. "You want to follow me back to the freeway?"

"I can find it," he says, slipping in. "I'd really like to see you again."

"Why?"

He shrugs. "I don't know. It was a cool night. I really liked getting fucked by you. Making love like that blows me away."

"You're too young for me, Rog."

"You're not so old."

"Old enough."

"I love your face," he says. "It's beautiful. All of it. I really mean that, Nick."

I jerk open my car door. "You better go first," I say.

That night, I don't go home after work but head straight for the park where I meet a guy, dressed in too tight jeans and a black shirt, whom I've seen before lurking in the bushes like a fox, always too eager and too needy. He lives way down in Long Beach, in a sort of semi-suburb filled with multiple rows of L-shaped semi-ranch houses ugly as egg cartons. Each of his rooms, even the kitchen, displays at least one large mirror, formally framed in that same old gold they use to decorate the china you can win at the county fair. The rugs are dark off-white, the furniture light off-white, and the walls medium off-white.

He offers me a brandy. I refuse, but he drinks two out of a bowl-sized snifter, and talks and talks. Apparently he's a comptroller for some new firm in Irvine, but I don't really listen. He turns on the radio to an easy-listening station. I ask him to turn it off. When he looks hurt, his sadness makes him almost handsome.

His eyes explore my face with that mixture of curiosity and revulsion I've seen often before. Maybe it was that look or others like it that helped persuade me, each time I'd recovered from my wounds, to return as soon as I could to the war. When he starts to ask me about the scars, I answer him by unbuttoning his jeans. After we're naked, he leads me into his bedroom where on a nightstand next to his bed lie several thick candles and a box of wooden matches. He lights one wick and hands the candle to me. Lying face up on his bed, he asks me to drip wax on his chest. "Make it look like yours, Nick," he begs.

I blow out the candle, quit the room, find my clothes in the living room, and leave even as he continues to scream at me for being an ugly piece of shit. I slam the door so hard several neighboring dogs yelp or bark.

Driving too fast back home, I find myself hoping Rog might be there when I arrive. But he's not. So I get mucho stoned for the first time in weeks and stay pleasantly high all the next morning. Seven overripe oranges sit in a row on the windowsill near the refrigerator, emitting an odor of decay, acidic and sweet. Gnats swarm over them, darting in and out of a swatch of amber sunlight. Outside the sky is patches of turquoise, silver, pewter, and pearl. I walk in the eucalyptus grove. Close to the shack, fuchsias that have dropped onto the ground overnight pop under my feet. The light is thick as mist. Back in the house, I grab one of the oranges. My thumb angrily breaks its skin. I suck out its juice and all the pulp that oozes off the rind. My face twitches as it does sometimes. I find my keys and head for the beach.

As I cut onto the Santa Monica, everything looks white. The green trees, bushes, and grass look white. The orange tiles and red bricks and brown walls look white. The clear blue sky is white. Not drained of color, but drenched in white.

I drive off the freeway and through an area where I've never been before. Having parked, I buy two churros from a small bakery squeezed between a noisy record store and a discount-clothing mart. I eat them too fast. Sugar and a glutinous grease coat my tongue. I buy a cup of coffee to wash them away. After I've drunk it, I taste in my mouth a peculiar mixture of too-long-chewed gum and sweat on male skin.

I rummage through dyed shirts tossed together in a large bin on the sidewalk, tank tops, I-shirts, V-necks, crew necks, and T-shirts, their vivid colors all in Spanish. The bright afternoon sun clarifies each one like a translation. Faded strips of purple, ruby, and chartreuse crepe paper hang from an awning, rustling like dry leaves in the air.

When a passing truck backfires, I jump. Two women are poking through piles of scarves in another bin. They roll their eyes happily at each other and forage deeper into the layers of scarves. One stretches an especially long white scarf up to the sun. Both grip a corner. It veils their faces like a sheet of ice. "You should buy it," I say.

Up the street young Chicanos talk and smoke a little dope. Their shoes are black and shiny, their trousers black and baggy, their T-shirts sleeveless, white, and tight. They're all beautifully sweating.

Across the street sits a small park by the side of a pond near a church. I rest on a park bench and sing to myself a verse of a hymn that Father Owens must have loved. He had his congregation sing it often, Mutti's strong voice swelling above all the others.

> Christian, dost thou see them
> On the holy ground
> How the hosts of Midian
> Prowl and prowl around?
> Christian, up and smite them!

Well, I challenge myself, are you a Midianite or a Christian, Andy? A Midianite, I answer easily, so I prowl and prowl around. The church's doors are locked, but an elderly gardener, at work in a bed of mums, agrees to open one. He wipes a muddy handkerchief across his brow and mutters, "You're a little late for church, son."

"I guess I am," I agree. "But better late than never, wouldn't you say, sir?"

"I might say so," he says as he opens the door, "or I might not."

Inside the church, the midafternoon sun is seeping through rippled milk-white glass windows and colors the walls pure honey. The ceiling is rose, the plaster cracks like the rust of petals as they fade. The light is as splendid as any light I've ever seen. I step back outside. The gardener locks the door after me.

I say, "Thanks."

The gardener tips his cap. "Come again."

Back in my car, I keep driving until I reach the ocean and a stretch of beach that's almost deserted. Where I decide to stop, a middle-aged couple is walking their cocker, a surfer is stripping out of his wet suit, but otherwise the place is empty. I stroll leisurely, enjoying the gritty, hot sand under my feet or the cool tide slapping gently over my toes.

The sky is blank and luminous, the horizon a silvery gray. The cliff behind me is a maroon so deep it's black. I find a small cove to hide in and wait for twilight when the horizon slowly thins and fades from sight. I pull out a joint from my shirt's pocket, smoke it as pleasurably as I've smoked any grass, and rest there contented for most of the night.

"Adelaide," I complain to my employer the following morning, "the next time you reveal my car's whereabouts to one of my smooth-talking Alabama cousins, would you please at least inquire whether he knows my right name."

She tapes another box of roses and hands it to me. "You mean that sweet boy lied?"

"He did indeed."

"But you knew him?"

"That's not my point."

"Well, if you knew him, what's the diff?"

I've been told I get mad too easily and stay mad too long. I grab the last boxes. "No diff, Adelaide. Sorry."

I work a full day but clock only a hundred and sixty-seven miles before it's over, pursuing a route that might have resembled a schizophrenic spider's web if it had been duplicated on a chart. My last delivery is to a sprawling plush new two-story house surrounded by high serpentine walls near Mission Viejo. The lad who answers the door looks as stoned as I was the day before or maybe I only woke him out of a deep nap.

"You Justin Shea?" I ask.

"Sure am." He accepts the box from my hands. "Come on in," he says, laying the box down on the bare floor. Inside, there's no furniture anywhere, only piles of cartons and wardrobes, barrels, and boxes. "We're just moving in," he explains. He finds his wallet on the mantel. "Here," he says, offering me a couple of singles.

"We're not allowed to accept tips."

He blushes. "Oh, sorry. I wasn't sure. I don't get flowers delivered to me every day."

"That's OK."

"Would you like a beer or something? The refrigerator's working, I hope. I could offer you a beer."

I check my watch. "Sure. Why not?"

So we both drink a couple of beers, sitting poolside, our legs dangling into the empty pool. Justin likes to brag. "I can't wait until the pool's been filled again," he says. "Maybe you can come back in a couple of weeks and take a swim. Do you like to swim?"

"I used to swim a lot."

"Yes, I can tell. Should I turn on the radio? We could listen to some music. There's one plugged in right over there by the porch."

"Quiet's fine."

"What's your name?"

"Harry. Harry Morgan."

"Really? You don't look like a Harry. What do you think of this place, Harry? Pretty fucking impressive, wouldn't you say?"

I finish my second can. "It's OK."

"It's better than OK. It's not mine, though. There's not one square inch of it that's really mine. It all belongs to my . . . you know." He blushes again.

"Was it your *you know* who sent you the two dozen roses?"

"You bet."

"Lucky you."

"I suppose so. I'd like to take a swim right now, wouldn't you?"

"There's no water," I remind him. "See?"

"You know that's not what I meant."

"Yep. You're right. So where do you want to swim instead?"

"Upstairs."

There's a naked mattress resting askew on box springs lying on an uncovered floor in a bedroom. He's out of his clothes in a second. When I start to screw him, he comes quick. It spatters his face and red hair. "Jesus," I exclaim and start to moan for effect without really feeling anything at all.

After I've withdrawn, he wipes himself off with a towel and tosses it into a closet. He dresses as fast as he stripped. "That was far out," he says. "But listen, Harry. Maybe you should go now. My old man could be getting home just about any minute."

I shake his hand at the door just as a glossy red Caddy convertible rolls onto the drive behind the van. Justin waves. Without moving his lips, he whispers, "You should know my lover is a famous plastic surgeon. He's fixed lots of the biggest stars. He does almost everything I ask. He bought this house because I wanted him to. I bet I could talk him into helping you without his charging anywhere near his usual fee. Think about it, Harry. You'd be almost perfect without those ugly scars."

His doctor backs out of the drive and open gate and parks on the street. I feel like slugging Justin but instead clench my teeth and head straight for the van, intersecting with the good doctor who passes me on the walk. "Thanks so much for delivering the flowers," he says. "Do you think he liked them?"

"It was my pleasure," I say.

"He's such a sweet boy. Justin," he shouts to him. "Isn't this the perfect house for us? Haven't the landscapers done the most remarkable job?"

"Sorry, Adelaide," I say to my boss back at the shop. "No offense." I hand her the keys to the van. "But I'm quitting."

"Andy! Why?"

"I've got to move on, Adelaide. I don't belong in fantasy island. I'm in a rut."

She pats my hand where it rests on her counter. "Caroline? Did you hear the news? Andy is leaving us." You might have thought I'd just asked her for a divorce. "Dorothy, Andy's quitting. Isn't that sad?"

Both daughters walk into the salesroom from the back room where they make the arrangements. "I'll work until the end of next week, if you like," I offer.

"That would be helpful," Caroline says.

"But it's so sad!" Adelaide exclaims "What are your plans?"

"I don't have any," I say.

Eight days later, I pack only what can fit in my car. I don't call my landlord. He already has my last month's rent. He'll discover I'm gone soon enough, and the furniture I bought at the used-furniture stores or Goodwill he can give to his next tenant, if he wants to, or sell.

I spend several months just driving around from state to state, not really wanting to get anywhere, working a week or two here or there all over the West, pumping gas where there is gas to pump, picking fruit, herding cows or sheep, even playing cowpoke at a dude ranch for a while. The day Tricky Dick finally resigns, I consider returning to California for a while, but instead pack up my few belongings and drive further south, crossing the border into Mexico, then heading for the coast once more.

I've hoarded a little cash, enough to survive in a run-down town where I rent an adobe hut on a cliff overlooking the gulf on the eastern side of Baja. One day, just roaming the beach, I meet a guy who tells me his name is Norberto Flores. I tell him mine is Bob Jordan, though why I lie when he knows only a little more English than I know Spanish, I couldn't say. We meet at my place maybe once or twice a week, the only times he claims he can get away from the demands of his boat and his wife and toddlers. *Toddlers* is the word he uses. I wonder where he learned it. But I don't ask because I don't want him to talk more than he already does, little of which I comprehend. He brings me truly exceptional grass. We fuck, we smoke, we lie quiet on my pallet. It's fine. "You're my Pilar," I say to him, counting on his not understanding.

But one Friday night, lying alone, unable to sleep, a full moon shining through the frameless, glassless window, I can feel blood. I'm bleeding. My whole left side is gushing blood again. Nothing will make it stop. I panic. Am I dying? The VC have caught us in another ambush. A machine gun is pinning us down. They're so close my grenade launcher is useless. The only way we can make it is to make sure they don't spot the flanker. Mickey Stiles starts firing at them with his pistol, but he takes his time because we're all low on rounds. Neither of us quits moving forward. It's crazy. Why don't they seem to be able to hit us again? But the mine throws us like a ball hit by a bat in the hands of a real slugger. Mickey and I keep on firing even after the blast rips through us. Mickey's leg is in shreds. The machine gunner tears through his chest. Lieutenant Wales kills the machine gunner. But it's too late for me. I'm bleeding and no one can stop it.

A body is blocking the light from the moon. "Norberto?" I say.

"I'm sick, Norberto. Or maybe it's just really bad grass. I think the last lid was bad."

"It's not Norberto, Andy." He walks through the wall and stands over me. "Here," he says. He's kneeling by my left side. "Here, I have bandages. Let me wrap your wounds. And morphine. You won't feel any pain at all soon, Andy. There," he says and stands back up. "A chopper will be here to pick you up soon. I promise. But I have to be going now, back into the jungle for good. I don't think they're going to let me see you again, Brother. So I guess this is good-bye. And good luck."

I doubt if Norberto will miss his strange, too eager gringo. He takes his pleasure where he finds it and finds it almost everywhere. I envy him. But I can't delay my departure just to say farewell.

I start to drive back north before dawn. The next night, I sleep on a beach in Del Mar. Late the following day, I reach San Francisco. "It's Sunday," I remind myself. Because it's so late and I'm running low on cash, I ask directions for Folsom Street at a gas station. Although he looks at me disapprovingly, the attendant tells me anyway.

"You look like a man who could use about a week's worth of sleep," a guy at a bar says to me.

I hate the music, the noise, the crowd. He's easily twenty years older than me, his hair already as gray as his eyes. "It's been a long drive," I admit.

"New in town? You'll like it here. It's fun." He holds out his hand for me to shake. "Bill Heaney. I've lived here all my life."

"Fred Henry," I say.

At the end of the second week, he asks me to stay permanently. He says he'd like me to be his lover. I respond, "You're too sweet a guy, Bill. You don't want me."

"I think I do."

"Sorry," I say.

But he helps me find a job driving another van, this time for

Rosetti Florists, and a cheap mother-in-law apartment on the western edge of the city. Two days after Saigon falls, I move in. Bill's bought a pickup's worth of used furniture. I want to say to him, to somebody, to almost anybody, "Listen. I was there. My brother was killed there. So was the first man I ever made love to. See these scars? Two purple hearts and a bronze star." But I don't say anything. I don't even tell Bill my real name, not even as he uncorks a bottle of champagne. With too many names, I've discovered, you're almost as anonymous as with none. Or the wrong one.

"How can you live here where it's always winter?" a guy I bring home one night in June asks me. "The sun never shines over the beach all summer long."

I hold him tighter, although I wish he'd leave. "The fog is what keeps me here," I say.

And it's true. In only a few weeks, roaming along its shifting edges, I've grown to love the ocean's summertime winter, how restless the water and everything close to it is. I may stand still and stare into the sea for a while, but soon the cold propels me to walk somewhere or to run, like the dogs or sandpipers or gulls. The dunes drift. The chilling fog hovers, retreats, and surges landward again. Everything is as reassuringly shapeless as the wind.

When I decide to stay in San Francisco for a few more months at least, I write Charlie, giving him my address. As always, I end my note, "How's Suzy?" because it's only my old mare I've really deserted by not going home.

A Friday night ten days later, I find in my mailbox a notice from the post office. I pick the packages up the next morning. It's from Charlie, of course. Inside, he's included a brief note explaining that he'd sent me the boxes only at my sisters' insistence. I leave them unopened on the floor for days, every so often glancing down at the scrawled *For Aaron Rose* on top.

Once or twice a week I invite Bill for dinner, a fancy name I give to the sandwich and salad I feed him. Sometimes I let him spend the night. Sometimes I don't. Sometimes he doesn't ask to stay.

It's a frantic Friday at Rosetti's and already past seven when I arrive home, grocery bag enfolded in my arms. Bill is waiting for me by the door. I'm just beginning to slice some carrots to dip in sour cream when he picks up one of the boxes from the floor and shakes it. "Who's Aaron Rose?"

The knife slices a finger of my left hand instead of the carrot. I lick the blood off, find a tissue, and wrap it around the cut. The tissue reddens from the blood.

I don't feel like lying. "My brother. Rose was his middle name."

"Was?"

"He was blown to bits in Nam six years ago."

"Fred, I'm so sorry." He sets the box back down.

I open the refrigerator door and put all the food I'd taken out for our supper back in it. "My name's not Fred, Bill. Fred is just part of a game I play. Fred Henry. Jake Barnes. Bob Jordan. Harry Morgan. Nick Adams. You get the picture?" He shakes his head. "It doesn't matter. It's a dumb game. Read some Hemingway sometime, you'll see. Or don't read him. It doesn't matter. My father hated Hemingway. Abominated him. Said he talked like the banker in our town who suffered some dinky, two-bit little wound during the Pacific war and never let you forget it in every macho thing he did or said. Said Hemingway's suicide was the only honest piece of work the man ever did. My father's father committed suicide, Bill. No one ever mentioned it. No one asked why because my family likes to believe it models itself on principles set forth by Seneca or the noble warriors of Japan. But by *family* I really mean my grandmother, of course. She was more like our mother, mine and my sisters' and Aaron's. My mother died when I was three days old. My sister Anna kindly told me when I was only six or so that I was the cause. She was right.

Christ, I'm jabbering, aren't I? No, worse. I'm crying. I'm crying, aren't I? And all because of those two damned boxes that I'm scared to open." I stumble around the stub end of the counter. Bill is holding out his arms. He wants to hug me. But I don't want to be hugged. I stare out the window into the late summer evening fog, dark and billowing like thunder clouds during August back home.

It takes me several minutes to quit bawling. "This is no good, Bill. I don't want to talk. I've said too much already. I'd like you to go. Please."

"No good? What's no good? I'd like to help."

"You've done all you could, Bill. I'm truly grateful for all you've done for me. But . . ."

"All right. I understand. I can't say this hasn't happened to me before." He pauses by the door, one hand holding the handle. "What's your real name, then? Or would you rather not say?"

"Andy. Andrew. Andrew Lane Odom."

"Andy?" He seems to be testing it in his head. "Andy? Well, Andy. It's been nice knowing you."

"It's been real nice knowing you too, Bill."

"Good luck," he says.

I wait for an hour to pass after Bill's left before I start to read what Father wrote for my brother. His handwriting is even worse than I would have thought and gets cruder as the pages progress. The last sheets contain only a few fragments of sentences each, all in a child's scrawl like letters written on a second-grade blackboard. By the next morning, I've read and re-read it all. I'm so tired when I go to bed I sleep almost without dreaming. But maybe the dreams that are almost not dreams are the ones that haunt you the most, like ghosts you know but can never see or touch or name.

Upon waking, I call Manhattan information, but of course there are too many Roses, Rosenbaums, Theodore or Joseph Roses, even A. Roses or Aaron Roses listed for the operator to give me the number of every one. Around noon, I drive to the library downtown, locate the directories, and jot down every possibility, however remote, on my pad. I don't know if Aaron Rose is alive or, if he is living, whether he still lives in Manhattan. But I need to see him. I want to see him. I have to try.

Back in my apartment, I begin with the few Aaron Roses. When someone answers the phone, man or woman, I inquire, "Is this the home of the Aaron Rose who might have fought in North Africa and Italy during the Second World War?" But all the answers are "No."

Nor did any of the Theodore or Joseph Roses know of any Aarons. And the other Roses knew only Aaron Roses whom I'd already called. I began to consider searching for Krauses and Greens. But the fifth Rosenbaum I speak to, an elderly lady whose weak voice quivers and strains like a voice heard over the wireless, recalls a Theodore Rose and his wife who years and years ago owned a bakery on Sixth Avenue perhaps and maybe Fifty-eighth Street. Or was it Fifty-fifth? "In any case it's long been closed," she says. "That's progress, they say. Call my sister Carol," she advises. "She'd remember better. She's much younger. Carol Seligman. Wait, I'll get you the number. She's got quite the memory, my sister Carol."

Carol Seligman's husband answers the phone but right away puts his wife on. "Theodore Rose and his wife Mikla," she says. "Yes, I remember."

"And their children? Aaron? Miriam? It's Aaron I'm really searching for."

"I used to see him in the bakery sometimes. A shy boy, uncomfortable behind a counter. But he had a sweet smile and rosy, rosy cheeks, when he was little. Everybody used to admire how little Aaron's cheeks glowed. When did I last see him? It must have been well over forty years ago, long before the war. Imagine that. I haven't thought of the Roses in years. It's such a pity how we lose touch."

"Mrs. Seligman, would you know if Aaron is still alive?"

"No."

"Or his sister Miriam?"

"Let me ask my husband. He may remember better." She sets the phone down. When she picks it back up, she says, "Wolinsky. David Wolinsky. My husband's name is also David, you see, and he and David Wolinsky were friends at CCNY right after the war. My husband says David Wolinsky dropped out of school to marry Miriam. So there you are. Miriam Wolinsky is who you're looking for. Good luck to you."

I get the number from information. But I wait to dial it. I check my watch to see what time it is there. I don't want to interrupt a meal. At first the number is busy. Then it rings and rings.

Finally someone answers, but not Miriam. A man. "Yes?" he says gruffly.

"Mr. Wolinsky?"

"You bet."

"Is your wife at home? I'm calling long distance. I'd like to speak to her."

"What about? Who is this?"

"My father was a friend of her brother before the Second World War."

"So?"

"My father left some papers for Aaron Rose to read. I'd like to see he receives them. I'd like to meet him. I thought your wife might know where I could reach him."

"She knows where he is, all right. He's right where he always is."

"He's alive then?"

"Miriam seems to think so."

"Excuse me, sir. What does that mean?"

"It means some of us think different. Let me put Miriam on the phone." He shouts out her name.

I hear footsteps, the phone changing hands. "Hello?"

"Miriam Wolinsky, the sister of Aaron Rose?"

"Yes. Who am I talking to?"

"I'm Drew Odom's son, Mrs. Wolinsky."

I can hear her gasp. "It's been so long. I didn't even know he had married. I never would have expected . . ."

"How could I get in touch with your brother, Mrs. Wolinsky?"

"Why, he lives right here. With us."

"Do you think I might speak to him?"

"Right now? No. That wouldn't be possible."

"As I explained to your husband, ma'am, my father, Drew, left some papers that belong to Aaron now. They have no value except to him. But I think he would like to read them."

"Drew's dead?"

"He died of a stroke over four years ago. He'd been in frail health for several years. It's an unhappy story, Mrs. Wolinsky."

"You were his only child?"

"No, not at all. His first son was Aaron. Aaron Rose, named after your brother, I've just learned. I've read Father's papers. I reckon I should have stopped when I discovered they weren't meant for my brother. I already knew they weren't meant for me, of course. But I'm glad I didn't stop. My sisters had them sent to me. Anna and Louisa, the twins. I was the fourthborn."

"And Aaron, the one named after my brother. Where is he?"

"He died in Vietnam. Mrs. Wolinsky? Are you all right?"

"There's so much pain in the world, isn't there? There's been so much sadness in my life and in Aaron's most of all. Now you call and tell me all this. After so many years of hearing nothing, now all this at once. I don't know what to say. But I can tell you it hurts. I don't even want to think how my brother will respond to the news that Drew Odom is dead."

"I'm sorry."

"I don't know what to do. I really don't."

"Would you like to talk to Aaron and call me back?"

"Yes. Tomorrow. Or the next day. I promise. Papers, you said. What sort of papers?"

"Reminiscences. Memories of the days when he and your brother were friends."

"Memories are all Aaron has. He may not want any more. But I'll agree to whatever Aaron wants. What's your name?"

"Andy. Andy Odom."

"You'll hear from me, Andy, one way or the other, rest assured. Just you give me your number."

But I don't rest, assured or in any other way. Miriam calls back early the next morning, shortly before I am due to leave for work. "Drew?"

"Andy," I correct her.

"Yes, of course. Sorry. My brother would like to meet you."

"Good. I'm glad."

"When would you like to come?"

"By the end of the month?"

"All right. You don't know the disaster that befell my brother, do you? No, how could you? Drew never knew because Aaron didn't want him to know. Well, that will have to wait. I look forward to meeting you in a few weeks. Imagine, Drew's son," she says and hangs up.

I book a cut-rate flight on a white-knuckle airline. But I still have to work overtime to pay for the ticket. I stint on food and other luxuries. I sell my stash of grass on the street. And I can stay at a Y or some cheap dive. I don't mind. I've crashed in some pretty crummy places when I've had to.

The Saturday morning before I leave, I wander the grounds of the Presidio and for the first time visit the halls of Letterman. I try to imagine my father when he wandered there. I try to imagine what he was really feeling. I read out loud to myself the names of a hundred soldiers carved into a hundred headstones. By chance, I pass the grave of another Odom, Frank Odom from

Massachusetts his headstone says. I walk to Lombard Street, buy a couple of dozen assorted flowers from a rival's shop, and lay them out like jewels of a necklace around his plot.

During both the flight and the bus ride into New York, I clasp Father's two boxes on my lap as tightly as I would hold them if they contained his ashes. And maybe they do. Maybe writing is just another sort of ash. Once in the city, I leave my bag in my room at the Y and immediately trek down to the Wolinsky's apartment on Avenue B near East Eighth Street, Miriam said, right across from Tompkins Square Park. "The Wolinskys aren't what the Roses once were," Miriam had remarked. The buildings' bricks look like they had all been salvaged from a coal bin and never dusted off. The park is a junkie zoo.

I walk up two flights and knock on the door of 315. A gray-haired lady answers, thin and stiff like a puppet. When I shake her hand, it feels weak and tense. "This way," she says, leading me down the dark hall.

Her small sitting room is crammed with furniture from her grandparents' generation, worn and bleak. The room smells of a resiny air spray and the moldy odor the spray has failed to conceal. Framed photographs cover the walls. In every picture, someone is smiling and too well fed. The men all display watch chains dangling across their bulging vests. The women all fill their blouses with European bosoms. Only one is thin and narrow faced as Miriam is now, her eyes bird round, bird black, and bird apprehensive. "That's Mother," Miriam says. "And there," she points, "standing next to her is Aaron when he was only seven or eight. Even in a black-and-white picture you can see how his cheeks glowed when he was a little boy. So much promise. 'Fingers like Rachmaninoff's,' Father would say to tease him."

I sit in a chair whose embroidered seat is now mostly only flecks of color and thread. "You have children, Mrs. Wolinsky?"

"'Miriam,'" she says. "Two daughters, Susan and Dinah. Both

grown. I miss their help at home. They loved Aaron, but now they almost never visit. David's locksmith shop is on East Fourteenth where it's been since 1949. Can you imagine? Twenty-six years working with keys. We've barely managed. I couldn't work, of course. Aaron's always lived with me. With us, I should say." She bites her lip. "I won't say it hasn't been hard because it's been very hard. Now we're getting old. What's there to look forward to? Only more hardship?" She takes a deep breath. "Can I offer you something, Andy? Coffee? A glass of milk? A cheese Danish? I bake them myself, almost as good as Rose's used to be." She glances at the boxes resting on my lap. "Those are for Aaron?"

"Yes. May I see him? Is he here now?"

"He's always here. He never goes out, except to the doctor's. Every time we go, I pray the elevator in the building is working. What I have to tell you now is very painful. Very painful. Even after thirty years, it's hard to talk about. Even harder every day to have to see. What must life be like for my brother? If anyone in this world should know, I should know. But I don't. I really don't have any idea. Maybe God knows. But maybe He doesn't. Or maybe He just knows too well. Aaron has no legs. No left arm. No left ear or eye. The war was already over. That's what I refuse to accept. The war was supposed to be finished for him.

"He and some soldier friends had taken a train to Lake Como on a leave. Aaron wrote me from there that its water was the most beautiful blue he'd ever seen, a blue so like sapphire that even after all those years of war it could renew your faith in God, he said, and nowhere had he ever heard such musical birds.

"Aaron was a composer. Not that he'd ever been performed. But he'd been composing since he was a boy. Perhaps Drew mentioned that fact in what you've read. But Drew wouldn't know how he continued to compose all during the war, writing music in his head when he couldn't jot down notes on the score paper he always carried with him when he could.

"After he'd first visited Como, he said he wanted to write a different kind of music, less pessimistic, even though all of history seemed to have conspired to confirm the deep pessimism that was already his nature. He wanted, he said, to be able to sing with the joy of birds. He wanted to write a music that might bring peace to the soul, he said.

"All those horrors he'd seen, had lived through, had learned about, because everyone had seen the pictures of the camps by then. Yet the simple songs of the birds at Como had elated him. If you were to ask me, I'd say my brother was too easily impressed by nature, too easily seduced. What did he know about birds? He was a city boy down to his bones. Birds were pigeons messing the street and rooftops or chickens on the dinner table. But by that lake, he said, all you heard was the music of birds. And that music was for him the meaning of peace.

"He was sitting near the lake in a little café popular with American boys. In a few hours, he was to catch the train back to Pisa where he was stationed. Seven boys were killed outright by the bomb. Two died later. Aaron and two others were severely wounded. A few escaped unharmed. Fascist partisans had planted it. It was never reported in the papers, of course. The authorities were afraid the news would only stir up more trouble. They feared repercussions. They feared reprisals. The war was officially over." She stares at my scars. "You've been wounded too, I see. It's a horrible word, isn't it, *wound*? Like the glint on the point of a knife." She doesn't stand up to show me the way but merely says, "Aaron's room is the one at the end of the hall. He's expecting you. Just knock."

After my second tap, he says, "Come in." His room is unlit except by the light coming from outside through a single window. Carefully made and covered with a red-and-white-check spread, his bed fills almost half of the space. An old TV sits on a straight-back chair, but it hasn't been plugged in. Several TV trays are folded next to it. No pictures, photographs, or mirrors hang on the walls whose wallpaper is yellow and dotted with brown patches like squash. A lamp with pink tassels dangling from a maroon shade stands in a far corner. Another corner is concealed by a folded hospital screen. There are no books or magazines, no records or record player. Yet the room is so small it feels cramped and cluttered by his wheelchair alone.

Sitting as if propped in it, Aaron faces the window, away from me. His hair is dirty white, like down. A small bald spot is pocked and splotched with dark scab-colored patches. He's wearing an oversized gray pullover and jeans folded at the end of each stump.

"Isn't it amazing what you can see happening right out in the open in that park?" he remarks. His one hand grasps his wheel-chair's push rim. Dexterously, he turns his chair around enough so that he can face me. I also turn, favoring my right side. "Yes," he says. "Yes, I can see the resemblance." His left ear is mostly just a bulbous scar and a lobe. His left eye has been sewn shut. His cheeks are chalky white. "It's uncanny, in fact."

I hold out the boxes. "Where should I put these?"

"It doesn't matter."

I set them down on top of the chest of drawers, next to the vials of medication. "They're not easy to read. Perhaps your sister will help you with them."

"No. I don't think so. I'll manage." His good eye studies me like an owl's. "Tell me. Did Drew have a happy life? Was your father a happy man?"

"We never talked much," I answer him. "Father was much closer to my older brother."

"Named after me, Miriam said."

"Yes. But none of us knew that. I just learned it myself. None of us knew there was such a person as Aaron Rose."

"No. No, Drew couldn't have told you, I suppose. And your brother Aaron? He was killed in Vietnam?"

"In '69."

"You fought there as well?"

"Yes. My brother Aaron loved music, too," I say. "He played the cello. He wanted to compose some day. He was majoring in music at the university until he was expelled for participating in an antiwar protest that turned violent. He was drafted. He was going to defect to Canada but . . ."

"But what?"

"It was my fault," I say. "I made him fight anyway."

"No one should ever make anyone fight. Not ever. But you look like someone who's learned that by now. Are you a music lover? Drew came from such a musical family. His grandfather, his mother, Drew himself. What instrument do you play, Andy?"

"None. I have a tin ear."

"Lucky you." He points to his right ear. "This is supposed to be the good one. But it hasn't heard any music for many, many years. Before the war, no one could ever have convinced me that it was possible for a human being to be so bored as I am all the time now. I look forward to oblivion. At least it won't be so boring. I can't stand music anymore. It's just another lie we use to trick ourselves into believing that life is a pleasure, that life has meaning, that it isn't a bore. Those junkies out there," he says, tilting his head toward the window, "those dope heads have the right idea. It doesn't matter whether the body lives or not. It's the mind you have to kill. But when only the mind is alive . . ."

"Could I visit you again tomorrow, Aaron?"

"Why should you want to? An embittered old man and his butchered body. No, your mission's been accomplished."

"Please."

"I'm suffering from another damned bladder infection. No antibiotic works anymore. I should go to the hospital. But," he glances up at my face, "talk to Miriam in the morning. See what she says."

After I leave, having given my thanks to Miriam, I stroll through the Village, get lost, and find myself in front of a bar where a couple of drag queens are standing outside the door, preening and fixing each others' wigs before they go in. I pass by slowly, like a tourist drawn by curiosities he's never witnessed before. Farther down the street I stop for a Coke and a slice of pizza. After I've finished my meal, I return to the bar. "What you have to do now, Andy," I counsel myself, "is fuck some cute butt and not think about anything."

I find an empty spot in a dark corner, where the dim light falls from the right, and linger there for over an hour with an empty beer bottle in my hand. My thumbnail has torn the label to shreds.

"Fear is only natural," Mutti had lectured me in the dairy the afternoon she advised me to take Aaron's place in the war. "We all are afraid sometimes. Just exert your strong Odom will, Andy. Make it as powerful as your body already is. The enemy doesn't matter. You're not fighting an enemy. You're fighting human nature. Terror infects everyone. In that way only are we all equal. But war, like music, like all great art, is what the best of us have created in order to be victorious over nature and over our lesser selves. Do you understand?" Smiling, she kissed my cheek. "I'm so proud of you already. And yet you're about to make me still more proud."

Was she proud of me still? How could she be when I'm always afraid? Why should I want her to be?

Two more drag queens walk in the door, both carrying purses, one wearing a wig almost as tall as she is. They wave to the others waiting for them at the end of the bar and call out their names: Miss C, Mavis, Roxie Heartbreak, Princess Meg, Norma Jean. They huddle together like bridesmaids at a wedding and talk loudly all at once.

A guy perched on a bench to my left is wearing a cowboy hat and vest, and chewing gum. When he smiles at me, he reveals a space between his front teeth as enticing as Charlie Sutton's. I hold out my hand for him to shake. "Jake," I say. "Jake Barnes. You busy tonight?"

He peers through the dark to the worst of my scars. I can feel them glow. "Sorry, Jake. I've got other plans," he mumbles and wanders off.

I quit the bar fast. Back in my room, I try to sleep, but can't. Across the street, a man is pulling down a shade. He stares into the darkness of my room as if he knows something that he shouldn't see, perhaps something very sad, is happening in it. Even after the shade is fully drawn, the man hovers against it as if it is a wall and he is a ghost struggling to pass through it. To where? To me?

When I wake, it's well past noon. Not waiting to dress, wearing just my shorts, I rush down to the end of the hall to the pay phone. "Miriam? I could be there in less than an hour."

"I don't know. I don't think so."

"Please."

"He cried most of the morning. He read it all last night, every page of it. I'd set it on a table and moved the lamp to light it as he asked. Then he read it again, he said, every word. When I put him to bed, he was sobbing. He just sobbed and sobbed, like a helpless child. And he is helpless, of course. Even David said it was the saddest thing he'd ever heard, like everything my poor brother has ever suffered had been reduced to one relentless sound.

"He's just now started to quiet himself. To calm down. I'm afraid seeing you again might hurt him even more. Surely others must have told you how much you resemble your father when he was young."

"No. No one ever has."

"Well, believe me, you do." She hesitates, breathing hard. "Try to be here before three. And please don't stay very long. I don't want Aaron to begin crying again just when David is getting home."

Miriam greets me at the apartment door. "He hasn't had much sleep," she warns.

I knock on his door. "Aaron?"

"Come in. Sit," he says, directing me to a chair not there yesterday. I push the chair closer to him. His hand touches my knee. Because I neither flinch nor ease my leg away, his touch turns almost into a caress, as innocent as it is intimate. His nose begins to run. I remove a tissue from the box on the windowsill and wipe his face. "An object of horror," he says, "a proverb among the people." He gazes out toward the trees in the park. "It seems your father truly loved me."

"Yes."

"The news comes late." A slight grin exposes a few teeth, yellow and worn. "We kissed."

"Yes. I know. I read."

"It felt enormous at the time. I misinterpreted it. To my grief."

"Aaron."

"What?"

I bend toward him and wrap my arms around his small, frail, vestigial body. Accepting my embrace, he places his arm over my shoulder and tugs me closer, his hand clutching my back. His lips are parched and cracked and rub like whiskers against mine. The kiss we kiss is a real kiss.

"Aaron," I say. He turns away as if afraid of what I might see.

"You must go now, Andy."

"Yes. I promised your sister I wouldn't stay long."

Miriam sees me out but asks no questions. Back on the street, I pass a bum. His filthy hands hold out a paper cup as monks used to hold out bowls for alms or rice. I grab all the change from my pockets and several bills from my wallet and pour it all in. "I'm so sorry," I say.

A month later, I pick up another package from the post office, this one from Miriam. Again I wait days to open it. Finally I feel brave enough and barely notice it's a Friday night. Miriam's note reads:

> *Dear Andy,*
>
> *Aaron asked me to send you this score that he completed in the days just before he left for the war. As you can see, he dedicated it to your father. Aaron understands that you don't read music. He says that's one reason he's decided to send it to you. It's never been performed and we all know of course it never will be. But Aaron has very little, almost nothing really. He asked me to tell you that it is his gift for your gift.*
>
> *Regards,*
> *Miriam Rose Wolinsky*

It takes me over a month to find another job. But at least it's a job I can like. The cattle ranch, with a small dairy farm in addition to it, is spread out over several hundred acres way up north of Sonoma, land which the Benedetti family has owned for over a hundred years. Angela Benedetti hires me, a tall woman in her seventies with a happy, weathered face and sun-cracked skin.

"You'll like it here, Andy," she says while standing on the porch of the white frame house, holding a bowl in one arm and a long wooden spoon in her other hand. "After I saw you ride that horse I knew you were our man. How old are you anyway?"

"Almost twenty-six. You think I could stable my own horse here some day, Mrs. Benedetti?"

"Of course you could. When do you want to start work?"

I shrug. "Everything I own is in that Chevy. I don't have any other plans. Right away."

"Do you have sheets and some towels?"

"No, ma'am."

"Let me give you some then. That old shack is pretty spartan,

Andy. You sure it will be acceptable? It's so far away from the rest of the houses and all of us. We never really imagined anyone would want to live there again."

"The rent's about what I can afford. I'm looking forward to a monkish life."

"That's what our son Michael said once. Michael's a priest in Boston. We rarely see him anymore, one of my two children who chose to leave home. When he was a child, I prayed every day Michael might become a priest. My only regret is that he must serve so far away. He was always different. More spiritual than the rest of my chidren. Even as a youngster he seemed to want less from life and more from God. And who knows? I suppose sometimes it is wise to strip life down to its bare bones. But I worship the saints. I don't want to be one." She laughs merrily. "You go ahead and move in, Andy. I'll have Paul or Carlo bring you some provisions later this afternoon after Joe and the boys get back home from San Luca."

"Sure," I say. "I'll do that, Mrs. Benedetti. I already have a name for her," I tell her. "Suzy Two."

"For her?" she says, puzzled. "For who?"

"For my mare," I say.

Michael Anthony Benedetti

From my seventeen-year-old seminary notes, 1967:

> Ubi Amor, Ibi Gloria Est.
> Love is sun.
> Glory is moon.
> Love, if seen, makes dark unless its light is reflected by
>   glory.
> Love loves the world.
> Et homo factus est.
> Darkness shines.
> Night is light.
> End of endless story.

The day after Gates Ogden left the priesthood to marry a woman he had been secretly meeting at her home in Worcester for, it was rumored, well over a year, Monsignor Lynch delivered the homily during the mass which he celebrated just for the priests. Like Father Ogden, we mostly worked as bureaucrats or petty functionaries within the headquarters of the archdiocese. Gates, like me, was a bookkeeper. His desk sat next to mine. He slept in a room down the hall from mine. We occasionally enjoyed being partners at bridge. Sometimes, especially when the weather was fine, we took long walks together all over Boston. But we never really talked. I told him about my life growing up on the Benedetti ranch, about all of my family—especially about my mother, my sister Catherine, and my brother George—about my childhood decision to enter the church, even about my having protested the war. In response, he told me about his comfortable early years in suburban New Jersey, the pleasure he had always taken in numbers, the rigor of his studies at Fordham, the confidence he found in a life of discipline. But, because there was no real feeling in what either of us said, we might as well have been informing each other about a distant and not too interesting relative. We liked working side-by-side. We always greeted each other warmly whenever our paths crossed. Up until a few weeks before his departure, we continued to take vigorous walks together several times a week and to beat all comers at bridge. But I didn't know him. I never suspected that he was violating his vows.

Father Leo discouraged friendship among his charges. "It is God's work," he would remind us, "to be friendly. But close friendships . . ." Winking, he'd wipe his hands across the front of his shirt. "Deep faith requires all the spirit's virtuosity, does it not? No virtuoso can perform at his best when faced with unruly, inattentive people fidgeting and coughing. Faith demands all our concentration. Every second of our lives, we must give it no less."

It was Charles Leo who had asked Monsignor Lynch for a copy of his homily delivered on the occasion of Gates's departure and who reproduced it to distribute to all of us. "What a brown-noser that little twit is," Gerry Pacini scoffed when he discovered a copy on his desk. Youthful, audacious, sharp, he liked stirring up controversy. He preferred the new mass. To him the Latin one was a relic of the past, as irrelevant as nuns' habits, eating fish on Friday, or the Legion of Decency. What difference did it make whether one received communion in the hand or on the tongue? Group recitation of the rosary was to him as rote as repetition of the multiplication tables. When Father Leo spoke reverently about the Fatima secrets and Mary's appearance in Medjugorje,

Gerry countered, "Superstitious nonsense." He argued vehemently in favor of contraception and the need for population control. He believed women should be allowed to become priests. He even questioned the need for celibacy and papal authority in matters that ought to be, he maintained, left to individual conscience. The church, he'd insist to anyone who would listen, must strip itself of all remnants of magic and outdated metaphysics. Since his first, noisy, impudent days among us, we knew he would not last. How could he? Father Leo loathed him.

"Listen to this idiocy," Gerry said to me, picking up his copy of Monsignor's latest homily. "God is not a loving parent, spouse, or brother," he read, mimicking Lynch's throaty roar,

> He is not a friend. He is a stern judge. Before Him and His laws, all of humanity must tremble, like ignorant savages cowering before lightning. Outside the Church, without its protective walls, no one is safe. Outside the Church's doors, all souls are lost. Seen from the perspective of eternity, we in our desperate creatureliness are mere specks, motes in Time's eye. Our souls cry out from the waste of our lives. Only the Church can save us. Only the Church can bind or loose.
>
> You, my sons, have vowed to live faithful lives, lives of celibacy, poverty, and obedience, of self-sacrifice, asceticism, and constraint, of conformity to God's revelation as it is sustained through history by the Church and its dogma. If our faith is a nuisance to the modern world, if our faith is alien to it, so much the worse for this modern world. If our faith is a thorn in the side of the modern world's flesh, then let God make ever more painful that wound until the body of mankind realizes it can never heal itself. The soul alone is faithful until death. For all heresy is born out of lust. All disobedience begins in the groin, fish spawn in a drying pond.

Gerry tore his copy and mine into bits and dropped them into a waste can. "We're priests," he declared, "not a tyrant's eunuchs. The day I was ordained, I don't remember the bishop's cutting off my balls."

"Gates broke his vows," I said.

"So what? You've never strayed?"

"Never."

"Not even before you took your vows?"

"No, not even then."

"For Christ's sake, you're a virgin. You're blushing. You are, aren't you? How old are you? Thirty-six? Thirty-seven?"

"Forty-three."

He shook his head in astonishment. "Well, for crying out loud. I mean, most of the codgers around here probably never had to resist temptation. But you, Michael . . ." He shook his head, puzzled and amused. "You know what this place needs? It needs someone to open up every window in every room on every floor until all the past's musty smell has been blown away. You want to get some fresh air? I've almost finished my work. We could sneak out the side doors. Or don't you want to risk playing hooky?" he taunted me.

"I promised Father Leo I'd have these books in order by tomorrow."

"Michael, for God's sake. It'll do you good to break a rule or two."

Because I'd grown up near the coast in Northern California, I knew something about fog and bitter winds blowing in over the mountains from the Pacific. But nothing back home had prepared me for Massachusetts' bleak midwinters or for air so cold that it knifed the skin like icy water. After blocks and blocks of walking against winds that pushed you backward like a strong arm, I was shivering. "Let's get warm," Gerry suggested, opening the door to a corner bar and directing me in.

A young couple were drinking wine in a booth across the room. Wearing a threadbare overcoat so long it dragged the floor every time he moved, an old man sat on a stool at the bar munching a burger. Leaning against the back of the cash register, the bartender watched a football game on the TV that hung from a beam over his head. To the left of the table where Gerry and I sat, a low fire crackled in a raised hearth. Its glow colored the left side of his pale face ember red.

When I ordered a coffee, the waitress said, "Certainly, Father." When Gerry ordered a draft and some beer nuts, she said, "Right away, Father."

"You're blushing again, Michael," Gerry observed.

"I don't get out much."

After the girl brought us our order, without any prompting from me, Gerry started to talk, fast and happily. Although he'd been born in North Bergen, New Jersey, he'd been raised mostly in Texas. His family had changed bases every few years until they finally settled outside Corpus Christi when his father retired, a twenty-year man. What he loved most about growing up in Texas, Gerry said, was playing football and baseball, driving sharp cars, and making love to a girl whose name was Sue Anne Starling. But Sue Anne broke his heart when he was not yet seventeen. His father made him stay in school until he was old enough for the army. Although he joined up immediately after graduating, he'd missed Nam, but he wasn't sorry. When his hitch was over, he enrolled at Texas/El Paso and barely finished after six hard years, most of his troubles, academic and otherwise, having their origin in another girl, Maria Elena Ibanez, whom he would have married if he had not found her, one night six weeks before their wedding, making love to his best friend Chuck Henderson on the bed of Chuck's pickup. His heart had been broken again, this time he thought for good. Degree finally in hand, he began to bum around the West, working odd jobs here and there until, late one spring, after a stretch of hard times, as close to destitute as he had ever been, he found himself begging for food at a Buddhist monastery he'd happened upon near Big Sur. They fed him and took him in. Working as a handyman at first, he stayed nine months and might have remained longer, observing all the discipline and meditating several times a day, but "I'm Catholic," Gerry said. "That's who I am. I don't want to void my personality. It's not absence I'm yearning for, but God. I found a seminary not too far away. After some initial misgivings, they accepted me. Once I'd been ordained, I asked for a parish. But someone in the hierarchy apparently thought I needed more taming. They sent me here. I'm willing to wait it out. For a while." He downed his beer and snapped his fingers for another. "So, Father Benedetti. Now it's your turn. Tell me your story."

But I didn't tell him my story. I never told anyone my story. I didn't have the nerve. I just told him the part I thought he might like. "I wasn't quite six, you see," I said, "not even six years old. I had never been so sick before. I've never been so sick since. All I could do was lie in bed, struggling for breath, and all I could see was that the fog wouldn't lift. My bed was next to a window. About a hundred feet across the yard, if only it had been clear, I could have seen a beautiful old acacia grove, five trees, each forty or fifty feet high. But the fog obscured everything. I couldn't even see the roof of the porch just below my window. I'd convinced myself it was the fog as much as the pneumonia that was making it almost impossible for me to breathe.

"Mother wouldn't leave the room. Even when the nurse or doctor appeared, she wouldn't go. If she ate or slept, I didn't see her.

"I was convinced I was going to die. Can a child not yet six form such a conviction? I was certain I was going to die and I was terrified. I kept staring out my window, praying for the fog to lift so I could see the trees.

"Mother told me later that the doctor had summoned an ambulance when, a little after noon, the fog started to break. Only that wasn't how Mother said it. 'Mary is parting her veil,' Mother said. 'Look how the trees glow from the splendor of Her face.' Mother fell to her knees. She lifted her rosary up as if she half expected it to have been transformed into gold and prayed. An hour later, my fever broke.

"When I was well, she drove me to St. Agnes in San Luca. In gratitude, we prayed the rosary all morning and half the afternoon. As we kneeled Mother made me promise I would be a priest when I grew up."

Pondering me, Gerry rubbed his right forefinger in the cleft of his chin. He leaned closer. "You don't believe, do you?"

I wouldn't look at him. "I don't know. I keep hoping obedience will be enough. I keep hoping the doubt will stop." Gerry grinned broadly. Why does a smile on some homely faces shine so much more brightly than it does on the most handsome ones? "I could use a friend, Gerry."

He rapped the table. "You have one."

Did I love him? Gerry would have responded that the love that moved the sun and the other stars to song also sang in us. But I think his love for me was so innocent of eros, so devoid of desire for me or any other man, that it made him reckless. Even within the walls of where we lived and worked he too easily grasped my hand or kissed my cheek. Perhaps he relished the insolence. Perhaps he enjoyed our being observed and silently judged. But I'd decided to retreat from his boldness days before Father Leo finally intervened. Father Pacini, he announced to me, had been assigned to another office in a different building. What had we done the months he had been watching us? I told the truth. We had talked. We had enjoyed each other's company. We'd walked. We'd attended a baseball game, taken a boat ride up the Charles, strolled through museums, gone swimming. Swimming? "Father Pacini loved to swim. He was strong," I said. Strong? Had we touched? "No. Of course not. Never. Certainly not."

"Nevertheless," Father Leo said. He instructed me in my duty. I obeyed. When Gerry called me to suggest we ignore the evil-minded, idiotic, medieval order that had separated us, I refused.

Two months later, while I was working at my desk, adding another column of figures, thinking about nothing but numbers, I felt Father Leo gently touch my shoulder. "Come with me," he whispered. I followed him to his office. When he instructed me to close the door, I did. When he suggested I might sit down, I sat. "There's been an accident, Michael. Gerry Pacini. God love him, he was rushing out into traffic to save a stray dog that had run into the street between two cars. The man driving the delivery truck swerved to avoid the dog, but he didn't see Gerry. The doctors tell me it's unlikely he'll survive much longer. But he's still conscious. He can still talk, though only with much pain. He's rejected all medications that might ease his suffering but blur his mind. He wants to be aware. His faith is great. He wants to see you. Of course you must go."

Father Leo drove me to the hospital himself, but stayed in the hall when I entered Gerry's room. A tube penetrated his nostril. Another was hooked to his left forearm. Large portions of his exposed skin were blue or purple. Even with the curtains drawn, the room was blindingly white. Some machine hummed and buzzed. "Sit," he said effortfully.

I sat. "Don't try to talk."

He closed his eyes. "OK." His face was bloated. He tried to smile. "What a cornball reason to die."

A pinkish froth bubbled out between his lips. When I started to stand up to find the button to alert a nurse or doctor, I sensed his body tighten. He opened his eyes again and silently directed me back into my chair. I was being told, "Don't try to help. There's nothing you can do. You needn't even pray. Just watch." So I watched. All that night and morning I watched Gerry Pacini die. Occasionally a nurse looked in. Several doctors visited. They probed and prodded and whispered in corners. Yet nothing seemed to disturb his concentration, not even when Father Leo gave him the last rites. The last breath I heard Gerry take was like a sleeping child's contented sigh in the middle of a dream.

When I quit the room, Father Leo was waiting for me in the corridor. I said, "You've called his family."

"They will be here this afternoon. His parents. Two of his brothers."

"I'd like to meet them."

"Certainly, Michael."

"We were just friends. But I never had a better one."

"I'm sure that's so."

"Listen, Charles," I said to him in the car as we drove away. "I need to go home. I want to return to California for a while. I need to think. Give me your permission."

"Think about what, Michael? What in Heaven's name is there for you to think about? You don't think. You brood. You're too susceptible, your vocation is too weak for you to leave right now."

"I'm not worthy," I said.

"None of us is."

"You know that's not what I mean, Charles."

"Despair is the subtlest sin, Michael, full of guile. You ought to be warier of it." As he steered with one hand, he withdrew a cigarette from a pack on the seat next to him and lit it. "You've never seen me smoke?"

"No."

"We should talk more, you and I. I like you, Michael."

"I'm not worthy," I repeated, almost savagely, my teeth chattering despite my efforts to keep them quiet. "I never have been."

Father Leo turned onto the street that led to our building. "I'll arrange for your leave tomorrow," he agreed.

Why did I go home? Perhaps I believed I was returning to a hallowed family living in a sanctified place. Even my brother George, Giorgio, despite his small and not-so-small rebellions, never really left home, however far he wandered away. Maybe home, like faith, can be lost but never forgotten. Maybe whoever has lost it will spend the rest of his life searching for it even in distant places where he knows home can never be found. Maybe home is like Heaven. Or maybe it's only a tiny speck of sand on heaven's shore.

Yet what is Heaven to a Benedetti? Bright sun and a little shade, a scattering of clouds drifting over golden hills, a fine grove of tall trees, robust wines and cheeses, perfect sauce, thick and garlicky, and, Mother would add, passionate, honey-throated, wind-swept, sea-borne, sun-lit song. De Lucia, Caruso, Gigli, di Stefano, Corelli. Ruffo, de Luca. Ponselle, Albanese, Tebaldi. All Italians, of course. "Heavenly," Mother would say.

Until a few days after my eleventh birthday, I never strayed far from home alone. Before then, whenever I would wander off, I could always claim I had been led astray by my brother George. My parents had eight children, five boys and three girls. Born three years after Isabel who had been born two years after Paul, I was the youngest. Joseph Jr. was the oldest, himself the father of two sons before I'd turned eight. Ten years older than I, ten years younger than Joe, Maria, with lots of assistance from Carlo and Catherine, helped Mother raise Paul, Isabel, and me. I loved all my family. All my family loved me. "A happy family," it pleased Mother to say, "is a fruit tree that blooms and gives fruit in every season and never sheds its leaves."

Yet for no good reason George was always riding off somewhere, whether on horseback or later on his cycle. Two of my brothers, Joe and Carlo, fought in the Second World War. When Joe returned from the Philippines, he married his high-school sweetheart, Alicia de Martini, from the neighboring valley. They settled in a cottage Papa had built for them in a grove of shade trees on the crest of a hill where the deer still roamed freely. Shortly after Joe married Alicia, Carlo married her sister Lucia. Though Carlo and Lucia first chose to live in an apartment over the drugstore that the de Martinis ran in San Luca seventeen miles away, they lingered in town less than a year. Papa built them a bungalow on another ridge. Lucia could stand in her living room and, looking across the narrow valley that separated them, wave at her sister Alicia standing in hers.

Eight years later, Paul married Kay DeBella and they bought a few acres seven miles from the ranch. But Paul continued to work for Papa just as he had always done, as did Maria's husband Jerry Buonaiuto and Jerry's two younger brothers, Tim and Tony. After Catherine's fiancé Rusty Worth was killed in a car wreck on the highway south to San Francisco, a Cadillac driven by a drunk driver having swerved across the road to smash into Rusty's truck head-on, she vowed she would never marry anyone else and pledged her life in service to the burgeoning Benedetti brood. Even Isabel insisted she would never leave home. "Any man good enough for me to marry," she declared to Papa, "marries us all." Only George abandoned the ranch.

Drafted into the army at the start of the Korean War, he simply vanished. Many years later we learned that he had been initially stationed in Germany and, once he'd decided to make the army his career, married a German girl. But shortly thereafter he'd been transferred to Okinawa where his German wife refused to join him. They were divorced. A few years later he married Nora Kavanagh from Berea, Ohio, a nurse in an army infirmary. They had two daughters, Connie and Kate. All this we learned from Nora only after George had been killed in Vietnam. The letter informing us of his death arrived only a few weeks before Nora and the girls.

Because of George, I determined to protest the war and was arrested once for lying down in front of the White House. Half a dozen other seminarians and two priests were arrested with me, all of us acting disobediently, repudiating the instructions of our bishop. One of the priests, Seamus O'Rourke, had seriously contemplated dousing himself with gasoline and lighting a match. The selflessness of the Buddhist monks, the purity of their sacrifice, had haunted him for several years, he said. His death could not be a sin if it was motivated neither by despair nor anger but by compassion. Fortunately, Father Markham dissuaded him. "Jesus did not choose to die. Remember His agony in the garden. Remember His despair on the cross, His certainty that He had been forsaken by His Father. Jesus suffered so piteously because it was His Father's will to which he yielded. All human suicide, whatever the motive," Markham had argued, "is an act of pride."

Lying on the cold, damp pavement, antiwar slogans draped over our bodies, heckled and spat upon by counterdemonstrators, we prayed aloud, "Agnus dei, qui tollis peccata mundi, dona nobis pacem. Miserere nobis, Agnus dei. Dona nobis pacem." But the peace for which I was praying, I couldn't help thinking, would come, if it came at all, too late for George.

It was George who showed me the best trails over the mountains and through the woods down to the ocean and the rocky promontory that jutted out into the waves like a fearless dragon, its mouth gaping open as if it meant to match the ocean roar for roar. Nothing for George was worth doing unless it promised the sweet taste of fear. He showed me how to climb the rock face near the summit of the highest hill behind the Worth ranch, how to explore the deep caves near the bay and to slink along their slick floors like a snake, how to pilfer grapes from the Cambereri vineyards just for the pleasure of daring the watchmen to chase us away.

One night, my arms wrapped around his waist, I rode with George on his motorcycle down to the river. We stole a boat someone had tied carelessly to a pier and drifted like escapees on a raft all the way to the ocean. Over still-smoldering driftwood left by campers, George cooked the hot dogs he'd brought for breakfast. When he offered me a toke of his grass, I refused. At noon, we hitched a ride back to his bike. Many warm nights,

George slept outside under the stars alone. Sometimes, he let me join him, a smooth curve in a rock our shared pillow.

The day George disappeared into the army, I followed a path he had shown me, trespassing onto the McLaren farm along a dry creek bed through golden hills jeweled with poppies. Finding the shell of a box turtle lying on a boulder, I carried it with me. When I reached the fire road, I squeezed through the fence's barbed wire, clutching the turtle shell to my chest. Curving around an oak grove, the road dipped down to a pond, its surface silvery and shiny like foil. Blackbirds were squabbling in an old walnut tree. A lizard scurried from rock to rock. I set the shell down on a stump, stripped, waded in, and paddled across. Climbing out on the other side, I lay in the shade of a boulder and fell asleep.

When I woke up, a bull was looming over me, his head three times the size of mine. He snorted and stomped his left hoof on the ground, stirring up dust. I had to work hard not to sneeze. His eyes met mine. His horns' sharp points flashed in the sun. I could smell almond in the air, the hide-like scent of sage, and burning leaves. The bull's saliva dripped onto my thighs. Its tail swished like a cat's. It snorted again, lifted its head, sniffed the air, stepped over me as casually as if I'd been a log, and lumbered up the path.

I slithered into the water on my stomach like a snake and, my arms flailing, swam across the pond. I didn't wait to dry before I dressed. Grabbing my turtle shell, I ran as straight as I could for home, not making a single wrong turn the whole long way. As I crested the last hill, our house far below looked as carefully carved and shone as white as the cameo of Our Lady that Mother always wore.

"What's that?" she asked me as I strolled into her kitchen clutching the shell.

"A present I found to give to George when he gets back home," I said, displaying it to her.

"Be sure to wash it good."

My fingers traced the shell's ridges. "A bull almost trampled me today," I bragged. "The McLarens' bulls are a lot bigger than ours. But I wasn't scared. I wasn't frightened at all."

"I don't want you wandering off like that anymore, Michael."

"Why?"

"Because George was George and you're you. Now scoot. I have to finish this stew for supper."

"Will you be with me when I die, Mother?"

She placed the lid on the enormous pot that was cooking over two burners and regarded me seriously. "What put that question in your head, Michele?"

"Will you?"

Every morning, every evening, Mother always led our whole family in prayers, her most fervent always addressed to Mary. Our Lady, she said, was our fairest flower. She was the rose before whom all the angels eternally danced and played. "O mater dei," she would end, "memento mei. Amen." She brushed my hair out of my eyes. "I'll be with all my children forever and ever," she said.

Despite her advanced years, it was Mother who chose to meet me at the airport after my flight back from Boston. As I drove across the Golden Gate, I said, "You're disappointed."

She nodded. "Yes. Of course."

"I was hopeless from the start, Mother. Everyone knew I never had the makings of a parish priest. I was worse in the classroom. I was no scholar. Thank God, Papa insisted I take all those accounting courses while I was at the University of San Francisco or nobody would have known what to do with me. I wouldn't have known what to do with myself. For nearly fifteen years, all I've done to serve God is mostly simple arithmetic. That's not a vocation."

"I've been praying for you," she said, sighing. "Ever since your phone call, I've been praying for you."

"I haven't lost my faith," I lied.

She glanced at me as, filled with shame, I stared down the old, too familiar road, every landmark a sign of my failure. She patted my knee. "You were the most pious altar boy I've ever seen."

"What do you mean to do here?" Papa challenged me in his den where Mother had directed me after I'd parked her car near the back porch. "No offense, Michael, but you were never much help on the ranch."

"I know. I could keep your books."

"Tom Mariano has been doing my books for years."

"How old is Tom, Papa?"

"Same age as me. A spry eighty-four. Where you going to sleep?"

"My old room."

"We just moved Kate and her new baby in there," Mother said as she walked into the den.

"It doesn't matter where I sleep. I'm used to austerity." Tears filled my eyes. "I'm sorry I failed you, Papa, you and Mother both."

Mother kissed my cheek. "You just need some time, Michele. You'll see."

I claimed the daybed in what used to be George's room, though it had long ago been converted into a sort of sewing room for many of the Benedetti women, a place for them to darn, sew, knit, embroider, and needlepoint, its walls covered with framed samples of Catherine and Kay's work in particular, with fewer pieces by Alicia, Lucia, Maria, Isabel, and the others. George had kept his room devoid of any decoration whatsoever, stern and functional. It had never been even a boy's room. It was unsettling to see it transformed into something frilly and cute, yet the disparity between past and present fit my mood perfectly.

After my sixth night home, Mother confronted me after breakfast. "You're not sleeping."

I rinsed my mug out in the sink and set it in the rack to dry. "Not very well."

Mother was chopping tomatoes. Once so abundantly thick and black, her hair, what was left of it, was like patches of foam clinging to the otherwise bare rock of her skull. Her face had thinned. Her eyes, although gay as always, had become darker and more beadlike, two small black pearls. Tremulously, she scooped up the tomato pieces and dropped them in the pot to cook. I stepped outside. Catherine was hanging sheets from the children's beds on the clothesline near the garage. Years ago, Papa had purchased two dryers, but Catherine preferred to rely on the sun because it made everything smell so much sweeter.

I handed her a clothespin from the bag hanging on the line. "I'd like to visit the cemetery at St. Agnes this morning, Catherine. Would you go with me?"

She withdrew one last sheet from the hamper. "Of course, Michael."

"Do you want to go into the sanctuary first?" she said after I'd parked Mother's car outside the church.

"No."

"George is over here," she reminded me as I marched through the open gate, "just at the foot of the pepper tree. See all those flowers? Nora still visits him here to talk to him once or twice a week. Isn't that lovely?"

I kneeled on the grass. Catherine lay a gentle hand on my neck. A squirrel scurried over the low stone wall. "In a few weeks, I'll be sixty-one years old. I'm not well, Michael," she said. "I can see the end. I can feel it coming. Mother and Papa don't know yet. I haven't told them, though of course they suspect. I'm glad you're home for a while. You and I, after all, are the only unwed siblings. I imagine I'll be the next one resting in this peaceful place. How lucky we've all been really. How blessed." I rose to my feet and gazed in wonder at her. "Drive me to the doctor's tomorrow, will you?"

She didn't want me to wait for her while she was in the doctor's office. "Go roam the streets of San Luca," she suggested, "take in the sights." But I wouldn't leave. While in the waiting room, she flipped through magazines. Her fingers drummed on a table. She opened and closed and opened her purse. She hummed to herself. She arranged and re-arranged and arranged again the billowy white silk scarf she always wore around her neck whenever she left the ranch.

"Well," was all she said as she returned to the waiting room. "They want more tests, I'm afraid. You'll drive me to San Francisco tomorrow, won't you? If either of them asks why we're going, just tell Mother and Papa we both wanted to take a walk around our old alma mater."

The next morning, her face looked powdered even though Catherine never used powder or any other kind of makeup. "I might be awhile," she said to me on the hospital's steps. She stared up the hill toward St. Ignatius's spires, then glanced back at me. "Michael, don't look so alarmed. I'm going to be all right. No matter what happens, I'm going to be all right."

After she'd entered the lobby, I headed straight for the Asian Art Museum, my refuge when I was in school close by. Whenever I thought I couldn't stand the loneliness anymore, I would walk there to search for repose in front of one of my favorite Buddhas. But what I admired even more was a large scroll that hung with other scrolls in a gray, dimly lit room. The garden on the scroll consisted only of a few fruit trees, their leaves still young though most of their blossoms had already scattered. A thorn bush jutted out of a little pile of rocks that sat near a meandering stream. An oriole perched on some brambles. A hare near the bottom of the scroll seemed ready to leap, but, near it, a pheasant was caught in a snare. An ancient man, his face mostly scrawls, sat cross-legged on the floor of a hut and stared up at some clouds. In the museum's note affixed to the wall next to the scroll, the calligraphy beautifully brushed down its left side was translated: "I have met a hundred calamities. I wish I could sleep and meet no more."

When I joined her at the hospital, Catherine said nothing. We rode back to the ranch in silence. About a hundred miles north of San Francisco, we passed a false-front diner with a red arrow flashing down on it and three or four double-trailer trucks parked in front. An airplane beacon swept the sky. Pepper trees and eucalyptus lined the road. The houses that sat scattered on a ridge, their windows lit by sunset, looked as if at any moment they might explode in flames. Catherine stuck her right arm out of the car to feel the rush of the wind stream. When she brought her hand back in, she rolled up the window, opened her purse, and removed her rosary, the one I had brought her from St. Anne's in Quebec ten years before. "Say it with me, Michael. Pray with me."

"Catherine . . ."

"Please."

So I did. Even after she fell silent, silent myself, I continued to pray.

As we walked through the front door of the house, Catherine untied the white silk scarf from around her neck. She was smiling. Mother was spraying the leaves of a massive philodendron that occupied half the entrance way. "We had no idea it had gotten so late," Catherine apologized. She kissed Mother on her cheek. "It's past my bedtime."

Papa was waiting for me in his leather wingback next to his desk in the den. His cigar lay smoldering in the big glass ashtray on top. The desk lamp's green shade deflected most of its light onto Papa's papers spread out across the blotter that he had not changed for years, ink and pencil marks scrawled all over it in an illegible palimpsest. "You've read the books? You've studied them?"

"Yes, Papa. I'm sure Tom Mariano has told you everything."

"I didn't need Tom to tell me. You think I didn't know already?" His right hand formed a fist. "What I don't know is how long."

"I'm not that smart, Papa."

"Pretend you were."

"You need to cut back, Papa. You employ too many people. You're too generous."

"They're all family, Michele."

"Actually only sixteen."

"No, no. They're all family. All of them. Everyone who works here. I still believe the land will sustain us. God will see us through."

"I wish I could share your faith, Papa."

"You're a priest, Michele. Even as Christ suffered his forty days of trial in the desert, Heaven was guiding him, the sun by day and the stars and moon by night. What would life be without faith, especially in times of tribulation?"

"I wasn't speaking as a priest, Papa. Only as an accountant. It's wise to be practical sometimes. Even the church knows this, as I can testify."

He reached for his cigar and puffed on it. "Practical? I've never been a practical man. Not even during the Depression. When everyone else was suffering, looking everywhere but to themselves for help, we worked. We worked until we prospered. Ask your mother. She'll tell you. So will Joe and Carlo and Catherine. During the worst years of the Depression, we were living in a garden. Don't tell me to be practical, Michael."

The next morning, I went on my first long walk since I'd been back. As I stood on the crest of a high ridge, far from the ranch, the horizon seemed to encircle the whole world like a thin gold belt. Resting against a knobby boulder, I took a swig from my canteen. A couple of hawks circled below, then soared higher and away. Did I hear the big cat before I saw it? It was crouched near a ledge facing me, perhaps thirty yards across a ravine. As it licked its paw, its tail whipped against a slab of rock. Then it became still as a statue, a lion carved by some ancient Sumerian or Chinese artisan from precious stone. I bowed to it. After a few seconds, ignoring me and my mere human gesture, it leaped from its ledge onto another ledge and wandered away.

I arrived home after dinner was done, but Isabel, Catherine, and Mother were all still working in the kitchen, cleaning table- and counter-tops, scrubbing the stove, sweeping the floor. A man I had never seen before was standing on the other side of the screen door talking to Maria. She noticed me. "Oh, here my brother is now," Maria said to him, pointing toward me. "Say hello to Andy, Michael."

He opened the screen door and stepped into the kitchen with-out taking off his cowboy hat. While scratching behind his ear with his left hand, he held out his right. "Andy Odom," he said.

I shook his hand and unsuccessfully tried not to stare at his scars.

"Andy's been working here for . . . how long has it been?" Maria asked him.

He released his hand from mine. "Almost eight years."

"He keeps to himself," Isabel said, "don't you, Andy?"

He blushed. "I guess."

"But we love you just the same," Maria said.

"I'd be so bored living by myself in that shack," Isabel said. "Would you like some water or a soft drink, Andy?"

"Michael's the brother who's a priest," Maria informed him.

"Your mother told me," Andy said.

"Maybe Michael could drive you tomorrow," Maria offered for me.

"I don't mean to trouble anyone," Andy said. "If I could just borrow a car for the day . . ."

"Nonsense," Maria said. "Michael hasn't anything better to do, do you, Michael?"

"Where am I going?" I asked.

"San Jose," Andy said. "2016 Keyes Street, Apartment 2B."

"We'll buy a map," I said.

"I went to San Jose once," Isabel said, "though for the life of me I can't remember why."

"It'll take four or five hours," Maria said.

"Is eight too early?" Andy asked me.

"Michael doesn't sleep anyway," Mother said.

"Eight's fine," I said.

Mother gazed out the window over the sink toward the acacia grove. Shimmering in the strong wind, the leaves were ablaze and the clouds were hovering over them bright as fire. She crossed herself and hummed a tune, "Mattinata," it was called, a song she liked to sing whenever she was happiest no matter what time of day it was, even at sunset.

The next morning dawned surprisingly raw and wet, although the rain fell halfheartedly, more like a late fall drizzle than an early winter storm. I finished eating the grapefruit wedges, scrambled eggs, and toasted panetone Mother had fixed for me and pecked her cheek as I slipped on an old denim jacket I hadn't worn in sixteen or seventeen years. I'd found it in the back of a downstairs closet, surprised to see how well it had survived. I was delighted that it still almost fit.

Mother was organizing the ingredients for the children's breakfasts that would follow mine. Most of the men had already eaten theirs, which Maria and Isabel had prepared, and, despite the weather, before light had gone to work with the herds. Mother cracked an egg into a large bowl. "I've never seen a man sit prouder on a horse," she said to me, "but since the day Andy arrived here in answer to our ad I don't think he's ridden off the ranch for more than an hour. Carlo told me he's fixed the cottage up really nicely."

"It's a shack, Mother. It was a shack when Old Bud McKinney lived there. I imagine it's still a shack."

"Old Bud wouldn't let me touch it either," Mother said.

I glanced out the window. "Here Andy comes now. He must have stabled his horse in the barn. I've got to get going, Mother."

She was humming a sweet, yearningly plaintive tune, nothing I could identify or remember. Probably it was a melody by Puccini. She loved every note Puccini ever wrote. I kissed her cheek again as she folded napkins.

Andy was waiting for me out of the rain under a sycamore. The brim of his cowboy hat dripped and his face glistened from the wet. He was wearing worn work jeans and a checked flannel shirt under an old windbreaker with a rip in one sleeve. More blue than gray, more silver than blue, his eyes focused not on me but on something behind me, as if I were being followed.

"We're going to take Mother's car," I said, "the Ford." Rusted in places, its paint faded, the car was waiting for us at the end of the drive where Mother had parked it last night. He grasped the handle on the passenger's side. "Be careful with that door. The hinge is loose."

The door, sagging, creaked open. As he sat down, the top of his hat squashed against the car's ceiling. He flung it onto the backseat.

Did he wear it out of vanity to cover his bald spot, his young man's tonsure? Was it only five months ago that I had strolled with Gerry Pacini in the Boston Fine Arts Museum through rooms filled with Greek antiquities? Gerry had lingered before one especially damaged torso waiting for me to join him. "Look," he instructed me. What was it he wanted me to see? "Have you ever seen anything more beautiful?" he asked. Andy's scars were ugly. Although wiry and muscular, he was bony like an old man. A mere wisp of yellow hair, like a dusting of pollen, circled the crown of his head which, like his scars, was pallid in comparison to his darkly tanned skin. When he caught me looking at him, I fumbled with the car keys, trying to find the right one. "Finally," I said, turning the ignition switch.

Neither he nor I said much all the way to San Jose. Silence is difficult, almost unnatural. But every time I started to speak, he'd glance away.

When we reached the city's edge, he pointed to a service station where we stopped so he could buy a map. The attendant at the station gave him directions. Back in the car, Andy wordlessly reviewed them on the map, then asked to drive the rest of the way. After so many hours of silence, the sound of his voice startled me. Most of what I loved about the mass was the long stillness of its ritual. When it was over—*Ite, missa est*—the congregation's lapsing into mere human speech invariably would sound to me like babel, nonsensical words. "What?" I said to him. "What did you say?"

"I'd like to drive now. Do you mind?"

"Be my guest," I said, stepping out the door. He slid over as I took his former seat. Not once did he make a wrong turn or lose his way. He seemed to know exactly where he was going. In less than thirty minutes, we were driving slowly down Keyes Street, reading street numbers.

He parked in front of an apartment building designed like a motel in the shape of an L. Perhaps at one time it had been a motel. Its three floors were bordered on one side by an outdoor walkway and iron railing. Perhaps, too, the building had once been painted red. But with time the red had faded to a grayish pink or flaked to reveal blotches of an ash gray. Its speaker turned to face out, a radio blared rock from a third-story window. Garbage bins near the street overflowed with trash, some of which the wind had scattered, littering the spindly hedgerows and grass. To the right of the complex stood a windowless warehouse, four stories high, every inch of it as black as the fire escapes that led out of black steel doors. To the left sat a small corner grocery, the lower floor of a Victorian whose upper windows advertised rooms for rent in both English and Vietnamese. Across the street was a row of bungalows, some less in need of repair than others. Small children were playing catch in the yards or hopscotch on the sidewalk. A barking dog, tied to the post of a porch, jerked persistently on its chain.

Furrowing his brow, Andy slipped a piece of paper out of his jeans' back pocket, checked what he'd written on it, and let the wind grab it out of his hand. "You don't need to go in," he said.

"How long do you think you're going to be?"

"I don't know. It depends." He opened the car's back door, picked his hat up off the floor, put it on, changed his mind, and tossed it back onto the front seat. "Do what you like."

I followed him up one flight of stairs, down the second-floor walkway past five apartments to the angle in the L where he turned left. Every window we passed had its shades or blinds drawn shut. On the next to last door, someone had printed Smithson in pencil on a three-by-five card and affixed it with tape under a roughly painted 2B. Andy pressed the buzzer. A dog in a downstairs apartment yelped. The thick draperies to the right of the door shook without being parted. Perhaps more than a minute had passed before Andy knocked, then pressed the buzzer again.

Although the boy who answered the door was tall for his age, his face was still a child's. His straight black hair fell in back below the neck of his T-shirt that he wore loose outside his cut-offs. His eyes and skin were almost Asian, just as his nose and jaw were almost European. Surrounded by burning votive candles, a foot-high wooden Buddha sat on top of a cabinet that rested against the wall directly behind him.

"You from school?" he demanded.

"No," Andy said.

"Social workers?"

"I'm Andy Odom."

The boy blinked, stepped back, and cried out, "Mom!"

"You know who I am?"

"Mom!" he hollered again, then turned back around to face Andy. "You're my father's brother."

A young woman, Vietnamese, opened a door on the other side of the room and walked in, wiping her hands on an apron. When the boy glanced over his shoulder at her, she grinned and sat down in a straight-back chair. Neither her apron nor her sweater fully covered the slip she was wearing. Her face was carved sandalwood, but her arms and hands, tense and restless, were constantly in motion. She pointed to Andy and nodded, then at me. "She's asking who you are," the boy reported to me.

"He's a son of my employers," Andy said to the woman. "A priest."

"Not really. Not anymore," I said.

"That's not what your mother thinks," Andy said. "He drove me here. Cam Smithson wrote my sisters a surprising letter about ten days ago. My sisters wrote me. You know about the letter?"

The woman nodded again. Old odors permeated the room's walls as if the smell of everything ever cooked in the tiny kitchen to its rear still clung to the plaster. Andy sat down on one side of a long couch, I sat on the other, and the boy crouched on the shag rug.

The woman's gaze was fixed on Andy's face. "I don't look like Aaron," Andy said. "I never did."

As her left hand traced the zigzag slashes of Andy's scars on her own face, the boy, watching her, said, "How were you hurt?"

"In the war."

She wept silently, wiping her eyes with the hem of her apron.

"She can't talk," the boy told Andy. "After my father's death, men came to her room. When they saw she was pregnant, they beat her, my dad, Cam, said. So he moved her to another place in the Chinese district, hoping she might be hidden and safe. But the same men found her just a couple of weeks after I was born. They beat her worse and cut out her tongue. My dad moved her again, into a room in a big house where Americans lived. After that, the men never came back."

"What men?" Andy said.

She shook her head. "She doesn't know," the boy said. "They could have belonged to either side, like her brothers." He wiped his nose with his hand, the first childlike gesture I'd seen him make. "My dad kept trying to get us out of the country. He refused to leave Saigon until he'd gotten us out of Vietnam. He'd taken a job in the American embassy so he could help us. I remember seeing the smoke over the airport when I was five. I'd never heard so much noise or seen so many crowds. Everyone was terrified. My dad reached us just in time and drove us to the embassy. People were crying and shouting and pushing and shoving, trying to get in. When the helicopter came, by the time he'd forced us on there wasn't any room for him. He escaped a couple of hours later, but landed on a different carrier. We didn't see him again for many, many months. But Dad used to brag all the time about his contacts. Even though he and my mom aren't really married, we were reunited pretty quickly, I guess. Mom wouldn't marry him. Dad asked her. But she wouldn't do it.

"Dad started being sick about a year ago. Ever since, it's been hard times. We've moved twice. I work when I can get a job. Right now, I sweep and clean out the grocery store next door. I try to go to school, but school is boring, and when Dad is real bad, like now, I refuse to go. Nobody'll hire Mom.

"My dad didn't want to write that letter. He's always been scared that if one of my father's family found out about me they'd try to take me away from him and Mom, try to adopt me or something. He wanted to write you, Andy, but he wasn't sure you were even still alive. Once he made the effort, your sisters were pretty easy to locate. He didn't know what else to do. He didn't know where else Mom and I could go. His own family disowned him years ago when they found out about us."

"Aaron must have wanted to keep it a secret too, I reckon," Andy said.

The boy's mother squeezed her son's shoulder and made a humming sound in the back of her throat, prolonged and mournful. When she'd ceased, the boy said, "She never told my father. She is very sad he never knew. But she hopes maybe he guessed."

Standing up, the woman grabbed Andy's hands, tugged him to her, wrapped her arms around him, and hugged him hard. Andy kissed her hair. "What do I call you?"

"Tu," the boy said. "Tu Loc is what my father called her. Cam named me Luke, after my mother."

"Tu," Andy said, squeezing her so tightly her feet lifted off the floor.

After he had released her, she smiled down at her son, breathing happily. "I think she wants me to tell you," Luke said to Andy, "that you hug her like my father."

"Like Aaron? No. No, I'm sure I don't, Tu," Andy said. He stiffened slightly and turned toward the door. "I'm not like Aaron at all. Excuse me. I need to step outside for a second. I'll be right back." As I started to rise to follow him, Andy ordered me, "You stay."

Bewildered, sad, Tu retreated to her chair after Andy had left. "Why is Andy upset?" Luke asked me.

"I don't know."

"You are friends?"

"We just met. He works for my parents on a cattle ranch and small dairy farm way up north. But I haven't lived at home for many, many years."

His mother nudged her son's arm. "Would you like some tea?" Luke offered.

"No, thank you."

"What's your name?"

"Michael. Michael Benedetti."

"It is good you're a priest because my dad is a Catholic, though he never goes to mass anymore. He had lots of friends. In the nice house where we used to live when he could still work, they were always visiting him or going out with him. But no more." Luke wiped his nose with his hand again and rubbed it on the rug. His mother swatted his ear.

"I'm sorry," I said, abruptly jumping up to leave. "But I'm worried about Andy."

Standing on the far end of the second-floor walkway, I could see him stomping back and forth in the warehouse's parking lot, his movements restricted by an invisible wall behind and in front of him. When I called his name, he neither quit pacing nor looked up.

"Andy!" I shouted at him again from the parking lot's driveway. "Why are you so angry?"

"I'm not angry, you dumb fucker," he yelled at me.

"You should go back," I said. "They'll misunderstand."

"What do you know about any of it?" he challenged me.

"Nothing."

"That's right," he said. "Nothing." But he relented and returned to the apartment anyway.

Although he knocked on the outside door, he didn't wait for a response but opened it himself. The inside door Tu had originally emerged from was open, though now a light shone in the room behind it. "Cam? You in there?" Andy said. "Let me talk to you, Cam."

"Come on. In," a voice, frail and halting, answered.

"Jesus Christ," Andy said as he entered.

"Yeah," the man agreed. "Fucking awful. Isn't it?"

I shut the door behind us. He was lying on a mattress stretched out on the floor. Next to it, a radio was playing classical music, a piece for string orchestra, very peaceful and gentle. Unpacked boxes lined one wall. Several, stuffed with clothes, sat open in a corner. Old sheets were strewn beneath the room's only lamp. A futon or pallet of a sort had been rolled up by the foot of the mattress. Crisscross lines of metallic tape sealed cracks in both windows. The air was as stale as a locker room's.

The small purple lesions that blotched his face, neck, and

forearms might have been fresh wounds, so raw they appeared when glazed by his sweat. His body twitched and jerked beneath the covers. His bright red lips were the only part of his face un-affected by the lesions that still showed any color. His eyes were as intent as a wild animal's frightened by headlights at night. His breathing seemed to require of him the effort of a bodybuilder lifting his heaviest weight. Each time he tried he became more exhausted.

"Luke's. Quite a boy. Isn't he?" Cam said to Andy. "He. And his mother. One. Insepara. Ble. You see that."

"Yes. I see that."

"Sorry. For not. Telling you. Before I. Had to. Afraid."

"Luke said."

"Yes. I know. My hearing's. Fine." Cam glanced up at me. "So. You're not. A priest."

"Right."

"Good. I may need. Someone. Who's not. A priest. Soon." He looked back at Andy. "Luke. Looks. A lot. Like Aaron. Doesn't he?" He coughed for ten or fifteen seconds, much too long. "I'm burning up. I've been burning up. For days."

"You want some water?" Andy offered.

"Just makes me. Thirstier." He shut his eyes. "We were. So young. Aaron. You. Me. All of us. Tu. Hell. We still are. Your brother's going. To make me eat shit. For taking. Such lousy. Care of. Them."

"I'll call Anna and Louisa tonight, Cam."

"It'll be peaceful there. Won't it. Andy?" Cam opened his eyes and stared up at him. "Promise me. Take good. Care. Of her. And Luke. I'm tired. Of this. So tired. Of dying."

Andy kneeled next to him and clasped his hand. "I promise."

"So glad. You came."

Only after Andy was certain that Cam had fallen asleep did he release his hand. He stood up and beckoned me into a corner. "You do know what's wrong with him, don't you, Michael? You look scared enough to know. Well, you don't have to stay here. I can easily hitch a ride back to the ranch."

"I don't want to leave."

"You sure?"

"No. But I'm going to stay."

"All right then. But try to stop shaking, will you?"

For a late lunch, Tu cooked some vegetables in broth and rice and brewed a pot of tea. We ate without talking. After she'd washed the dishes in the sink, Andy dried them. "Tu?" he asked her as he placed the last cup in the rack. "May we stay here for a few days?" She pointed at me. "Yes. Michael also," he said.

Since Cam and Tu couldn't afford one, Andy and I used the pay phone inside the corner grocery. Calling first, I asked Catherine to let Mother and Papa know I might be away at least several more days, but didn't bother to explain why. Then Andy phoned his sisters. "I haven't spoken to either of them in, Jesus, I guess it's been thirteen years," he said to me after he'd hung up. "Why is it that voices don't age at all until people are really old? Anna sounded just like she did when we were all in high school. Do you suppose this place sells anything worth eating?" he asked while selecting different cans from the shelves. He carried several filled sacks back to the apartment.

"We'll need some changes of clothes," I suggested as we climbed the stairs. "At least of underwear. A shirt or two. Toothbrushes. Razor."

"You go."

"I don't have any money, Andy. Not enough."

"There must be a real cheap store somewhere near this crummy neighborhood." He set the two bags down on the walkway, extracted his wallet from his back pocket, and handed me a fifty. "Buy whatever you think we need."

I slipped the bill into my wallet. "What size shirt? What kind of razor? Boxers or briefs?" Had I blushed as I asked?

He squatted to pick the grocery bags back up. "Boxers, 32

waist. Shirt medium. Razor, you choose. Color of toothbrush, you choose. OK?"

During the afternoon of our second day in the apartment, I whispered to Andy that maybe someone should call a doctor, but he looked at me so fiercely that I didn't risk the suggestion again. Night and day, asleep or awake, Tu spent nearly all her time in Cam's room, often kneeling by his bedside as if in prayer. She wiped the sweat from his brow, the spittle from his lips. She held his hand. With her fingers, she combed his hair. If the little radio lost its signal, she adjusted the dial or the antenna so the music would play clearly again. She let Andy prepare all the meals and did not appear surprised at how well he cooked curried potatoes or spicy fish.

Luke showed us the pile of books he'd borrowed from the city library and bragged about how many he'd already finished. Yet, even as he read, whether lying on the couch or floor, his attention never left Cam's room; his door was always left open. If any of the candles surrounding the wooden Buddha went out, drowning in the melted wax, he'd immediately adjust the wick so he could light it again.

For exercise, Andy and I went for long walks, although never together. Once the days had warmed and brightened, Andy would run for miles and return so sweaty that he'd have to take a shower in the tiny bathroom next to the kitchen. I didn't question why he risked running barefoot over city streets and sidewalks.

During the late afternoon of our fourth day there, while Andy was out, Tu knocked on the floor in Cam's room. She paused, then knocked again. I didn't understand. "Dad wants to see you," Luke said to me from across the room where he lay on his back reading a novel about horses called *King of the Wind*.

Tu was holding Cam's head up, trying to encourage him to drink some broth from a cup. He opened his eyes. Tu beckoned me closer. Cam tried to speak, but his voice was fainter than a whisper. "Does he want me to hear his confession?" I asked her.

"Don't be. Absurd," he said more distinctly. His right forefinger tapped the blanket. "Listen. Pray. Want to hear. Prayer. Someone. Not really. Who doesn't. Believe. Like Verdi. Good man, Verdi. Free me. *Libera me*. Understand?"

I'd never administered last rites. In every way I'd been no good as a priest. But it wasn't ritual Cam wanted from me. I'd understood at least that much from what he'd said. Yet I made the sign of the cross anyway, and as I prayed the Our Father I saw his lips moving in silent repetition of my words. After I'd finished, I kissed his cheek, savaged by disease. His body shook. It trembled. He started to cry.

"Cam," I said. "Please listen. I promise you. You shall soon be eternally everything who are now nothing at all. Like orient and immortal wheat or the eternally green tree you shall live from everlasting to everlasting. Neither your love nor your desire for love shall ever die, Cam Smithson. And what is strangest of all is that this shall truly come to pass. Amen."

His lips ceased quivering. I kissed them, made the sign of the cross again, and stood up to leave the room. Whose words had I spoken? Not my own. A pain like a fire burning in my head so blinded me that I stumbled through the door and across the living room and almost fell out the other door onto the walkway. I bent forward, certain I would faint, and grasped the railing to recover my balance. When I opened my eyes again, everything was light. Yet I could see the tiniest details of everything wherever I looked: each petal of a geranium that grew in a windowbox in a house across the street, the peel in the bark of the eucalyptus down the corner, the silver shimmer beneath the red of the Stop sign on the other corner, the beads of a child's bracelet dangling on her arm, the orange tail feathers of a bird that perched on the warehouse's fourth-floor fire escape, every pore in his face as Andy raced up the stairs.

He shook me. "What's happened?"

"I don't know."

Luke stepped out the door of the apartment onto the mat. "Mother said . . ." He started to cry.

Andy embraced him. "OK, kid. It'll be OK."

Tu lay on the bed next to Cam as if she were trying to keep his body alive a little longer with her warmth. Luke and I waited on one side of the bed, Andy on the other next to the radio, which was still playing. Listening very carefully, Tu lifted her head off the pillow and glanced at her son. "Turn up the volume," he told Andy.

It was cello music. Listening intently, Andy smiled. His smile changed to a grin. Cam breathed ever more shallowly. His body shuddered, but it gave no other sign. After several minutes, Tu rose slowly out of bed. She reached for her son's hand and led him out of the room.

Andy was still grinning. "I think he's passed," I said.

"Yes."

"Andy?"

"Shshsh. It's almost over."

When the cello finished playing, he stooped over and clicked off the radio. "What was that?" I asked. "Bach or something?"

"The Fifth Cello Suite. I used to have to listen to Aaron practicing it all the time when we were kids. That might have been him. That could have been Aaron playing. He was pretty awkward on his feet, Aaron. But he sure could make that cello of his dance."

"I don't understand," I said.

"Hush, Michael. Not now," he said. "I'll explain some other time."

The day before Campbell Burke Smithson's funeral, Andy and I drove back to the ranch to change into more suitable clothes and, without speaking to any of my relatives except Catherine, immediately returned to San Jose. After Cam's death, Andy had notified the coroner and made arrangements with a funeral home. I called a priest I once knew since Tu insisted that Cam be buried out of a church and in holy ground. She was not a Catholic, she was not even Christian, but Luke left no doubt that it was what she wanted. Father Collins agreed to say the mass himself and asked Tu and Luke only kind questions. The three men who'd removed Cam's body, however, had dressed themselves from head to toe in protective clothes and covered their faces with masks. When Andy saw them arriving, he tried to keep Luke from also seeing, but Luke broke free. He would have struck out at them, I was certain, if Andy hadn't reached him in time and pulled him back.

"I'll pick you and Luke up day after tomorrow," Andy reminded Tu after the funeral as he escorted them from the car back to the apartment. "Saturday night at ten. Be all packed and ready to go, OK? Our flight takes off right before midnight." He tousled Luke's long hair.

"Why can't Michael go too?" Luke complained.

"He could, but he doesn't want to," Andy said.

"This is for family," I said at the door. "But I'll be driving you to the airport, remember? I'll say good-bye then."

"I think you should go too," Luke grumbled. "Why do we have to live so far away? We won't know anyone there."

"You'll know me," Andy said.

"But you're not going to stay."

"You can't live here any longer, Luke. There's no money. You'll like my sisters. It's a big house with lots of land. You're Aaron's son. You belong there. It'll be home."

"You think so?" Luke said hopefully.

Andy hugged his nephew, then Tu. "I'll see you Saturday, ten sharp."

Andy and I rode to the ranch almost as quietly as we had driven to San Jose on the first day. But the silence had changed. Even though during our days together we'd seldom talked, we were no longer strangers. Or, if we were still strangers, we were strangers who had shared many meals, slept on the same floor, been startled awake by the other's dreaming, and smelled the other's breath and sweat in the close air of a small room. Strangers who had been present together in the presence of death, who had come to love the same too grown-up boy and his terribly harmed mother. After Andy had parked the car exactly where Mother had left it for us to use on the morning we'd first departed, he hopped out and tossed me the keys. I nearly dropped them in the dark. "Thanks," he said. "I'll see you Saturday evening, I guess."

"You sure you don't want me to drive you to your place?"

"I'd prefer to walk."

"Until Saturday, then."

He didn't move but gazed up toward the starry sky. "It's so much more beautiful here, without all those city lights. Look," he said pointing. "There's Orion. There's his dog. Out hunting. My favorite constellation."

"It was my brother George's favorite too, just as winter was his favorite season."

Andy started to head up the path. "It's late. I'll get Suzy from the stable in the morning."

"It's a long walk, Andy. It'll take over an hour."

"I know. But it's such a beautiful night."

"Yes, very. All the lights are out. In Papa's house. Joe's. Carlo's. Everyone's. There's not a light on anywhere. There's not even a moon. Just the stars. When I was a kid sleeping out here with George, I used to frighten myself by imagining how many and how far away they all were."

"Do they still scare you?"

"Of course. More than ever. How about you?"

"Not usually."

He quit walking and turned and faced me in the dark. "The house is back that way, Michael."

"I need to leave the keys in a tray on the table in the front hall. Mother wants to use the car in the morning."

"I'll walk you there."

The front door was unlocked. It was always unlocked. The house had never been locked, not since Papa had built it. No Benedetti ever locked his home. I tiptoed across the threshold and left the car keys in the tray. Andy was waiting for me when I stepped back outside.

"You're coming back to my place, then?"

"Is that all right?"

"I've been alone a long time, Michael."

"I've been alone all my life."

"How old are you?"

"Forty-three."

I could sense his pondering that number and its implications. "You'll be my first priest."

"I've never slept with anyone. I won't know what to do. I don't even know how to begin."

"Not to worry, Michael."

But I did worry, all the way to Andy's cabin. I started to pant and then worried more thinking Andy might believe I was even more out of shape than I actually was. I tripped over a tree root that, despite the night, I should have seen and over a rock Andy had tried to kick out of my way. The cry of an ordinary hoot owl sent shivers up and down my spine. As we descended the trail that led to his place, I started to sweat and my palms were wet.

He opened the door but, once inside, didn't turn on a light. "There's the bathroom," he said, pointing to his right. "I built it myself, put in all the pipes. It's not much, but it's better than Luke and Tu's. Use it if you need to. I'm going to start a fire."

It was already burning when I walked back out. "This is it," he said, "this is my home. There's a closet on the other side of that door and the stove and refrigerator are hidden behind that plywood divider. And this is my bed," he said, sitting down on what in the dark looked more like a cot.

"I'm cold," I said, warming my hands over the glowing pot-bellied stove, the cabin's sole source of heat.

He stepped behind me, laid his head in the nape of my neck, and hugged me. "Calm down. You're shaking like a sick dog. I'm not going to hurt you. I promise." He unzipped my jacket, un-buttoned my shirt, turned me around, grabbed my shoulders, and kissed me. When he stepped back, his smile looked crooked. Why hadn't I noticed before how his scars could distort his smile?

We had both been sleeping on a floor for so many nights that a floor with a softer rug on it felt almost like a bed. Why was something I had desired for so long so painful and arduous for me to accomplish? I fumbled and groped and had to be shown how to use my body. In every respect except age, I was like a naive, in-experienced teenager thrashing about in the backseat of a car. Yet slowly, patiently, wordlessly, Andy taught me how to touch, where to linger, what to caress, what to say and what not to say with lips, chest, hands, thighs, hips, cock, ass. When his tongue circled inside my foreskin and he asked me to do the same with his, I felt ashamed. His body and my body suddenly were too real. Why should love be so crude, so coarse? But I liked the taste. His penis was not large, smaller than mine or the few others I'd seen erect, but in me it felt huge. My bowels burned with pain. He would move faster, slower, then faster again, asking, "Am I hurting you? I don't want to hurt you. Am I hurting you?"

And I'd reply, "No. No. No," until I began to blaze. My whole body burned with the pain until it burned away. For an instant it was gone and I was gone and Andy was gone. There was just this sun everything had become, though just a few moments later it was night again.

He hugged me as he slept. But I didn't sleep. I couldn't sleep. I felt too grateful and afraid. In the morning, dressed only in my shorts, I sat on the little cabin stoop to watch the dawn, wishing it were true that making love was how the body prays.

He squeezed the door open behind me. "Aren't you cold?"

"Yes."

"Want to take a shower? There's almost enough room in it for both of us. It'll warm you up."

"Look how beautiful and fresh the green hills are this morning. The whole valley's shining like a lake."

He ran his fingers through my hair. "Go back to Carolina with me. Come with us on Saturday, will you?"

"I don't have any money."

"My sisters do. They're paying for the trip. I'll just add your ticket on." He squatted behind me and kissed my shoulder. "Michael? I was just wondering. Do you read music?"

"No. Don't you?"

"My sisters and I refused to learn. I wish I hadn't. Eight years ago, a man important to my father gave me a score he'd composed. It's a long story, the story of my life, I guess. I'll tell you about it soon. I want to have it performed. For eight years, I've been saving money. Just recently, I checked all the costs again. I've saved almost enough. I'm almost home.

"I'm going to take the score with me to Carolina to show my grandmother. It won't matter, but I'm curious what she will say because I have no idea what it sounds like. In the meantime," he said. He thrust his arms under my armpits and lifted me up.

His need startled me. How could I be the object of such desire? He wrapped his arms more tightly around me. "You in me this time," he breathed into my ear, "this time, your body in mine."

Early Saturday morning, before our flight that night, I visited Catherine. Since her illness, my sister often preferred the seclusion of her room to the bustle of the rest of the house, especially on weekends when all the children passing through it at one time or another were full of laughter and youthful spirits. Even long before her fiancé's death, Catherine had always been the quietest, the most solitary of the siblings yet, all of us agreed, the most completely loving. Open displays of affection, however, or anything suggestive of sentimentality could make her squirm. At family parties, she'd often sit apart from everyone else, close to a door or window where she'd watch us, smiling radiantly, joyously. Although she'd never miss any festivity we celebrated, she chose never to participate fully either. Except for Mother and Papa, she was the most important member of our family. Yet she was alone, and, except for her faith, perhaps nothing was more serious to her than her solitude.

I had little doubt it was selfish of me to want to tell anyone in my family about what had happened between me and Andy. Wasn't I merely a middle-aged man who, flush with an utterly unexpected first love, needed to prattle and gush about it like an adolescent girl, like one of my more voluble nieces in fact? Still, I wanted to tell. I wanted to talk about it.

Yet when I reviewed the members of my family in my head the only one I thought might listen to me with any sympathy or understanding was Catherine. She removed her wire glasses, laid her book on her lap, and listened to my story without once changing her expression in the slightest, appearing throughout interested, almost hopeful, and unsurprised. When I'd finished, she smiled sweetly and gazed out the window toward the barns. The light reflecting off their roofs brightened her face even more than did the sun's direct rays. "I barely know Andy, of course," she said. "We've rarely said more than a polite hello. Mother's extremely fond of him, but she's remarked how she worries about him. 'A troubled boy,' Mother has called him, and about people's troubles Mother is rarely wrong. But, Michael, don't say anything to anyone else for a while, will you? Mother and Papa's love for us is as nearly boundless as human love can be. You know that as well as I. But it cannot tolerate discord, can it? And what you have told me would be to them more inharmonious, I suppose I could say, than your decision to leave the priesthood. But you never had a real calling, did you, Michael? Don't allow them to confuse the two, thinking you left one so you might have the other. You're glowing, dear brother, and it makes you look quite goofy and altogether adorable." She touched my arm gently. "You have my blessing, Michael."

"Thanks, Catherine."

"Don't be silly."

"But I'm feeling silly. I'm feeling so silly and foolish that I want everyone's blessing. The whole world's."

"Oh, Michael! Please!" She laughed merrily. "Perhaps it's for the best that you'll be away from the ranch for a few days, you and Andy both." Without diminishing, her smile became more enigmatic, like that of someone remembering a moment of joy she'd promised another to keep secret forever. "I think all human happiness must be a little like this book." She tapped the binding of the one that lay in her lap. "I wouldn't bother to finish it if it weren't a pleasure to read. But it would be very foolish of me, wouldn't it, if I read it only to pass the time, for distraction, especially when, by all accounts, I've so little time left. Pleasure, excitement, joy, elation, they're all really only metaphors, aren't they? We have to learn how to read happiness and delight as profoundly as sorrow or grief, don't we?" Her eyes sparkled so brightly I wondered whether my dearest sister knew more about pleasure than she had ever confided to anyone.

Carlo's two younger sons again agreed to take care of Suzy while Andy was gone. When Mother passed down the hall close to where I was packing, she wished me a safe trip without inquiring about my reasons for going. Papa was smoking in his den, reviewing the quarter's bills. "Those storms last year," he speculated, "maybe it was those endless storms last year that are still hurting us." When I shook his hand good-bye, he grumbled, "You should be going back to Boston where you belong." Maria insisted on fixing me a hearty early dinner, and Isabel sliced me a piece of her fresh-baked custard pie.

Dusk's last light was fading when I picked Andy up by the side of the old fire road that approached within a quarter mile from his cabin. Because of stop-and-go traffic after an accident on the highway just south of San Francisco, we were late arriving at Luke and Tu's and reached the airport with only minutes to spare. On the plane, Luke asked to sit between me and his mother, but even before takeoff he was already asleep, though neither Andy, Tu, nor I slept a wink on either that flight or the two that followed.

It was Charlie Sutton, not Andy's sisters, who met us at the airport. From Andy's description, I recognized him immediately as he strode down the concourse to greet his old buddy with his broad, gat-toothed smile and sprawling arms, three fingers missing from his right hand. He gripped Luke's right hand with his left. "I'm Charlie, an old friend of your uncle here." Tu cowered slightly in his eager embrace. "Ma'am," he said, then noticing me, "Who's this?"

"My friend Michael. Michael Benedetti," Andy said.

"Well, for Pete's sake," Charlie said, scratching his cheek. He took Luke by the hand. "Why don't you and me go grab y'all's luggage?"

The three suitcases and Tu's boxes barely squeezed into the trunk. Luke, Tu, and I crowded into the backseat while Andy sat up front. As we drove out of the airport parking lot, Andy asked, "Where's Anna? Or Louisa?"

Charlie took a right turn onto a faster road. "They don't leave the farm much, hardly at all anymore. So, when Anna phoned me, I said I'd be glad to take a little drive." He slapped Andy's thigh. "We've missed you, buddy. How long's it been since you even wrote me a letter?"

"A long time."

"Damn straight. Too long."

"You haven't changed much, Charlie."

"You know I have. I've got four kids now, Charlie Jr., two sweet girls, and a brand new spanking baby boy. Appears like you've lost just about all your pretty-boy golden hair, buddy." His free hand thumped the dome of Andy's head. As Charlie drove onto a ramp that led onto a four-lane highway, its median grassy and wide, he said, "Ain't this something?" and speeded ahead. "Built it more than ten years ago. There've been lots of changes around here, boy. More than I care to count. Wait'll you see."

Over an hour passed before we turned onto Odom Road, the entrance to the farm marked by an imposing sign. "It's been re-paved," Andy commented. "Widened too."

"Pretty fancy, isn't it?" Charlie said.

"There are so many trees," Luke said.

"Wait'll you see it in springtime, kid," Charlie said over the back of the seat. "Prettiest damned place you'll ever want to see this side of Heaven."

"They've torn down the old bridge," Andy observed as we approached the new one.

"It'd just about rotted away," Charlie said.

"Jesus," Andy exclaimed as we reached the driveway to the house. "It's blue. Whatever made them paint the house blue? And why those fancy shingles, Charlie? Where's Mutti's garden gone?"

"A winter storm nearly wiped it out about five years ago, so Anna built a new one over on the other side of the house. Built a big, fancy greenhouse too. I hear she really loves that green-house. Breeds hybrids, experiments with grafting. You're proba-bly not going to recognize a single worker on the place anymore, Andy. All the old ones are gone, retired, or left to look for differ-ent work when your sisters started to modernize seriously. My cousin Jesse Hamlin works here now and says it suits him just fine."

Charlie parked the car near a walkway and, having hopped out, opened the trunk to remove the luggage. Tu slid out her side, Luke followed her, and I stepped out of mine, but Andy didn't budge. "It's huge," Luke enthused, as Tu nodded anxiously.

Charlie slapped him on the back. "Biggest house in the county still. Your aunts make sure of that."

One of the sisters stood in a window and called to the other. "Andy," I warned.

"Yeah. I know," he said, but still wouldn't move.

Charlie lifted some luggage onto the porch. I carried the rest. Wearing a plain blue dress too matronly for her face, the sister who had been standing in the window walked out the front door. Her long yellow hair had been tightly braided and circled her head like a tiara. The knuckles of her fingers, tightly clasped together, touched under her chin. "Anna!" she called into the house. "Anna, come!"

Dressed in work slacks and a baggy sweater, her hair cropped close, Anna strolled out of a different door, one closer to where Charlie had parked the car. She stared long and intently at Luke, who didn't flinch from her gaze. "Yes. Yes," she said. "There's no doubt. You're my brother's son."

"I agree. I agree completely," Louisa said.

Anna drew Tu to her and kissed her cheek like a sister. "Thank you for bringing him to us."

"We are overjoyed to see you both," Louisa said, hugging Luke. "This moment is a dream neither of us would have imagined even just a few weeks ago."

"Andy," Anna said. "Are you all right? You don't look well."

"I hate that blue. It belongs in a swimming pool."

"We think it's pretty. You'll get used to it."

"Mutti must have had a fit."

"We haven't met," Anna said to me.

"I'm Michael. Michael Benedetti. I came along for the ride. I hope you don't mind."

"Of course not," Louisa said.

"I'll help you haul all this luggage into the house," Charlie offered.

"There's no need," Anna said. "You mustn't give us one more minute of your Sunday, Charlie."

"Glad to do it," Charlie said.

"Charlie's leaving now," Anna said to her brother.

"Where's Mutti?"

"I told you on the phone she's not been well for some time. She's in her new room, what used to be the parlor. We transformed it into her bedroom when it was obvious she needed one downstairs. We built another bathroom for her close by. She's quite content, I'm sure. She's eager to see you. Don't be pigheaded, Andy. Charlie wants to leave."

Slowly, Andy opened the car door. "You've redecorated the inside too?"

"Of course," Anna said. "We've changed everything."

Charlie jumped into his car. "Catch you all later." He waved heartily as he backed down the drive.

After Charlie's car disappeared down the road, Louisa said, "We thought we'd give Tu Mutti's old room and Luke you should have Aaron's, of course, and you yours, Andy, while you're here. I suppose Michael could take the back guest room. It has a wonderful view of our new garden, Michael. It's a very pretty little room really, though a bit spare right now. We didn't know we'd be having the pleasure of your company, you see. Andy didn't choose to tell us."

"No," Andy said. "That arrangement won't work. Michael sleeps with me."

"Oh," Louisa said tremulously.

Luke grasped his mother's hand and whispered louder than he intended, "See?"

Anna glowered at me, at her brother, at me again. "Interesting. Well, Andy." She picked up one of Tu's boxes to carry up-stairs. "Who would have thought?"

"Not me, for one," I said, wondering how vividly I was blushing.

After he'd laid our suitcase down next to the bed, Andy groused, "This isn't my room. I want you to know that. This is not what my room ever looked like. It's only the room where my room once was." He kicked the door closed and, grabbing my shirt, yanked me to him, kissed me fiercely, then turned away to-ward a window. He jerked on a cord to open the curtains. "If it has to be this dismal a day, I wish it would rain. I wish it would storm." With a finger, he wrote "Aaron" on a windowpane. "You Benedettis hide all your dead in faraway churchyards, don't you? We Odoms keep ours at home. Let's take a walk, Michael."

Two imposing cypresses stood guard on either side of a gate that creaked as we opened it. Every grave was decorated with flowers. "There's my father's," Andy said, "and there's Mother's right next to him."

"Your ancestors enjoyed admonitory Latin inscriptions, didn't they?"

A harsh wind shook the leaves of a house-high, cone-shaped magnolia. "Excuse me," Andy said and circled halfway around its skirt, out of my view. A single raindrop splashed my face, then another and another. In a few seconds, it was pouring, the rain gripping the skin as cold as sleet. But I didn't call to Andy be-cause I believed I knew where he was. I could see him tracing the letters of his brother's name carved into marble. I could hear him praying, saying his brother's name over and over as he fingered the petals of a rose like the beads of a rosary. In my mind's eye I could see him. In my mind's ear I could hear him. But I also knew that what I saw and heard were undoubtedly fantasies, not what Andy was saying or doing at all.

I waited for him, getting wetter and wetter. When he came back into view, he slipped on a down slope of the slick grass and was able to check his fall only by grasping hold of the sword-bearing arm of a statue that stood on a black marble pedestal. He laughed out loud. "This one was shot in an ambush during the Civil War. You'd never know it from the way he's holding that sword behind him, getting ready to order the charge. Meet Great-great-grandfather, Michael. His nose and mine are almost identical, aren't they?" he said, posing so that I might observe how his right profile reproduced his forefather's.

"Let's go in, Andy. I'm soaked to the skin."

"In a minute. Follow me. I want to show you something."

I read the name on the headstone aloud. "Aaron Rose Odom." At the foot of the grave someone had placed a rifle, barrel down, in a soldier's boot and crowned its stock with a helmet.

"Crazy Charlie." He shook his head. "Well, there's no sense in my letting it get ruined by this rain. Besides, I don't want Luke to see it." He disassembled the memorial, gathered its pieces, and cradled them in his arms. "Someday I may tell him about his father and me, about why Aaron's here. But not now."

We climbed to the house's second floor by outside steps and entered through a door at the end of the second-floor hall. Luke was racing down it as if he were running the forty-yard dash. "I've never seen so many rooms. But it's so empty," he said. "Where are all the other people?"

"It's Sunday," Andy said, "a day of rest."

"Mom has a really bad headache," Luke said. "I don't think she likes it here. You two are dripping all over the rug." He turned to race the other way.

"Luke?" Andy hollered after him. The boy stopped fast and spun around. "Do you think you could be happy here?"

He shrugged. "It depends on Mom." Dashing down the hall, he almost collided with Anna who was carrying fresh towels and sheets in her arms.

She stared at the rifle, helmet, and boot Andy was still hold-ing. "Why did you bring those home with you, Andy? What for?"

"They're Charlie's," Andy said.

"Oh?" She sighed heavily. "Well, keep them out of my sight. By the way, Mutti's already met Luke. She's proclaimed him a very clever boy, quick and smart. Dinner's at six every night. Our cook insists on being home by seven-thirty, without fail. Grandmother wonders why you're avoiding her," she said and marched into a room just a few steps away.

Andy and I stripped out of our soaked clothes in his bathroom. He pulled back the shower curtain. "Plenty of room." He grabbed my butt and drew me into the stall. "It'll prepare you for Grandmaw," he said.

For my presentation to her, I dressed in a shirt and tie I'd borrowed from Paul and a pair of Carlo's wool slacks that fit better than I would have thought, some of my lingering muscle substituting for Carlo's emerging flab. I donned one of Carlo's best jackets. "I'm ready, I guess."

"Try to relax," Andy said. "My grandmother can smell fear."

"So you've said."

"There's no reason to be scared of her."

"You are."

"That's different. I'm family."

He paused outside her door downstairs for several seconds. Then he took a deep breath and tapped on the door, but opened it without waiting for an answer. I followed him in. His grandmother sat in a wheelchair. A thick blanket covered her lap and legs. Several shawls were draped over her shoulders. A turban like a silent-screen star's crowned her head. She glanced up at Andy and laughed. "Son, you're almost as bald as I am. Doreen!" she ordered a woman in a nurse's uniform who sat in a corner chair reading *Cosmopolitan.* "Bourbon for these two gentlemen and myself. See what old age has accomplished, Son? It's made me thirsty. I've never been so thirsty in my life."

Her grandson bent to kiss her forehead. "How are you really, Mutti?"

"Bored. Bored. Bored. They even took my piano away. I couldn't play it anymore. But I enjoyed looking at it. Anna said they needed the room for that ridiculous bed over there. Nonsense."

"I see they haven't moved Great-grandfather. He's still glaring down from above."

"They wouldn't dare." She winked at me. "You know, it used to be rumored in town that I was his love child. But now that I've managed to outlive all the old gossips and biddies, I'm told no one spreads that story anymore. More's the pity. All my life, even after my marriage to his son, I've wished it were true. Sit down, Andy, your fidgeting is making me uncomfortable. You too, whoever you are," she commanded me.

"This is Michael," Andy said.

"Michael Benedetti, Mrs. Odom," I said. She ignored my offered hand.

"Benedetti? Have you ever heard any decent Italian music since Scarlatti?" she challenged me. "Because there isn't any. Not a bar."

"You'll like him, Mutti," Andy said. "You'll have a lot to talk to him about. Michael's a priest."

"Andy," I protested. "Please."

She regarded me dubiously. "You are, are you?"

"Technically, yes, I am, but . . ."

"Technically, technically. What does that abysmal word mean?" She'd pronounced it as if it were fit only to spit. "Horowitz was technically a great pianist. Heifetz was technically a great violinist. I suppose I am technically still alive. Would the both of you please stop looming over me? There's a couch right behind you. Sit! Where's Doreen?"

I sat on one end of the couch next to the arm, but Andy, rather than choosing to sit next to the other arm, sat down next to me, provocatively pressing his right thigh against my left. If I tried to move a fraction of an inch away, he squeezed even closer.

The nurse brought us our drinks generously poured into tumblers that rested on a tray. She served Andy's grandmother first, then Andy, then me. Mutti lifted her glass as high as her diminished reach allowed. "To life," she said. "As you can see, I still can claim one limb that almost works. So, Michael, tell me. Have you ever noticed how all novels are too long? Novels are like symphonies. They're garrulous. I've never known one that oughtn't to have been shorter. Do you like Haydn, Michael?"

"I don't know much about music, Mrs. Odom."

"Aren't all Italians born singing? Well, let me tell you, even Papa Haydn went on too long. The secret to art is to know when to call it quits. You should have learned to play an instrument, Andy. Then you could play something for me now. Radios, record players are poor substitutes for real music. Aaron had true talent, I think, but he wasn't ambitious enough to have established a career. But who knows? He and Drew and I once played an Archduke that was nearly perfect, almost as good as the Brahms op. 99 that Andrew and I once performed to no audience but ourselves alone. How have you been, Andy? You look tired."

"It was a long night's flight. It's been a long day."

"You know that isn't what I meant." Her elbow banged the arm of her wheelchair. "I despise this contraption. I don't sleep at all anymore. 'Sleep no more. Macbeth has murdered sleep.' Wouldn't I like to, just for revenge?"

"Do you still read, Mutti?"

"Read? Oh yes, I can still read. But I don't bother with anything new. I dislike everything new. You've seen how Anna and Louisa have transmogrified this house, inside and out. They waited until they'd safely imprisoned me in this room before they began their hideous transformations, let me tell you."

"Do you still like to read music?"

"Yes. Occasionally. What's this about, Andrew?"

"Not much. By chance, I met an older man about eight years ago, a composer. He'd been wounded in the Second World War. I did him what he thought was a favor and in return he gave me a score of something he'd composed. I thought I might like to try to arrange to have it performed. I brought it with me. I'd like to know what you think."

"I'll be tactlessly honest, if need be," she warned.

"I know that."

"Then I'll do it. What's this man's name?"

"No one's ever heard of him, but you might recognize the name, Mutti. Let's call him Anonymous until you've read what he's written."

"You've become cunning, Andy. I rather enjoy that. I agree." Andy put his arm over my shoulder and drew me still closer. His grandmother's eyes glittered. "But don't bother to try to shock me. Classical emotion between men has always intrigued me, provided it is noble and Apollonian and devoid of all Dionysian vulgarity." She sat back in her chair, as proud of herself as anyone could be. "Bring me that score. I'll have it read when next I see you. Doreen," she called out, "pour us another drink. My grandson's home. I want to celebrate."

Andy released his grip on me. "No more for me, Mutti."

"No? Too bad. I suppose you'll want to leave now. Well, leave then. I can't say I blame you. I've become an old bore, haven't I? Just ask Doreen. But, before you go, I must tell you that, if that boy is going to live here, he will have to take the Odom name. I'll make no other demands. But that one I insist upon. You understand," she said to me, "despite what my darling granddaughters have done to this house and this farm, they both still belong to me." She winked mischievously at her grandson. "I could surprise them and leave it all to you, you know. I still might, Andy."

"If you left me anything, I'd give it to Anna and Louisa anyway, so you might as well not bother."

"Fool. You've become a bit of a fool, Andy. I don't enjoy that at all."

"Maybe so." He kissed her cheek. "I'll bring you that score right after supper."

"Andrew?" she called to him as he opened the door. He turned back to face her. "I've loved you most of all."

"I know that. I've always known that, Grandmother. I've loved you, too," he said as he retreated into the hall.

"What's going on, Andy?" I said to him after we'd returned to his room. "Why am I, why are we on display? I feel like Exhibit A."

"Sorry. You're right. It was a desperate gesture, badly executed and insulting to you. You can't provoke my grandmother. You can't scare her. She's right. There's no use trying. I shouldn't have come. I should have just put Tu and Luke on that plane without me. Without us."

I snuggled next to him, our heads resting on the same pillow. "I haven't slept in what feels like days. My head is dizzy from three crowded flights and one waterless, iceless, and I'd bet a hundred and ten proof whiskey. How long have we known each other? Two weeks? Or is it more like two days? OK, so what? Who knows why, but suddenly I feel blessed with conviction. I know I want to be with you the rest of my life, to live with you and sleep with you and love you all the rest of our days." The frost on the windowpanes might have been snowy hills jutting up into a beautifully pure black night. "Andy?"

His fingers gently scratched my back. "Listen, Michael. Two or three times a week I wake up in the middle of the night in shock because I'm bleeding. My nose, ears, mouth are all oozing blood. It's seeping out of my ass. And everything inside me, all my bones and muscles and organs are dripping blood. My skin is sweating blood. I don't want anyone else to have to live with that."

"I love you, Andy."

"I'm grateful. I think I love you too, Michael. But I don't know much about love. I thought I loved my brother, but I couldn't have, could I? I thought I loved my grandmother. I thought I loved . . . listen to that old owl hoot, Michael. Tomorrow I want to show you my woods and the river, all right?"

Late that night, close to morning, several telephones rang at once in different parts of the house, shrill and insistent. But no one answered them. "A wrong number," Andy assured me. "No one would ever deliberately call the house at this hour. No one would dare." But the persistent ringing had alarmed us both, and neither of us fell back to sleep but instead we waited impatiently for the birds' first songs.

But dawn came slow. Even before the sun rose, Andy and I had fixed our breakfast and left the house just as the cook arrived from town. The bed of her banged-up pickup was piled with logs for the four fireplaces. When the sun finally appeared, it painted the whole sky winter-white, the clouds sparkling like fresh snow. Over the entrance to the dairy, tall letters cut from large milk pails spelled out ODOM SISTERS DAIRIES. They swayed in the breeze like huge wind chimes, bonging and clanging pleasantly against one another. Workmen were leading cows to pasture. From inside the buildings we could hear the sound of engines whirring smoothly.

We hiked all morning, sometimes along the river's winding banks, more often following only the still accurate maps imprinted in Andy's memory. Whether we were trekking through thick forests or across open fields, Andy never lost his way. He showed me hidden creeks, secret woods, untilled fields. He told me the name of this tree, that bush, this bird, that wild animal's track. He found us delicious nuts to eat. We explored dark caves and rushing streams. I was the tourist, he the native guide. And like most guides he became more real, more vivid with every new thing he showed me.

Yet, however far from the house we had hiked each day, Andy would always make certain that we turned back in time to reach his home by dinner. Unlike the other two meals, dinner remained an Odom ceremony, even though Andy's grandmother no longer participated. Instead, she took her meals alone, assisted by her nurse. In the dining room, Anna sat at one end of the table, the end, Andy informed me, once reserved for Mutti. Louisa sat at the other. Luke, we were told, would sit across from Tu. I would sit across from Andy. Our dinners were as friendly as they were orderly. Yet our conversations were seldom more than chitchat and small talk, strained and dull. Occasionally Tu and Luke would communicate through a furtive glance or smile. Everyone was ill at ease, especially Anna and Louisa. They politely directed questions to each of us in turn and always appeared interested in the answers. But they inquired only about matters of fact or taste. What work did Andy do on the ranch? Did he like it? Where had he lived before? Had he liked it there as well? Did California suit Luke? Did it, they would inquire through her son, please Tu? What were Luke's favorite subjects in school? What did he want to be when he grew up? Whom did he most admire among his contemporaries? Had I enjoyed what I'd seen of the farm? How would I compare it to my parents' ranch? How did it affect the dairy cows there to graze not so far from so many cattle raised for slaughter? Had Andy noticed the improvements in the stable? Question after question passed from one sister to the other and back again as if each were reading off a cue card the questions they'd previously agreed upon. They never directly talked about themselves and responded to our questions even more tersely than we did to theirs. No one talked about Mutti. None of the Odoms mentioned their father or mother. Aaron's name was never spoken.

Yet Anna and Louisa clearly adored Luke. They doted and fawned so uncharacteristically, Andy said, that it made him want to laugh. In response, Luke followed one or the other of them everywhere they went, whether to the dairies, the fields, or the garden and greenhouse. They hugged him and kissed him and brushed his hair. They gifted him with almost every small object he'd admire, praising his taste: a tiny carved wooden horse, a fish etched and painted on glass, a nutcracker in the form of a dancing bear, a leather change purse with a leather pull string. One night, just before bed, he brought us a small toy box he'd found and laid out all his new treasures on our bed for us to envy. He was thrilled when Andy told him the old toy box had once belonged to Aaron.

Every day, Tu looked more dismal and proud. When Andy cautiously asked her what it was she really wanted, her gestures alone made it clear that she believed Luke must stay and she must leave. When Andy inquired, "How will you live, Tu?" her face ceased being her own. She'd put on a mask that she wore for most of the rest of the day. Whenever we invited her to join us on one of our hikes, she declined by kissing her fingers and delicately touching us both just beneath our eyes. She spent most of her days and nights alone. Several times we saw her walking only a few hundred feet away from us, but when we called to her she did not acknowledge us. One afternoon, returning from her travels, she was clutching close to her bosom a beautifully shaped stone, a curiously curved twig, a fragment of an animal bone, a leaf that rot had spared. Luke had said that Cam had told him that Tu Loc was the name she assumed when she began to work for money from the Americans. Since Tu was also the name his father had known her by, she chose never to reveal her real name or to tell anyone about her life before those times. She visited Aaron's grave always alone, though one afternoon her son followed her. After she'd left, he discovered beneath his father's stone another much smaller, but more beautiful stone, a lovely twig, a fine piece of bone, a whole brown leaf, and he brought me and Andy there to show us.

The morning after our interview with Andy's grandmother, Anna informed us that Mutti had fallen suddenly, seriously ill. When Andy snuck into her room to see for himself, he found her lying in bed, frail, gaunt, feverish, and vulnerable. After Doreen, who had left the room for a smoke on the porch, caught him there, she scolded him and shooed him away. Every morning early, every afternoon late, a doctor appeared from town and always left with no report of a change. Although Andy clearly was worried about her, he said nothing to me. But his relief was obvious when several hours after supper on the last day of our visit Doreen reported to him that his grandmother was much better and wanted to see him right away.

"You've been summoned," I said. "You go alone this time. I'll just be in the way."

"No," he said as he changed into a fresh shirt. "I want you there with me."

She was sitting up in bed, her neck cushioned with many pillows, all soft and white, her maroon turban matching the maroon trim on her blue silk robe. On a bedtray was spread the score Andy had asked her to read. Her face was sallow, still waxy from illness, but her eyes glinted like crystal. Andy bowed and kissed her offered hand. "Each time I pry open death's iron door, God slams it in my face. I don't deserve such insults from the Almighty," she said. Regarding me crossly, she demanded, "Why are you here?"

As I turned to leave, Andy shoved me back into the room. "Michael stays."

"Very well, if you insist, but I don't think I care for this new stubborn streak, Andrew. It's like a child's. If you wish to defy me, fine. Defy me. But do it with some spirit." She slapped a hand down on the manuscript, held a few sheets up in the air, and shook them angrily. "As for this dreck, this Slavic self-pity, this Semitic sentimentality, this maudlin whining, this formless, tawdry romantic mush and hum, this preposterous assemblage of vaudeville tunes fit only for some crooner in blackface, destroy it. Whoever wrote it will benefit most not from any performance but only from its destruction. You understand?"

"Yes, Mutti. You've been completely clear. You've always been clear."

"Burn it." She swept the sheets off her tray onto the floor. "How much better the world would be if only more such trash were thrown into the fires that refine everything into oblivion." Sinking deeper into her pillows, she forced the tray away from her lap and ordered Andy to set it down on the carpet, next to her wheelchair. "Step closer, Andrew. I have something very important to ask of you."

He leaned over her, hovering, his shadow on the wall stooped like an old man's as he listened intently. As he gripped a post to stand back up, the bed creaked. He shook his head angrily. "No."

"You refuse? Me?"

"Yes. I do."

"You can't refuse. It is your duty." She clutched his shirt. "I loved no one more than that great and noble man," she said, pointing to the life-sized portrait on the wall. "No one. I owe all my life to him, my very existence, everything precious life has meant. But, when he asked of me what I have asked of you, I didn't falter. I didn't hesitate for an instant. I did what he expected of me. Out of love. Out of devotion and gratitude and love. You used to shine, Andy. The old Odom fire burned so bright in you and you alone. Why did you let it burn out?" She glared at me. "You, priest. This is what I think of humility." She spat on the floor. Why did so common, so vulgar a gesture appear in her so majestic? She might have been an ancient queen dismissive of a poor peasant who had dared to approach her person.

"I'm not a priest," I objected pointlessly.

"You can't fool me. You reek of clericalism and submission and alarm. But the noble soul needs only form. That's all it requires of God. Just form," she declared, her words not so much spoken as willed into being in defiance of her body's ruins. "One Bach fugue, even the least wondrous, suffices to account for all suffering. Do you understand, priest? The brave don't need prayers. They don't need hope. They only need someone to give them the gift of their death."

"Don't blame Michael for my refusal, Grandmother. He doesn't know anything about it."

"I would have given you everything, Andrew. Everything." She beat one arm weakly against her covers. "If only there had been just one spark left. Just one spark and not everything in your soul gone to ash. You might have freed me. Then everything would have been yours, as by all rights it should have been." She turned her face away from him and to the wall.

Andy kissed her cheek, but she did not move or in any other way acknowledge the gesture. Squatting awkwardly, we gathered the sheets of the scattered score off the floor and attempted to reassemble them in order to make sure no pages were lost. I handed the last sheet I'd found to Andy. He flipped through the stack and slipped it in where it belonged.

"Michael and I will be returning to California tomorrow morning, Grandmother," he said near the door. "I'll say good-bye to you before we go."

Her fingers explored the bindings of several books that sat in shelves across from her bed. "You mustn't bother," she ordered him.

Back in his room, he stared out the window toward where, if it had been light, he could have seen the cemetery. "She wants a Roman death. I'm to hold the sword. She quoted the family motto to me. In Latin, of course. She whispered to me the secret means by which she'd killed my great-grandfather. She's right. It would be very easy and almost painless and leave no sign. I've done it before. I was trained to, during the war. Aren't my family's traditions enviable, Michael?"

"I can't pretend to understand them, Andy."

"Are you scared, Michael, scared I might still do it for her?"

"Let's go to bed," I begged. "Just stay here with me until it's time for us to leave."

"Death is so simple really," Andy said. "Any soldier could tell you that. Once you get the hang of it, once you catch on to its few simple little tricks, there's nothing easier."

"You're frightening me, Andy."

"I'm a scary guy. That's what I've been trying to tell you, Michael. It's not my fault if you haven't wanted to listen."

After midnight, without having knocked, Tu slipped into our room. She stood by the foot of the bed, her body as alert as a garden statue in the glow of moonlight. We both sat up, although because we were naked neither of us got out of bed to turn on a light.

Andy said, "What is it, Tu? What's wrong?"

She started to hum. The melody repeatedly turned downward, its pitches at the end of each phrase bent and strange. It was a faraway tune, neither happy nor sad, of some distant place, some long ago time. Perhaps, I guessed, a song of farewell. When she was done, she covered her eyes. Before either of us could respond, she'd vanished from the room. Had she already sung it to Luke?

"Do you have any money at all, Michael?"

"No."

"This evening, Louisa said to me that she and Anna have become so accustomed to solitude that she's certain Luke will find them quite dull in a very short time. 'Have we been selfish?' she asked. 'Please don't misunderstand. We haven't meant to be. It's so strange how loneliness suits us. Except to accomplish our work and chores, we hardly ever speak even to each other anymore. Luke has been a delight, of course, but Tu . . . that poor woman, Andy. It wouldn't be right. For so many reasons, it wouldn't be right. It would be like a prison for her here. But what else can we do? We owe it to Aaron and the peace of his soul.'" He inhaled the cold night air and massaged my tense shoulders and back. "I've saved eight thousand five hundred dollars and sixteen cents. To have the score my grandmother so happily loathed performed some day soon. I suppose I could steal some of it back to help us get started, until you and I have both found jobs." He got out of bed and put on his shorts. "I'm going to wake Luke. I want to talk to him."

It was almost dawn before Andy returned and crawled into bed. He draped his arm over my side and nestled in the curve of my back. His breath wasn't warm but chilly like the night air. "Luke said yes," he reported. "I assured him he could visit here whenever he liked. That pleased him and Tu. It looks like we'll be living in San Jose, Michael. That's where Luke told me Tu wants to stay."

I hesitated. "Andy?"

"She was waiting for me. She'd ordered Doreen out, I guess, knowing I couldn't disobey because I never had. I stared down at her in the dark, but she didn't move or flinch. She never acknowledged my presence in any way. But I knew she knew I was there. I couldn't do it. I tried. Several times I tried. But just as my hands began to touch her flesh I yanked them back. I couldn't do it not because I didn't want to but because I wanted to so bad. But, if Grandmother's going to walk laughing into her tomb, as she always said she would, she's going to have to walk there on her own. Michael? You've stopped breathing."

"I do that sometimes. I'm OK, Andy. I'm fine."

Before Charlie arrived in the morning, Luke, Tu, and Andy visited the cemetery one last time, their first visit together. Anna invited them into her greenhouse to pick flowers to place on Aaron's grave. I waited for Charlie with Louisa on the verandah. Both of us sat on the porch swing. The suitcases and boxes were already on the stoop, two more than we had brought with us. The morning was so balmy it might have been early spring.

"Grandmother used to complain all the time that my sister and I were afraid of life," Louisa said, breaking the silence between us, "that we were afraid to live it to the full. But I've never wanted to live life to the full, have you?"

"I don't think I'd have the nerve," I confessed.

"We've been very successful at business, of course, Anna and I. We make an excellent team. But that's not what Mutti meant. I used to dream of a romance during springtime in Tuscany." She giggled. "That's a secret, Michael. Please don't tell Andy. I find Mediterranean men to be so lovely and robust and alluring, don't you? Oh, my," she blushed. "I think I may have completely lost what little skill at polite conversation I'd ever known. I'm certain I've missed a lot in life, maybe even the best parts of it. But I'm really quite content. Do you love Andy, Michael?"

"Oh, yes."

"Andy isn't easy to love. He never was. But I love him too. So does Anna in her heart of hearts. You will tell him so, won't you? He wouldn't believe either of us."

"I'll try."

"Good." She took my hand. "I hope my sister and I haven't appeared rude. I must go in now. I've baked some cookies for Luke and I want to wrap them."

"Well, Luke," Anna said to him after Charlie had appeared and Luke, Tu, and Andy had returned from the cemetery. "We were very pleased to meet you, Nephew." She handed him the cookies that Louisa had just handed her, wrapped like Christmas treats.

"Mother wasn't happy here," Luke said to both sisters. "I couldn't leave her."

Anna patted his head. "We know."

Andy stooped to pick up the last box, filled with Luke's treasures. "We'd better hustle," Charlie hollered from the driver's seat.

I stepped onto the walkway. Andy followed me, but paused as I continued ahead. Turning back, he said, "I'm sorry."

"Yes," Anna acknowledged. "We know."

"I wish I could talk to Father," Andy said. "I've tried. Maybe now I can."

"Only Aaron ever really could, Andy. It was the music," Anna said. She clasped his shoulder. "Take good care of Luke. And Tu."

Honking the horn, Charlie shouted, "Hey, Andrew! Let's get going, gang, what do you say?"

Once Andy had joined us in the car, Charlie backed slowly down the drive. Just as he began to turn onto the road, Andy's grandmother's nurse threw open the front door to the house and raced down the walk, yelling, "Wait! Wait!" She knocked on his window until Andy rolled it down. "Here," she said, forcing an envelope on him. "I almost forgot. She would have killed me." She stood back up. "No one pays me enough for this."

Cows were crossing the road from one pasture to another. A flicker drilled a tree high overhead. After Andy had opened the envelope and read the note, he crumpled it up into a ball. "Got a match, Charlie?" Charlie handed him a lighter from his coat pocket. Andy lit the paper and dropped it, burning, onto the pavement. As Charlie drove forward, a gust picked up the black ash, swirled it about, and scattered tiny pieces of soot behind us.

Late that night, back in San Jose, Andy and I once more slept on the floor at Tu and Luke's. The next day the four of us hunted for a new place to live. By afternoon, we'd rented a small duplex near the university, not too far from downtown. Luke and Tu chose the left side, we took the right.

By the time we moved in, Andy was working as a substitute driver for UPS. He'd stabled Suzy on a farm less than twenty miles away, close enough for him to ride her several times a week. After a long month looking for a job, I was hired by a small accounting firm whose offices sat over a Paulist bookstore in an old brick building downtown. I chose not to notify the archdiocese of my whereabouts and made all my family promise to stay mum. At the beginning of the new semester, Luke enrolled in a new school. Anna and Louisa had offered to pay his tuition to a private one. Luke liked the prospect at first. But, after a long talk with Andy, he decided to say no. He seemed to enjoy the new public one well enough. With Andy's encouragement, Tu had begun to learn sign language at a special institute. One morning she handed us a long note written in her own hand. "How long have you known how to write, Tu?" Andy asked.

She took back the pad and pencil. "Cam taught me. In Saigon."

A week after Easter, Andy flew to New York again to arrange for the concert. After he'd discussed his plans with Aaron's sister Miriam over the phone, she advised secrecy in the preparation. "He'll only worry," she'd said. "He'll only fret. Let's spare him that."

Andy found a conductor by attending cheap concerts in New York for a week. After each one, he'd approach its director with his proposal. One, Max Appleman, finally agreed, even before he'd read the score because he'd been so moved when Andy told him Aaron's story. After he'd read it, fired with enthusiasm, he hired the tenor first, a young cantor with some experience singing opera. "A young Jan Peerce!" Max had gushed to Andy. Andy reported to me over the phone that he didn't have the heart to tell Max he'd never heard of Jan Peerce, but Miriam had and she was excited. The three instrumentalists were all friends of Max. After Max had reviewed the score with them, a small, largely amateur chorus from Brooklyn agreed to learn it. For a modest fee, Andy rented an auditorium belonging to the synagogue next door and arranged with a printing shop to print posters and programs. He called several newspapers to place ads for the event the week before the third Wednesday in June. Max offered to solicit several critics he thought would attend.

Andy had just returned from New York the Sunday before when Catherine appeared at our door early on a Saturday morning. She was holding a philodendron with a broad blue ribbon tied around its pot. She handed it to me. "It began as a cutting from Mother's."

"How nice, Catherine. Thank you." I set it down on the floor and glanced out to the Ford on the drive. "You drove yourself?"

"I've been given a gracious reprieve, if that's what I should call it. Even my doctors agree. All in good time, I suppose. Right now, I feel quite wonderful and very strange." She stepped in. "This is very nice, Michael."

"Small."

"Tiny, I'd say. Here," she said, opening her purse and offering me a package. "From Mother."

I unwrapped the tissue paper. "My first catechism. And the rosary Aunt Anita gave me when I was confirmed. She won't give up, will she?"

Catherine pinched my cheek. "Why should she? Now, show me the rest of the place. And when might I meet Luke and Tu?"

As I opened a drawer to put the rosary and catechism away, our phone rang. Andy rushed into the kitchen from the back-yard to answer it. "Anna," he said. "Yes. What is it?" Although I had turned away from her toward Andy, I could sense Catherine watching me as I listened to Andy listening to his sister. Many long minutes passed before Andy said, "Anna, don't cry. You never cry. Never. Please, Anna, tell me what she said. Are you certain? I don't believe she meant you, Anna. She wrote the same word down on a slip of paper and sent it to me via her courier Doreen just as I was leaving the farm. Yes, that's the truth. Of course it was a terrible thing for Mutti to do. I know how frightening it must have been for you to have to listen to her. But I'm sure she wasn't addressing you, Anna. You said yourself she was almost raving. Maybe she was thinking about me. Or maybe, just maybe, she was condemning herself. I know that's not likely. But think what it might mean, Anna, just think of what it might mean for all of us if it were what she was saying. Try to stop crying, Anna. And, Anna? Do me a favor. Wait until next Saturday to bury her, will you? I want to be there, but I can't afford to miss any more work."

"I'm so sorry, Andy," I said to him as he entered the living room.

"Hello, Catherine. My grandmother," he explained to her. "Apparently she had a bad death. My sisters are very upset."

"What was her name?" Catherine inquired.

"Elisabeth Reinertz Willingham Odom."

"I'll pray for her," Catherine promised.

"Thank you, but I don't think she'd want you to." Andy sat down on a rugged old couch we'd bought at Goodwill and rubbed his face. "Her last word was coward, Michael. She couldn't stop saying it over and over. Coward, coward, coward. I'm certain she meant me. I could have spared her the agony."

"Catherine?" I glanced back over my shoulder.

"Yes. I understand."

Only after she had quietly closed the door behind her did Andy start sobbing.

It is early evening on the fourth Saturday of May in 1984. Tu has recently decided to dedicate her life to flowers, planting, growing, nurturing, and arranging them. She wants to make a career out of them, and, because she is very talented, I think she'll succeed. Already she has shown her arrangements to a few shops where she left her name and phone number. We are all hopeful that soon one might call. She is kneeling, crouching over her narrow plot in one corner of our backyard. As she weeds, she shakes the dirt off the roots before she sets them aside on a sheet of newspaper.

Squinting in the half-light, Luke lies on the grass reading an illustrated book from his school's library on tropical fish. When he sees a picture of a fish he particularly admires, he claps his bare feet. He is saving every week from his allowance to buy a ten-gallon tank for his room.

Andy is planing a door that rests on two sawhorses so that it will open and close more smoothly. He is wearing only shorts and sneakers. His desolate beauty thrills me.

I'm grilling vegetables and fish fillets over a large hibachi for supper. Rice is cooking in the kitchen behind me.

The acacia are golden in twilight. Scared by a cat that lurks on a fence, a blackbird, flapping its wings furiously, flies out of a tree. The sky is a cloudless silvery rose. I follow the bird's flight until, smaller than a speck, it vanishes from sight.

In the kitchen, I spoon the rice onto plates, bring them outdoors, and pile them with grilled fish, mushrooms, onions, sliced carrots, potatoes, and zucchini, and chunks of green and red peppers. Tu and Andy wash their hands with the garden hose. Luke doesn't bother. Sitting cross-legged on the lawn, watching the twilight dissolve into night, we eat without talking. A neighbor turns on his backyard floodlight. When we've finished eating, Andy gathers the plates, cups, and forks to wash in the kitchen sink. "A feast," he says to me as he strolls through the open glass door.

I stand up to scratch my knee, which is itching from the grass. Luke is describing to Tu a girl whose name is Jo Lynn. He has just met her, during the last days of the semester. He says he's in love. His mother in turn frowns and giggles merrily.

Another cat leaps over the fence into our yard. Its teeth pierce the body of a bird it's just pounced on. Tu seizes the cat by its neck and forces its mouth open until it drops the bird. She holds it tenderly in her hands as, dying, the bird flutters and trembles. Once its heart has stopped beating, she digs a grave for it with her trowel and buries it.

When Andy walks back outside, he kneels next to her. Luke tells him what has just happened. Andy waits until she has stopped shaking before he puts one arm around her shoulder. "Tomorrow we'll plant some bulbs there," Luke says.

Can any loss ever be redeemed? The neighbors switch off

their floodlight. A crescent moon is rising over the trees. Its waning edge is as smooth as the lip of a cup. Andy shivers. Luke rubs his sides against the air, chilled by a touch of fog in the west. The four of us stand in a row to admire the moon. It could be an ancient barge riding the sky like a sea. I am so happy I can almost believe we might all embark on a boat like that someday and sail hopefully to who knows where.

Joshua Aaron Rose

I hurt. I always hurt. If only pain would turn its countenance away from me, if only it would leave me alone, if only I might not see its face for a day or two, I might find a little rest, some peace, succor. But even as I sleep it grips me. It rips and tears my flesh. It gnaws on my genitals.

It's a hot, muggy June day, the miserable kind of day when flakes of the city cling to your sweaty skin. The heat magnifies everything. Like a megaphone, it amplifies all sounds. The square is a racket: guitars, drums, a couple of saxes, people shrieking, police whistles blowing, horns honking, a jackhammer attacking cement. Uselessly, I clap my hand over my good ear. All afternoon, I struggle to suppress the urge to scream.

Early evening, Miriam enters my room. As she starts to unbutton my shirt, I ask, "What are you doing?"

"You need to look nice," she says. "You're going out."

I hate surprises. Why shouldn't the unexpected frighten me? I grab the rim of the wheel of my chair. "It's almost six. No doctor would see me this late."

"We're not going to the doctor's, Aaron. This time, it's something nice." She tosses my dripping shirt onto the floor, wipes my torso with a towel, and slips a colorful silk shirt on. "There," she says, buttoning it. "That's better."

My teeth clench. "Where are we going?"

David knocks on the door but as always walks in without waiting for a response. "Is he ready?"

"He's in a foul mood. He's been snitty all day," my sister reports to her husband.

I want to say, My right stump is throbbing, my left side is being torn by pincers, my bladder is full of sharp rocks.

David says, "Maybe he's not up to this."

"This what?" I demand.

"Frankly, Aaron," she says, drawing a line with her hand across her forehead, "I've had it up to here." Poor Miriam. She's suffered too. "It'll be a very nice surprise, I promise you."

David pushes me out of the room. I never go out except to talk to another pill merchant, high-priced frauds in white coats. My brother-in-law has double-parked his car in front of the building. As he backs my chair toward it, Susan and Dinah greet me. They both kiss my cheek. "Hi, Uncle Aaron," they say as one. They're grinning like children with a secret they're bursting to tell.

David lifts me into the passenger seat in front. I ask, "What's going on?"

"Be patient. You'll see soon," Miriam says, beaming.

We cross the Williamsburg Bridge and slowly drive through heavy traffic down Bedford Avenue in Brooklyn. At a big Catholic church, David takes a right, continues down the street for a few more blocks, turns left at a graffiti-infested playground, and five minutes later parks in front of a synagogue. Sunset reddens the sand-colored brick of its dome, but the same light reflected off its huge Star of David hurts my eye. David and Dinah carry me out of the car and seat me in my chair that Miriam has just unfolded. "We're going to temple?" I ask.

Dinah squeezes my shoulder, an old gesture of fondness I've never much cared for. "You could say so."

We move past the synagogue and pause at a broad walkway that leads to a school. It might be any school, gritty and black, although the sun's last rays still flicker in its upper windows. Down the street, outside a pizza parlor, three handsome boys dressed in sleeveless T-shirts and jeans that cling to their crotches like swimsuits flirt with four beautiful girls wearing billowing white blouses over ass-grabbing black skirts and stiletto heels. As they notice us approaching, they turn their backs. Across the street, a sickening bright green neon sign flashes over a discount-clothing store, discoloring the faces of all passersby.

"There's the door we want, I think," Miriam says to David.

The corridor inside could be the hallway of any public school. The same lockers might have lined any wall. The walls might have been deliberately painted the same watery cocoa. Monitors might have been guarding any entrance way.

A willowy, white-haired gentleman stands by a table next to a door and hands out fliers or perhaps a program of some kind to everyone who walks in. Dressed in the sort of black suit only ushers or undertakers ever wear, he is all smiles and courtesy. As we pass in front of him, he coughs nervously. We turn left and disappear down another, more poorly lit hall.

"Miriam?"

"All in good time, Aaron. You'll know soon enough."

Dinah giggles. "It's a concert, Uncle Aaron."

"Hush, Dinah," her sister Susan says.

"Concert? What sort of concert? I hate music. I hate it."

"Be patient just a few minutes longer," Miriam pleads. Her eyes look scared.

"Patient?" I snap. "Me?"

Susan pats my shoulder. "Don't be upset, Uncle Aaron." I dislike her pity. I dislike all pity. I dislike the way it lies. "We should go in now," she says to her mother.

"Peek in the door," Miriam suggests. "See if the auditorium is dark yet. I was told to wait until it's dark."

Susan checks. "It is," she reports.

"Good." Miriam takes a long, deep breath. "Well, then. Let's go in."

There's a space for my chair in the fifth row on the right side. David and Miriam sit to my left, my nieces behind me. After we're seated, Miriam excuses herself. When she returns, she touches my side and regards me nervously. "Oh, Aaron, I hope we all haven't made a huge mistake. I do hope this pleases you."

The auditorium is less than half full. About forty men and women, all wearing black choir robes over their street clothes, march in file onto the stage and take their places on the bleachers, the men in back and on the sides, the women in front and in the middle. Three men in dark suits follow them in, one carrying a violin, another a cello. The third sits down in front of a baby grand. A young man with a cherub's pink round face and a boyish grin stands in front of the choir. As the conductor enters with his score tucked under one arm, the audience applauds. He bows more grandly than the plain environment should allow and, standing rigidly erect, lifts his long arms. As his right arm moves, the violin plays its tune. Mikla's song, I used to call it. I mutter, "My God."

"Yes," Miriam whispers. "Yes."

How much do I manage really to hear? While the tenor sings his first solo, "I am the man that hath seen affliction by the rod of his wrath," my right stump throbs and throbs. A sharp pain presses against my chest. My whole left side's on fire. What did the boy who wrote this music know about suffering? I can't remember. I wouldn't want to guess.

How long does it last? An hour maybe. Too long. "Look, Uncle Aaron," Dinah directs me as the performers take yet another bow. "The audience won't stop applauding."

I do look. Who has come? All friends of the performers undoubtedly. No wonder they applaud. David stands up, grips the handles of my wheelchair, and pushes me down the aisle, up a ramp, and onto the stage where he abandons me. "David, don't you dare!" I holler into the wings. Even the choir, the instrumentalists, the tenor, and the conductor are applauding me. What could I do? I lift my right arm and wave. Cheering, the whole audience stands as one. Could they really have liked it? Someone steps across the stage behind me and places roses in my lap. He kisses my cheek. I look up at him. "Andy?"

As the lights of the theater come up, the applause slowly dies away. All the performers exit backstage, the audience out the rear doors. The conductor touches my chair. "It's been a great honor, Mr. Rose." He shakes my hand.

"Thank you."

"I'd like to see more of your work. I'd like to perform more."

"There isn't any more. I destroyed it all, all except this. I should have destroyed it."

"That's a pity, Mr. Rose."

"Why?" I challenge him. But he doesn't respond.

Andy beckons some people in the auditorium to join him on-stage. Headed by a tall boy, they march up in a line and form a semicircle in front of me. "This is Luke Smithson, my brother Aaron's son," Andy says introducing me to the boy first, "and this is his mother Tu Loc." She grins at me soberly, a fierce and appealing glint in her eyes. I do not pretend to understand but shake her hand anyway.

"I'm Aaron's sister Louisa," another woman says, stepping forward.

Much more than Andy does now, she resembles her father. "You look like Drew," I say and at once wish I hadn't.

She curtsies. "Why, thank you, sir. My sister Anna would have come too but she was reluctant to leave the farm unattended. Your music was very beautiful, Mr. Rose. It touched my heart."

"Did it?"

"Yes," she says, blushing. "Very much."

Andy combs his fingers gently through my hair. "This is Michael, Aaron." He tenderly grips the back of the man's neck. "Michael Benedetti, Aaron Rose."

As Tu Loc gestures with her hands, Andy interprets. "She is

very happy to have heard the music by the man after whom her Aaron was named." Although she nods emphatically, both she and her son draw closer to Michael. They all look anxious to leave.

I say, "It seemed very strange to me. Not mine at all."

"Aaron would have enjoyed meeting you," Louisa says. "He composed music too, you know."

"You're behind this, aren't you, Andy?" I say to him. "Well, I have a real favor to ask you." He bends closer to listen. "Wheel me to the men's room, boy. I need to pee."

After Andy rolls me back into the front hall, my cousin Samuel and his second wife and their two teenage daughters who have driven in from Trenton greet me, as do Judith and her son and daughter-in-law and their little baby boy who had all taken the train from Plainfield. "It was lovely, Aaron, just lovely. Beautiful, beautiful," they repeat over and over.

Andy and his group head for the door. "I'm flying to Italy tomorrow," Andy's sister announces to me. "All by myself. Isn't that daring? Rome, Florence, Perugia, and Rapallo. I couldn't be more excited."

"Italy can be very beautiful," I say. "When do you return to California, Andy?" I rub my hand against my chest in a vain attempt to still the pain that strikes and strikes against my ribs.

"Tomorrow also. We all have jobs to return to. Three days were all we could get off at the same time." He kisses my forehead. "Thanks so much, Aaron."

"I would like to have seen more of you, Andy. I really would."

"Next time," he promises.

"You're as lousy a correspondent as your father."

"I'll try to do better."

"I'd like that. Thanks, Andy. Thanks for this night. I mean that."

"You look more than usually glum," David observes as he lifts me from the car and sets me back down in my chair underneath a streetlight outside our apartment building across from Tompkins Square.

"Do I?"

"You're disappointed?" Dinah asks.

"No."

"It's those drums," Miriam says, staring off toward the sources of the worst of the noise. "All day, all night. It's more than anyone should have to bear."

Since May 13th of 1945, whenever I see my face in the mirror or look at my missing legs or arm, I say, "This isn't my body. That can't be me." But of course it is.

If the war had left me more nearly whole, what might I have done with these thirty-nine years? What might I have become? What pleasures might I have enjoyed? Whom might I have loved? If not Drew Odom, what man or men? Who, if anyone, might have loved me?

"You'd have been better off dead," David remarked to me shortly after I'd been carried into his home and immediately, uncontrollably peed in one of his beds. He apologized later, of course. David is not a bad man. But he's never stopped believing what he had said. Doesn't he understand that every day I think the same thought? The dead don't know what they've missed, but I know little else.

Again and again, Miriam has counseled me, "Be patient. Have patience." Patience for what? During the first months after I'd been returned to New York, I thought I might be able to live a tragic life, reading tragic plays, listening to tragic music, thinking about tragic art. Tragic wisdom would comfort my pain. It would instruct and console. But no wisdom came. The pain goes on and on.

"You can still make something good out of your life. You could still write music," Miriam used to say. "You have one good arm, one keen ear, your mind, your soul. It's enough." She was right about the arm and ear, of course, and maybe even about my mind. But she was wrong about my soul. It fled from me, appalled by what it saw as I lay in my hospital bed in Italy after it had already seen too much.

During the week after the concert, Miriam scans the daily papers in hopes of finding a review. But there is no review. After almost a month has passed, Max Appleman phones. "Who needs a review?" he says. "It was wonderful music. Many, many composers might struggle a whole lifetime and not write one such glorious score."

"I didn't write it, Max," I say.

"Don't talk nonsense."

"But I didn't," I protest. "Some kid did, not me."

"You'll change your mind. Wait until you hear the tape."

"What tape?"

"You didn't notice the microphones? Didn't Andy Odom tell you? He insisted we tape the concert. He wants to have a record made. With your permission, of course. His sister has agreed to pay for it."

David and Miriam rent me a tape player. Alone in my room, I listen as if for the first time. It's always a terrible shock to see or hear a ghost, especially if the ghost is the spirit of your own young self, long dead. What could possibly live on?

Very late that night, when even the park has grown still, I believe I can hear just beyond audibility the first hint of a new melody. In the morning, I ask Miriam to buy me a hundred sheets of music paper. All day and the next day and the day after that, I sit in front of a little table with the score paper spread out before me and a pencil in my hand. I wait.

Do I have patience for nothing? I pray to God. I pray to my pain.

Max Appleman

"How?":

A Conductor's Notes on Joshua Aaron Rose's
A Lion in Secret Places

Isn't all song, even the most despairing, a kind of hymn? But if God does not listen, if He will not hear, why does anyone sing? Yet what is more necessary to us than songs?

In Hebrew, *Lamentations* begins, "'Eikhah yashvah badad ha'ir." "How doth the city sit so solitary." Jerusalem lies in ruins. God has destroyed and abandoned His Holy City. Since Sumer, haven't men repeatedly mourned their ruined cities, lamented their solitude, grieved at how the Lord their protector has been more like an enemy? Now even the beauty of Israel is rubble. Mothers eat their children to whom they can't give suck. Covered in ritual ash, mourners lie dead in the dust. Priests have been murdered in God's sanctuary. The prophets are blind to vision. There is no Torah. The joy of the whole earth has been pitilessly cast down. Their bodies litter the streets. What prayer is there left to pray? Only qinoth, threnoi, threni, elegy, dirge. Only lamentation.

But hasn't the Lord covered Himself with a cloud so that our prayers and songs might not pass through? How might our songs of woe and sorrow pierce this cloud and reach Him? The poet of

Lamentations knows the futility of prayer. Yet he prays. Prayer is pointless. Yet prayer is endless. Prayer is as necessary as song.

Joshua Aaron Rose wrote *A Lion in Secret Places* over four decades ago when he was still a very young man. After the Second World War, he wrote no more music. Until this evening, none of his work has ever been performed in public.

Could a young composer have chosen a more difficult poem? *Lamentations* is one of the most formal books of the Bible, every chapter except its last structured by an acrostic principle based on the twenty-two letters of the Hebrew alphabet, from Aleph to Tau. Is this not a magical form, an appeal to ritual? Surely many composers who have set portions of the poem to music before have thought so, composing music for the Hebrew letters with which the verses begin as well as the Latin translation of the verses themselves, as Krenek and Stravinsky have also done in our own time.

But Rose in his work repeatedly departs from traditions established for its musical realization. He sets neither the Hebrew nor the Latin translation, but instead prefers the English of the King James Bible. He does not observe the selections of the poem that the Roman Church arranged for its Tenebrae services during Holy Week, but instead chooses to write music for almost all of Chapter Three, the most personal of the lamentations. (He concludes his work before the terrible call for vengeance against one's enemies with which the third chapter ends.) He thinks of the poem not as an intricately formal ritual but as a personally expressive lyric, not as a disciplined ceremony but as an emotive song.

So it should surprise no one that there is not a hint of sonata form in his work, even though it is equally obvious that this piece, roughly an hour in length, is really a symphony divided into four clear movements: an Adagio, an Andante beginning, "It is of the Lord's mercies," an Allegro beginning, "Who is he that saith," and a Largo sostenuto beginning, "I called upon thy name." Does not sonata form require the conviction that no opposites exist that cannot be overcome either through argumentation or by artistic and spiritual vision? A sonata's drama always ends happily. But a prayer, praying, can never end. Like true song, praying is infinite. And Rose's masterpiece is everywhere a prayer, one which finds its form in its melodic expression as song weaves into song. *A Lion in Secret Places* is in fact a rhapsodic Symphony of Songs in F minor.

If F major is the key of celebration, rejoicing, and holiday, F minor is the key of lamentation, a mournful, particularly Romantic key. Yet *A Lion in Secret Places* is not a Romantic composition. Its bold harmonic progressions and modulations, its dissonances, its rhythmic energy and freedom, its fury and despair, its fire and almost inconsolable melancholy belong to our own time.

The beautifully aching violin solo with which the work begins, marked *cantabile*, might be a Russian or Jewish folk song, full of longing and loss. Yet it also echoes Barbarina's rueful cavatina in *Le Nozze di Figaro*. (So much of Rose's work is lyrically operatic, operatically dramatic.) As the violin continues to play its keening F minor tune, the tenor starts to sing along with it: "I am the man that hath seen affliction by the rod of his wrath." Yet this man, who is so completely solitary, suffers not only for and with his city, but from it. "I am their music" will be his last words. He is their butt, the pipe on which they play, the object of their scorn and derision. Yet is he not also one of them? For seven verses this solitary man and his fiddle sing alone. Only when, crying and shouting, he laments that God shuts out his prayer do the piano and cello join them as together they repeat the music for the whole of this despairing, accusatory verse three times.

If God will not listen, if He cast us down, is He not also secretive and cruel, a bear lying in wait, a ravenous lion in secret places? "He hath made me desolate," the tenor sings as F minor and F-sharp minor collide bloodily in a series of convulsive chords in the instruments.

Not until verse eighteen does the chorus enter with the words, "My strength and my hope is perished from the Lord." Throughout the next two verses, Rose's music becomes increasingly agitated and dissonant, but with the words, "This I recall to my mind, therefore I have hope," the composer introduces a new melodic turn, an almost unbearably lyrical F-sharp minor theme, worthy of Schubert, which slowly drifts into an even more tender G major over trills high in the piano. With that trilling, all else grown silent, the first movement ends.

The tenor remains silent throughout the choral second part, which is unified by a repeated, almost stalking four-note figure that surges upward through two fourths and a minor third. As the sopranos and altos sing, "Yet will he have compassion according to the multitude of his mercies," one hears a new melody, serene and confident, in what must certainly be F major.

But this movement also ends with a question. As the piano sounds a repeated F major chord, the cello articulates an uncertain phrase in F minor. The Lord destroys me. Yet the Lord is good. The Lord is just. Yet the Lord has thrown me down. How Lord, Rose's music is asking on bended knee, can this be?

Choral ostinati often accompanied by percussive fifths in the piano dominate the allegro third movement. Rhythms shift suddenly, erratically. Each melodic phrase seems short of breath, ever more desperate. The harmonies are recurrently twisted, and the work's most terrifying dissonances are heard as the chorus proclaims, "Thou hast covered thyself with a cloud." The whole movement consists of dangerous, angry music addressed to a dangerous, wrathful God. After the chorus stops singing, the trio plays in unison a theme based on a five-note descending scale. But at every repetition it returns at this wrong pitch or that wrong pitch so that the effect is grotesque, almost inept, yet always artful.

But in the last movement as the tenor, now singing unaccompanied, calls upon the Lord's name "out of the low dungeon," the music restores the whole piece's opening melody, now in a heart-stopping variant in F major that the chorus sustains as they sing "Fear not" over and over. After they have sung their last "Fear not," however, the tenor once more sings alone, still unconsoled and mindful of all the wrongs done him, all the injuries he has suffered and continues to endure from his enemies. Though the piano trio joins him for a few bars, the piano first withdraws, then the cello. Finally not even the violin plays. He is utterly alone. "I am their music," he sings to the five-note descending scale sounded before at the end of the previous movement, although now barely whispered.

But *A Lion in Secret Places* is not yet over. After a few bars of silence, the trio plays a strange little figure. It could be, but isn't a children's monotonous playground round. A canon? Over it, the tenor chants, "'Eikhah? 'Eikhah?" The chorus joins the plea. "'Eikhah? 'Eikhah?" "How? How?"

Once more there is silence. When the trio begins again, we hear for the last time the work's opening tune, now wordlessly vocalized by all the singers including the tenor in a gorgeous, glorious consonance. Each time the tune appears about to end— each time it would seem to approach a place of rest—it beckons us forward, onward, upward. Finally, somewhere off in the distance, far away from us, it continues, although now unheard by anyone except God, if God does hear it. One can only hope. Over these last few bars, the composer has written *morendo*: *dying*.

Acknowledgments

I learned of the story of Major Charles Whittlesey in *There's a War to Be Won* by Geoffrey Perret. My source for the passages from Tacitus is Michael Grant's *Readings in the Classical Historians*. My listening to recordings from the Metropolitan from the period prior to and during the early years of the Second World War has been greatly enhanced by Paul Jackson's *Saturday Afternoons at the Old Met*. Much of the Chinese material in the book I've derived, after the manner of pastiche, from Arthur Waley's *The Book of Songs*. The words for Cam Smithson which Michael Benedetti prays, a prayer whose words Michael knows are not his own, owe everything to Thomas Traherne.

For their kind responses to it while I was completing this novel, I'm grateful to Steve Arkin, Gerald Coble, Sam Crowl, Susan Crowl, Forrest Gander, Michael McGrail, and Richard Parks. My thanks, too, to Kurt Beaver, Jon O'Bergh, Elizabeth Spinner, and Bob Stephens.

The text of *How the Body Prays* is set in Berling,
a typeface designed by the Swedish typographer and
calligrapher Karl-Erik Forsberg, issued in 1951
by the foundry from which it takes its name, the
Berlingska Stilgjuteriet in Lund, Sweden.

This book was designed by Wendy Holdman,
set in type by Stanton Publication Services, Inc., and
manufactured by Friesens, Canada on acid-free paper.